DAWN IN THE SHADOWS

SHIFTERS OF MORWOOD: BOOK 3

CHARLENE PERRY

Cover by Charlene Perry

Published April 14, 2021

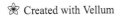 Created with Vellum

DAWN

*S*ome days, I love my job.

Taloned feet touch the ground as goosebumps prickle over my skin. He lands with surprising grace, considering his bulk. Wide, leathery wings fold tight against a backdrop of emerald scales as his head sways from side to side, surveying the pristine courtyard outside HQ.

A few people stop and stare as the massive dragon crouches to let Elite Gideon slide out of the saddle, while others pay no attention at all. Still others give him a wide berth, their faces twisting with annoyance.

This is the reason I eat bagged lunches and bottled coffee instead of enjoying the full-service cafe provided for HQ employees. Even the crisp spring air won't keep me from catching a close-up look at Tarek.

He's incredible. Nearly fifteen tons of solid muscle, covered in iridescent green scales that can stop a bullet. Wide, emerald eyes and wings able to carry him as high and as far as he wants to go. And even though I always suspected it, now I know for sure; inside that dragon is a man. I've never seen him do it, but if Tarek wanted, he could shift into human form.

The thought alone sends a fresh wash of shivers over my skin.

The remaining half of my sandwich can wait for later. I pack it away, then swing my bag over one shoulder.

Time to execute my plan.

I've chickened out of this more times than I can count. Today could be my last chance. If I let it slip away, I'll regret it for the rest of my life.

With my eyes focused on the ground in front of my feet, I walk a wide arc around the courtyard. A deliberate path that will pass within ten feet of the dragon. It'll be the closest I've ever dared to get.

Five. Four. Three. Two... Like the klutz I am, my shoe hooks the edge of a raised grate. I stumble as my bag slips from my shoulder, odds and ends tumbling from the unzipped pocket as I scramble to contain them.

A broad shadow falls over me.

Not daring to breathe, I look up to see his enormous head tilted toward me with one wide, emerald eye staring down. I close my mouth.

"You okay?"

The deep voice nearly gives me a heart attack, as steady hands grip my arms and help me to my feet. Elite Gideon scoops the rest of my scattered belongings into my bag, then holds it out to me.

"Dawn?"

I grab the bag and clutch it to my chest, unable to take my eyes off the dragon that's within arm's reach.

"Yes, I..."

I've never been this close to him. He has a smell. It's subtle, but I'm sure it's him. Woodsy, maybe, like leaves. But not fallen leaves. Fresh, green leaves. Do those even have a smell?

"Don't worry about Tarek," Gideon slaps a hand on his snout. "He's just a big teddy bear."

A low, rumbling growl travels from Tarek's deep chest and

into my bones. I want to touch him, but I keep my hands clasped on my bag. Attempting to pet a Shifter has always been off-limits. Now that we know they're people, it's a different kind of inappropriate.

"He's beautiful."

Gideon laughs. "He says you're quite handsome, yourself."

I cover my mouth with a hand, but I can't stop the smile. It might be the oddest exchange possible, but he just spoke to me. Through his Link with Gideon, but still. It totally counts. I wrack my brain for all the things I've imagined saying to him.

"Thank you." I look at Gideon, too, because I mean it for both of them. "For everything you did and still do. Thank you."

I clutch my bag a little tighter. Forcing my feet to move takes a monumental effort. Before I've taken more than a step, Tarek moves his head close enough that I can feel his warm, smoky breath on my face.

I lift my hand. A silly gesture, considering... He presses his nose against my palm.

Time stands still as his warmth soaks into my skin, heating my entire body. I move my fingers, feeling silky smooth scales. He pushes against me, and I run my hand along the side of his face. The world fades away as I close my eyes and let the weight of this moment sink in.

This isn't an animal I'm petting. This is a man letting me touch him. I open my eyes and lean forward, pressing a fleeting kiss to his cheek.

"Thank you," I whisper against his skin.

He answers with a low rumble.

I step away. Elite Gideon's watching with raised eyebrows and a boyish grin. There's nothing more to say. This moment was the pinnacle of my existence.

It's all downhill from here.

We were all taught that Shifters are nothing more than intelligent, highly trained animals. Don't make eye contact. Don't get too close. Don't try to interact. A Shifter, like a guide dog, is a working animal and requires a wide berth.

Now, the entire world knows what I always suspected; Shifters are people.

I glance back as I walk away. He's still watching me.

After stuffing my bag under my station, I take a deep breath. I kissed Tarek. Maybe he thinks I'm crazy, but I don't care. I'll be doing far more in my daydreams. Later. Right now, I need to stop staring out the window and focus on work.

I log back into my terminal and offer a practiced welcome to the next in line.

Working the front desk at the Headquarters of the United Army of Terran Protectors: Solar One Division has been a dream job. Even though I'm typically a bit socially awkward, this job lets me slip into a different personality. I love greeting familiar faces in the morning, helping newbs feel welcome, and catching snippets of conversations far above my pay grade.

There's also a steady stream of Shifters. At least, there used to be.

I glance past the woman in front of me as she digs through her purse for ID. Gideon's strapping his legs into the saddle. An instant later, Tarek spreads his wings and leaps into the air.

"Terrifying."

It takes me a moment to realize the woman's talking to me. She holds out her identification while looking over her shoulder toward the front doors.

"Excuse me?"

"Six months ago, everything was normal. As it should be. Then those things... I just can't imagine."

It's a conversation I've been baited into one too many times. I type double-time to get her into the system. An accountant transferring from Moridian. Just a few more keystrokes and she'll have her pass.

"Do you know they allow them to *marry* humans?" She's leaning over the counter, whispering like we're sisters in some juicy gossip. "I mean, seriously... what are people thinking?"

"Welcome to HQ, Ms. Canning." Handing her the documents she needs, I gesture toward the elevators at my right. "Head up to the sixth floor. They'll get you settled in."

She nods curtly, clearly unsatisfied with my lack of participation in her little rant. It's not my place. The official government stance is one of support for Shifters, but people like this are impossible to reason with.

"At least the Terran Defenders are standing up to this nonsense. Lord knows the Elders won't. They're even letting those animals call themselves Protectors."

Oh, hell no.

Just over six months ago, I was sitting at home enjoying my day off when the emergency broadcast came in on my comm. Shots fired at HQ. A five-second clip from a shaking comm showed Tarek high above the buildings as he dove to crash through the glass dome at the top of HQ. A breath later, fleeing with something clutched against his chest.

I ran the six blocks to work as the Solar started locking down. My credentials got me past the barricades, but they'd already sealed the building. No one in or out. I had to watch and wait like the rest of the world.

After an endless week, they finally released the details. An assassin had killed four Elders, leaving only Elder Tobias and Elder Tanikka. Tarek and Gideon had brought him down.

A few weeks after, they announced there would be significant changes to the Shifter program. From that day forward, Shifters would be considered an independent race, entitled to all the rights and protections afforded any other sentient species.

They are not animals.

"Where the hell have you been for the last six months?"

A manicured hand flutters to her chest as her painted eyebrows lift in tandem. "Excuse me?"

"Shifters are people. This planet is their home. You fear them because you haven't taken a moment to try and understand them. The Terran Defenders are terrorists. If you support them, maybe you should take your fancy ass somewhere else."

There. Fuck it. Her gasp of shock and quick retreat to the elevators is highly satisfying. I don't care if she reports me. I'll gladly accept the consequences. Maybe now she'll think twice before vomiting her hate.

I was in the crowd the day a brindle wolf and a black panther stood in front of the press and shifted into men. The crowd erupted with gasps and even some screams. Then one of them took the mic. I've re-watched his speech so many times since, I know it by heart.

My name is Damon. I'm a Shifter. Because of our unique abilities, my species was taken from our planet and sold into slavery. No one, including ourselves, has questioned our role in the universe. We've been happy to serve and protect the planets we now inhabit. This is our home. We will remain here and defend Earth as we have done for over a century. But we are no longer content to remain as animals. We are people.

How can anyone still view Shifters as less than human? I guess that's the nature of our species, if history is any indication. We're always willing to see ourselves as superior to those we don't understand.

I motion to the next in line, shaking off the encounter and pasting on my public face. "Welcome to HQ. How can I help you today?"

"The blue-haired pixie has a wicked mouth."

What the- "Excuse me?"

The temperature in the room drops a few degrees when I look up at the man who's now leaning an elbow on my station. He's wearing a simple button-down shirt, but the line of implant tattoos on his neck is as clear as a badge. The thought of that stuck-up accountant reporting me was one thing. Being overheard by an Agent is another.

"Don't worry, Blue. I won't tell." He winks, and I want to sink into the floor and disappear. "You're always so polite. It's nice to see you let loose. Kind of sexy, actually."

He flexes his biceps, and I definitely don't roll my eyes. At least he's not upset by my outburst, though I'm not really sure this kind of attention is any better.

It's always the hair. My short, blue cut seems to be a creep magnet. I don't care. It suits me. Uncomplicated, but unique. Feminine without being girly. Blue. Because I like blue.

"Thank you, Agent, I-"

"Agent Thomas. Call me Daniel." He winks again, and I force a smile instead of a cringe.

"It was inappropriate for me to speak to her that way. I'll talk with my supervisor." No, I won't. But I'd rather him think I'm that committed to remaining professional. "Is there anything I can assist you with today?"

He grins but doesn't whip out any of the raunchy comebacks I'm certain lurk behind the mischievous expression.

Thank fuck. I don't do Agents. Not that I don't like sex, or the killer body that usually comes with the uniform. Agent Thomas is definitely the full package; tall and muscular, attractive features, dark hair, and crystal blue eyes.

"The only assistance I need is your company at dinner tonight. Any plans, Blue?"

What the hell? He's clearly not getting the hint that I'm not crossing any professional lines. I might only be a receptionist, but dating within the workplace is a dumb idea.

"I'm flattered." No, I'm not. But he just saw me go off on some random accountant. I don't want to piss him off, too. Men can be such babies. Or maybe it's just Agents. "I have plans. I'm dating someone. I have a boyfriend."

Not rejecting you. Just already taken. I hold my breath, but he nods and seems to accept the fib.

"That's too bad. Look me up when you get bored." He gives me yet another kind of sexy, but way overused, wink. I wonder if that move makes other women fall all over him? Mercifully, he moves on, evidently not having needed my assistance at all.

The day drags on until six o'clock finally arrives and the last person in line is tended. I guess Miss Accountant didn't report me after all. I still can't believe that there are people who share her opinions.

Shifters have just as much right to be Protectors as their human counterparts do.

After that public speech, the Elders announced that all Shifters wishing to remain in the Protectors could do so. They'd be required to complete the final Academy exams in human form, and undergo the same rigorous security checks. Shifters and humans would work together as partners, making the United Army of Terran Protectors stronger than ever.

Shifters disappeared from the ranks as they stepped away to complete their requirements, then slowly trickled back in. Morwood forest was declared Shifter territory, giving them the space to nurture their own culture.

Not everyone was pleased with the changes, not by a long shot. There were constant debates on the news between pro-Shifter and anti-Shifter factions. There was talk about the Shifter 'invasion' and accusations that they'd assassinated the Elders.

An active-duty Shifter Protector was gunned down in human form outside HQ by a group that called themselves the 'Terran

Defenders'. More acts of terrorism against Shifters followed, until the organization was found and shut down.

Things seem a bit calmer now. At least on the surface. The Terran Defenders returned, though their tactics have changed to less public displays of aggression. There are a few thousand active-duty Shifter Protectors worldwide, some in the field and some with desk jobs. Tarek is the most visible here, though he always stays in his dragon form.

It's only made me more curious about him.

Which is why I'm heading home to chill while obsessively replaying my close encounter with the legend himself. The last item on my bucket list is complete. With my bag slung over one shoulder, I pull out the sliver of metallic paper that's tucked in my pocket. The embellished font against my fingers sends a rush of anticipation through me.

As interesting as this place has been over the last six months, it hasn't changed my plans.

TAREK

*H*ow would she react if I shifted?

It only goes one of two ways with humans; either they're fascinated by the transformation or disgusted by the unnatural display. I bet Dawn would find it cool.

She scrambles to pick up the weird junk that spilled from her bag as I hover over her, waiting for her to notice how close she's gotten. I don't make a habit of crowding people, but this girl has me curious. I've seen that shock of blue hair and the brilliant smile that goes with it many times through the windows or across the courtyard. Haven't had the excuse to introduce myself, since I never use the front door.

Gideon's quick to come to her aid, talking to her with that comfortable ease he always has around people. A skill I haven't exactly mastered. But despite his legendary charm, she's not looking at him.

She's looking at me.

G puts his hand on my face. He calls me a teddy bear, but I growl to make sure she knows I'm anything but. Instead of taking a cautionary step back, she gives me one of those stellar smiles. I almost smile back, but flashing these pearly whites won't exactly have the desired effect.

"He's beautiful."

Shit G, we might have to take this one home.

I'm not kidnapping a woman for you.

You owe me. I saved your life.

"He says you're pretty handsome yourself."

Do not expect a smooth ride home.

Dawn covers her mouth as another radiant smile consumes her. Fuck, I want to shift. I want her to smile at me like that when I'm in human form.

"Thank you." Her smile fades as she looks from me to G and back again. "For everything you did and still do. Thank you."

Huh.

She steps back, but I can't let her go just yet. I lower my head. Close enough to smell a hint of sweet citrus. Close enough that she can touch me if she wants.

She lifts her hand, and I push my nose against it. There's only the faintest pressure from her small palm against my thick skin, but it's the look on her face that warms me to my core. She runs her hand along my face, her eyes drifting shut for a moment before she leans in to kiss my cheek.

"Thank you." It's a whisper meant just for me. I reply with a low tone that brings the smile back to her face.

Then she's walking away, and I'm left speechless.

Shit. Maybe we should take her home.

That was... unexpected. A trip to the Solar is rarely as pleasant as this.

Most people would rather Shifters have stayed as we were; nothing more than weapons controlled by our masters. Others think there's no place for us here, peaceful or not.

Thanks to those asshats, any time spent in the cities is a constant show. We have to work harder, talk smarter, and turn the other cheek. There's always a bystander ready to film our fuck-ups, or a vigilante looking for an excuse to end us.

I don't shift in public. The moment they get my face on camera, my private life is over. I still like to have a drink in peace now and then. Maybe catch a show.

I thought I'd love being a Protector once I was given the same rights and responsibilities as any other. But I hate the city. I hate the politics. I just want to hole up in the Meadow, build houses, and play with the young. Heck, I'd be down with settling in with a female... maybe having some young of my own.

You okay, brother?

I tilt my wings, slowing our flight. *Sorry, G. Zoned out.*

I swear I can feel him roll his eyes. *You liked her, didn't you?*

I growl, dropping about twenty feet so his stomach lands somewhere near his throat.

I'll take that as a yes.

You'd have to be blind not to notice that woman. But G doesn't get that I'm not a raging mountain of hormones. Sure, I like the idea of finding a mate someday. That doesn't mean I'm desperate to bed every desirable female I encounter.

I've never given much thought to any female. Never experienced the attraction that makes men do stupid shit to earn just a moment of affection.

My desires are simple; protect the people I care about, protect the Meadow, and enjoy the life I've worked for.

For most of my years, I've lived in my animal forms. Working at Gideon's side, I never questioned my place or my purpose. I was happy, I think. Content, at least. I guess I never really thought much about me, only we.

It was all a lie. I knew it the moment I saw Damon take his human form. That day changed everything I'd taken for granted. Everything I thought I knew about myself and the world I lived in. It set me free.

Even so, sometimes I feel more animal than man. As much as I appreciate the autonomy and my new Meadow family, I'm just as content when I'm following orders or wandering the forest as a grizzly.

The afternoon sun is dipping behind darkening clouds when we arrive at the Meadow. The heavy scent of freshly turned earth and roaring cook-fires greets us, and the moment G slides out of the saddle, I'm in human form and heading for a meal.

I don't make it far.

The horde ambushes me, and I'm helpless to do anything but sit on the ground and take the abuse. I wrestle and growl and hug until each has had a piece of me. Some literally, considering the scratches and teeth marks on my arms.

"Go on, kids. Give Tarek some space."

The young scatter at River's command, only a few lingering for an extra pat.

"Watch what I can do." One of the youngest of the BioSol kids, Ash, holds up two little hands, waiting for me to acknowledge I'm watching.

"What can you do, pup?"

She covers her eyes with her hands and spins in a circle until she stumbles and faceplants in a fit of giggles. I glance at River, who shrugs her shoulders.

"Did you see me?" Ash picks herself up, watching for my reaction with dancing eyes.

"That was epic. You made the whole world spin."

She squeals with delight and throws her little arms around my neck. I hug her tight, then shoo her away to join her friends.

"She cherishes your praise." River steps close as I push to my feet, taking my hand to inspect the scratches that'll be gone in a matter of minutes. "Your attention means a lot to all of them."

"I love the little shits."

She laughs, her hand moving from my forearm up to my

bicep. "It's good they can look up to you and the other men. They deserve father figures they can be proud of."

"I just hang out with them when I'm here, which isn't as often as I'd like."

A smile wrinkles her freckled nose. Her gaze meets mine, and something new flashes in her caramel eyes. I think she's attracted to me. I hadn't considered that before. River's exactly what I need. She's a good mother, even though she doesn't technically have any young of her own. If I settled down with someone like her...

That's the life I want. Long days spent building houses and improving the Meadow. Work that leaves me tired at the end of the day but never tires me out, if that makes any sense. Nights spent surrounded by a real family.

I reach to tuck a strand of dark hair behind her ear. I should kiss her. This seems like a moment; an opportunity to show her what I'm thinking.

Her eyes drop to my mouth.

I lean in.

Fuck, what am I thinking? I can't kiss River. If I want her to play the leading role in this fantasy life, I need to start by being honest. If she wants a mate who enjoys kissing and... she's going to be disappointed with the life I can offer.

"River, I don't-"

"Oh! Gosh, Tarek, I..." She shakes her head, her cheeks flushing pink. "Don't even... just forget about that. It's been a day."

She turns to walk away, but I reach for her arm. "Tomorrow. I'm working on a house at the eastern quarter. If I finish in time, I'd like to chill with you and the horde. If that's okay?"

She smiles and gives me an exaggerated nod. "Your companionship would be most welcome." She points at my forearms. "Maybe wear long sleeves."

Tomorrow, I'll lay it all out for River. If she's looking for a mate, if she's willing to try being partners... maybe this'll be the start of my next chapter.

Maybe she'll laugh at the idea.

I eat my fill at the nearest cook fire, not really caring what the fare is. I should jump in to help with some construction, or move some lumber, but I'm not in the mood for people.

The sky's mostly clear. The storm clouds seem to be moving farther east.

I head for the edge of the Meadow, shift into my dragon form, and push off into the solitude of the sky. I climb until the Meadow is small against the vast expanse of Morwood, then head north, away from the cities and thoughts of human life. Over the mountains, where the air currents keep me focused on the simple act of flying.

Hours pass and the wide mountain range has long faded into endless green when I spot movement on the horizon. Banking left, I coast on a warm updraft as I keep one eye on the aircraft. It's unusual to see a plane over Morwood. There are no low-flying flight paths ovehead, and only the occasional jet passing far above.

Heat blooms in my chest and travels up to my throat, my instincts kicking in a moment before my brain. The object changes course like no machine ever could. I pivot, dropping into a steep dive to gain speed before levelling out and pumping my wings. The pursuit proves unnecessary, as the other dragon mirrors my movements and the distance between us closes twice as fast.

We pass so close that the wind from his flight nearly throws me off course. He's smaller than me, but not by much. His body is long and slender, almost serpentine.

I flare my wings and turn. He's done the same, and we circle one another slowly. Observing. His dark scales are a shade of brown that's almost orange, with a hint of darker stripes along his back.

He dives, and I follow. Angling toward one of the many rivers that cut through the forest, we splash down in unison and face each other with flared wings and swinging tails.

Fire burns in my throat. I want to throw it into the air and roar until he lowers his head, but I fight the unfamiliar urge. A distant memory of Hope mentioning a third dragon Shifter comes to mind, but the sudden territorial aggression of my dragon form makes logical thoughts hard to grasp.

I take a step toward the other. He lowers his head, tucks his wings, and twists until the pale underside of his neck is visible.

Her neck.

Something new heats my body. The fire in my chest spreads through my veins, all but consuming me with an impulse I can only feel. I want to bite her. Not to pierce scales, but to dominate. I want to pin her beneath my superior weight. I need to...

The slick rocks of the riverbed make for unsteady footing as I push backward. Closing my eyes, I attempt to block out the sight of the female offering herself in submission, but my dragon's instincts pull me to her like a magnet.

I push off the ground, forcing my wings to carry me as high and as fast as they ever have. I don't look back. I aim for the city and fly at full speed for two hours before my dragon loses its hold on me and allows me to shift into the far smaller form of a hawk.

AGITATED

he rush of victory has me leaping off the couch to do a happy dance. Hell, yeah. Friendly neighborhood receptionist by day, stone-cold sniper by night.

"I take it that means you won?"

I trip over my feet, instantly regretting my uncoordinated imitation of a twerk.

"Liam! Shit, I didn't hear you come home."

"Don't apologize. That was... enlightening."

My roommate's grin is a little too warm, and I don't miss the way he sweeps his eyes over me.

Hell. I like the guy, but he knows I'm not into him that way. I roll my eyes and flash a smile that lets him know I'm taking his comment as a joke.

I'm wired. And not just from the game. Today, I spoke to Tarek, and he spoke to me. He let me touch him. I kissed a *dragon.*

Today was epic.

I retreat to the kitchen to grab a cold soda, tossing a treat at my gaming buddy. Rocco catches it in the air, waving his tail in appreciation as he takes it back to his bed to eat.

He's the best foster we've had yet, though he'll be one of the hardest to place. Ex-Enforcer dogs aren't known for making great family pets, but this boy doesn't seem to have any distressing quirks from his old life. He's just a big teddy bear.

"How was work?" I ask, attempting to distract myself from diving into another dragon-filled fantasy.

"The usual." Liam shrugs, leaning against the counter and popping the top of his own fizzy drink.

Liam's a Code Wizard. That's the title I gave him the day we first met. He was a customer at the cafe I worked at when the computer system crashed. It was me alone against a growing lineup of disgruntled, under-caffeinated suits. I was ready to walk out or burst into tears when he slid across the counter and worked his magic. He even stayed to help me catch up with orders.

He asked for my number, just in case I had any more tech emergencies. We got to know each other a little over text, played some couch co-op, and discovered we both loved volunteering at the local shelter. He even taught me some basic programming skills.

When I found this apartment and needed a roommate, he was my first call.

"You know you can do better than that place. They don't pay you half what you're worth."

"And you know I don't care. It's easy money, and it gives me plenty of time to work on private contracts."

Liam's private contracts usually involve all-nighters hunched over his laptop, with me supplying enough delivery pizza and fresh water to keep him alive. The only time he gets fresh air is if we're fostering a dog at the same time and it's his turn to walk it.

I suppose he won't be able to take in fosters once I'm gone. I finish the last of my soda and reject the thought. He'll make sure his next roommate is up for the shared responsibility, too. He'd never get along with someone that doesn't like dogs.

My comm vibrates, the screen lighting up with familiar digits. It's weird enough to be getting an actual voice call, but I'm pretty sure that's my mother's number.

"Hello?"

"Dawn, sweetie, Auntie Renee passed away. Her heart, again."

I take a deep breath. Still trying to catch up on the fact that my mother is calling me after... how long has it been? Nearly two years?

"Thanks for letting me know, mom."

"Of course, sweetie. I'll call your sister now."

"K."

I disconnect and stare at the black screen.

"What was that all about?"

"My mom. She said my Aunt passed away."

"Oh, shit." Liam steps toward me, reaching like he'd grab me for a hug.

With a quick side-step, I dodge his advance and head back to the sitting room. "Want to co-op?" The invite to play should make it clear I'm not in the market for a shoulder to cry on.

"Are you okay? Did you know her?" Concern for my emotional well-being twists his features.

He doesn't get how my family works. I don't think he's ever gone a day without talking to his parents or siblings. If I told him how long it's been since I talked to Mom, he'd probably have a heart attack.

"I'm good. It's fine. Yeah, I knew her. My sister and I lived with her for about a year when I was eight, and again when I was thirteen. I guess we were close."

He looks shocked by my admission. The truth is, she was more of a mother to me than my own ever was. That was a long time ago. It's been over ten years since I even spoke to her.

"Dawn, it's okay if you need a minute to process. I can give you some space, or we can go out if you just want to drink."

"Liam, seriously. I'm not that delicate. People come and go, that's just life. If I got attached to everyone I ever knew, I'd spend all my time wallowing."

"Shit. That's the saddest thing I've ever heard."

Holy hell. Why do I need a roommate, again? "Liam..."

"If you never have someone you can't live without, you're not really living to begin with."

"What's that supposed to mean? We're talking about an Aunt I haven't seen in a decade and you're making it sound like we're debating my love life."

"Maybe it's related."

"I don't see you happily attached to anyone. You seem perfectly content with your single status."

His eyes drop. "I enjoy being single. That doesn't mean I don't want to find someone just for me, eventually."

I huff out a laugh that sounds more like a snort. Where the hell did this wonderful conversation come from?

Liam shakes his head. "Nevermind, Dawn. Sorry about your aunt. I'm heading to bed."

The jarring thud of his bedroom door marks the official end of whatever that was. I don't understand that man. He can be so emotional over the strangest things.

He's a good guy, though. He also kind of has a point. I should be upset about Aunt Renee. I am upset, on some level. It's sad that she's gone. It would have been nice to see her again. But that's just life. People come and go, and getting attached would only make it hurt more. I never want to be so dependent on another person that my own life would grind to a halt if they left.

I hate these thoughts. Damn Liam and his touchy-feely vibes.

I pace the room a few times, consider taking Rocco out for a walk to clear my head, then opt instead for another round of kicking ass.

I play hard and lose every skirmish for the next two hours.

That's it. I'm done saving credits. Tomorrow's the day. I'm putting in my two-week notice and getting off this rock.

"YOU DID THE RIGHT THING."

Tanikka's reassuring tone does nothing to dampen my anger. Maverick has a fading bruise across his neck from the boot that could have ended his life. The latest attack against Shifters. If he'd fought back, he wouldn't have a mark on him. A man deserves to put a fist in the face of someone who jumps him in the middle of the fucking night.

"Thank you, Elder."

Tanikka and Elder Kareem take turns thanking Maverick and Troy for their service, stressing that they did the right thing.

Gideon and I keep our mouths shut.

It's not right.

I know, brother. I know.

"As difficult as it is, your commitment to not engaging these terrorists is crucial to our efforts." Tanikka looks at me like she can tell I'm ready to combust. "The moment you give them what they want, the moment you throw a punch or retaliate in animal form, they'll have the footage they need."

"It's a delicate balance," Elder Kareem chimes in. "The Shifter partnership has many supporters, but also many opponents. We fear that with fuel for their propaganda, the Terran Defenders will have the leverage they need to tip that balance against you."

The Terran Defenders. Such bullshit. They introduced themselves by gunning down Fury in human form in broad daylight.

They managed a few more near-fatal attacks before they were caught. Amateurs with more ammo than brains.

After five months of silence, they've re-emerged with less firepower and more stealth. The Shifters who are attacked all report that at least one of the masked assailants recorded the show with a comm.

They haven't gotten to me yet. Good thing, because I don't know if I'd be able to play nice.

"We don't need to be here." All eyes turn to me. I don't make a habit of speaking up unless I have something to say. "Morwood is Shifter territory now. We've got plenty of space and a complete lack of human bullshit."

Gideon nods. I know he hears me. He might have been a career Elite for most of his adult life, but he'd be perfectly happy never having to leave Hope's side.

I hold Mav's stare. He already knows I'm fed up, and I don't think he'll be too eager to disagree after this.

"I know, Tarek." Tanikka walks up to me and rests a hand on my arm. Her crimson lips are pressed into a thin line. "You don't need to stay. You don't need to put yourself at risk like you do. But we all know what will happen if Shifters retreat to the forest. It'll heighten the fear and mistrust, and lead to greater conflict. Maybe not in our lifetimes, but in our children's, or their children's. We owe it to both our species to fix this."

Goddamnit. That's why she's an Elder, and I'm just the muscle. I nod, and she smiles.

"Then we need to do more."

"What do you have in mind?"

I cross my arms and look past her. The Atrium is a wide, open space full of history. Its glass dome is the highest point on the Solar, offering an unobstructed view in all directions. Beyond the artificial atmosphere, dark clouds are churning. Moridian is getting drenched with spring rain, but on this hovering chunk of metal the air is deceptively calm.

There's no sign that six months ago, Gideon riddled the place with bullet holes, and I smashed the dome to shit. Sitting and waiting for the good guys to solve our problems didn't work back then, and it won't work now.

"We need someone on the inside. Someone who can infiltrate their ranks and get us some hard intel."

Everyone nods, but agreeing and acting are two different things. It's not the first time I've made this suggestion. I'd do it if I could, but taking a new human form isn't easy. I'd never be able to hold it. A Blender implant would let me change some superficial things like eye color and skin tone. Not nearly enough for the long-game undercover work we need.

"We're looking into that option, Tarek." Tanikka's never too proud to take a suggestion into consideration, but I'm tired of waiting for her to *look into it*.

"I want them taken out. I don't care what the risk is." Troy's been quiet until now, but I can see the tension in his stance. He's just as pissed off as I am. "This is the second time I've rolled over for those assholes. They wanted me on my knees while they took Mav to the brink. They deserve to die."

Maverick is nodding. "We could have taken them all out and destroyed the comm in seconds."

"You know they're likely streaming," Gideon says.

"Someone's going to snap. It's just a matter of time before they push the wrong Shifter too far."

"You're absolutely right." Tanikka lifts her chin, looking at each of us in turn. "All I can do is ask you, please, don't be the one who gives them what they want. It's a cruel thing I'm asking of you, but as the victims in this you are in a unique position to gather intel. If you're targeted, pay attention. Words, accents, scents, clothing... anything that can help us learn more."

"I can just grab one. If I'm attacked, I can shift and bring one here."

Tanikka shakes her head. "Please don't. Think of how they can spin that image. Give us more time. We will find them."

I nod, and Tanikka offers a grim smile. It's the way any disagreement ends with her. She's smart and gives a shit. She's rarely wrong, and when she is, she's the first to point it out.

She's also very intuitive, and when everyone else takes their leave, she asks me to hold back.

"Are you okay, Tarek?"

"Of course, Elder."

She clasps her hands at her waist, glancing down for a moment and looking uncharacteristically unsure. "I know you feel strongly about this, and for good reason. But I've never seen you this agitated. Can I count on you to be patient?"

Agitated. That's one word for it. I haven't felt right since that female dragon fucked with my head. Didn't sleep at all last night, trying to figure out what to do about her.

"I'm good."

Every animal form comes with its own instincts and temperaments. The dragon was always a little different; vague and hard to interpret. Never uncontrollable. When I discovered my human form, that new awareness woke something in the dragon, too.

Most of the time, the change is hardly noticeable. There have been moments when I've been ready to return to human form, but the dragon pulled me to the sky instead. Moments when the urge to hunt nearly drove me to a herd of deer for a quick meal.

I've been making excuses for it, but that encounter with the female is impossible to ignore. I'm not the only one in the driver's seat.

ANGEL

*T*his city really is something.

My block is all but deserted, but the sounds of traffic from parallel streets echo off the metal buildings. The sky above is inky, though it's certainly far from dark. The Solar always glows, day and night.

As much as I appreciate the architecture of the inner city, the real view is on the edge. With the glow of the Solar at my back, I'll be able to see Moridian spread out below with the glint of the ocean far on one side, and the blackness of Morwood on the other. It's a place to get some perspective; a reminder of how small I am, or maybe how big the world really is.

I'm not having regrets. No way. I'm leaving, and I couldn't be more ready. Tomorrow's my last day of work. I feel guilty about leaving them in the lurch, but I can't stomach the idea of an emotional goodbye. I booked a two week vacation, and by the time they realize I'm not coming back, I'll be long gone.

They'll survive. I'm good at what I do, but I'm also replaceable.

Metal towers give way to quaint, metal houses as I leave the government district. Those end at a swatch of park, complete with grass that feels nothing like the real thing, and trees that never change.

The edge is just on the other side, but when I'm almost there, my heart sinks. Between the park and the edge is a wide, open lot. A black SUV is parked in the middle. Someone else wanted to do some midnight sightseeing, I guess.

I didn't come here to socialize. I could wait, or I could walk another mile to the next shipping yard look-off.

Voices reach my ears, and I crouch. Too many video games. Still, I tighten the hood of my black sweater around my face, not wanting my blue hair to attract any attention. I creep a little closer and peer past the fake brush.

Holy hell.

A group of masked Agents surround a man on his knees. No, not Agents. Their gear isn't quite right. There's six of them, circling and taunting in voices too low for me to hear. One of them kicks the kneeling man in the back, but he only grunts. Another punches his head, and he sways.

I cover my mouth with both hands. Why the hell isn't he fighting back or running?

I scramble for my comm, pulling up the camera to record the scene. There's nothing identifiable about the attackers. They're all dressed in black imitation tactical gear and full face masks. Even the vehicle is blacked out.

The man on the ground is bodybuilder big, wearing a white t-shirt that's stretched to accommodate his heavily muscled chest and thick arms. His blond hair is about shoulder length, tied back from his face. He's wearing black pants and heavy boots that look more like authentic tactical gear... Oh fuck.

He's a Shifter. A Protector.

He's not defending himself because those assholes are the Terran Defenders, and if they get footage of him showing any kind of violence, it'll be viral in seconds. Sure enough, one asshole is standing off to the side with her comm held high. They all have at least one gun strapped to their bodies. The Shifter must know it's pointless to run.

One of them throws another punch that lands across his jaw, snapping his head to the side. He leans down, spitting blood as strands of hair fall loose around his face. His fists are clenched so tight, I'm not sure he's going to hold back much longer.

I wish he would give in and put them on the ground. They might get the video they want, but mine will show the full story.

He says something, his voice reaching my ears as a low rumble. One of them kicks his lower back, and the Shifter's face twists in pain. Another kicks him square in the crotch. He goes down to his hands with a roar, and I'm on my feet before logic overrides my anger.

"Hey!" I shout, holding my comm high as they all pivot to look at me. "Fuck off assholes. I'm uploading this now."

I walk toward them as the Shifter pushes back up to his knees. When his eyes meet mine, something pulls in my chest.

"Get out of here. Please." His voice is raspy, his expression pleading. I stop my approach.

Two of the masked men start toward me, and I clutch my comm even tighter. The Shifter tries to rise, but stumbles. He's hurting. Three of the men jump him, pushing him to the ground as the two on their way to me speed up.

"Back off. The Protectors are already on their way."

My threat only earns a laugh, as the two men break into a run. Fear kicks in, and I bolt. I'm not nearly fast enough. An arm hooks around my waist, pulling me off my feet.

This is the moment where all my training should kick in. Countless hours playing MMO's and first-person shooters should give me some sort of real-world instincts, right? Apparently not. I flail and kick and curse, but my back slams against the side of the SUV.

A hand grips my neck.

"Who the fuck are you?" The voice is a growl in my ear as I struggle to breathe. "Are you one of them? Are you an animal under that pretty skin?"

I shake my head as much as I can. The grip on my neck loosens, and I gasp to catch my breath. He grips my hood and pulls it back, then goes completely still.

"Well, isn't this a treat?"

Oh, fuck. I don't like the sound of that. Or the way he leans in closer, the rough fabric of his mask brushing against my ear. He smells like something dusty. Hay, maybe, though it's been years since I lived near a farm.

I focus on the Shifter. He's staring back at me with calm confidence. With impossibly green eyes... it can't be. He shakes his head, almost imperceptibly. He doesn't want me to fight back.

"She didn't upload shit." The chick with the comm is scrolling through mine. So much for my video. Not that it caught anything to identify these assholes.

"You know this animal? He your pet?" Farmboy tightens his hand on my neck.

I keep my eyes on the Shifter. His steady gaze is the only thing keeping me from freaking out. "I don't know... I don't know what you're talking about."

"Come on. She's not a Shifter. Let's get out of here."

He ignores his friend. "You sympathize with them? You want to save them?"

My virtual combat skills might have failed me, but my hostage scenario training won't.

I look away from the safety of green eyes, and stare into Farmboy's cold, blue ones. They're paler in the center, with flecks of darker blue on the outer edge of the iris. I do my best to commit the pattern to memory, in case I ever see this asshole in a lineup.

"Are you fucking this animal?" He lets go of my neck, tracing a finger along my jaw.

"I don't know…" I widen my eyes in mock suprise. Ignorance is more believable than denial. "That's a Shifter?"

He laughs, and the other assholes join in. I glance at the Shifter, and he's looking at me with suspicion in his narrowed eyes. I swallow the guilt, hoping desperately that I get the chance to explain myself to him.

"Come on, dude. Let's get out of here."

The gloved hand returns to my neck, this time with a light brush of fingers from my ear to my collarbone. I shiver at the contact, taking every ounce of willpower not to break his nose with my head.

"Don't worry, Blue." He whispers the words into my ear, and I shudder at my least favorite nickname. "I wouldn't hurt you. I'm just trying to look tough for these fools."

Sure thing, asshole. I can't swallow without feeling the ghost of his grip on my neck. He brushes against my ear one last time, and my stomach turns at the almost affectionate gesture.

He backs away, turning to the Shifter whose calm expression looks a lot more pissed off than it did a moment ago. "Get the fuck out of here, animal. We're done."

Two of the other assholes draw their weapons and step closer. He stands stiffly, glancing at me only briefly before slipping smoothly into the form of a hawk. With a few flaps of his wide wings, he's up and gone.

I don't want to be alone with these people. I blink away the sudden sting behind my eyes. Thankfully, with the Shifter gone, they don't linger.

"See you later, Blue."

I don't move a muscle as they pile into the vehicle and it rolls quietly out of sight.

The lot's empty. My body's numb. I don't know if I'm cold or warm, but my hands are shaking and my skin feels damp.

The edge is close. It's the reason I came here, but I don't really care about the view anymore. I feel small enough already. I should haul ass home, but even though I'm sure it's perfectly safe, I can't help but think this is the only place I know for sure *they* aren't.

I sit on the ground and tuck my knees up to my chin. Even though the air is cool, the Solar's ground is always warm. The shock will pass. I just need a minute.

I knew this sort of thing was happening. Everyone at HQ's been briefed about the Terran Defenders and their vendetta against Shifters. Seeing it firsthand is a different story.

I reach for my comm where that bitch dropped it on the ground. It's unharmed, but a quick scroll through confirms my video's gone. I should call someone. Maybe the Enforcers. Maybe Liam.

"You okay, Dawn?"

I snap my head toward the voice, the motion causing a stab of pain across my throat.

The Shifter's back. He's looming over me, and when he crouches down, I scoot a little farther away.

He knows my name.

I focus on his emerald eyes, soaking in some of the reassurance they gave me earlier. His lip is split and there's a faint bruise coloring his jaw. The hits he took to his back and... other parts play through my mind. I close my eyes.

"Better than you," I say, my voice a bit raspy.

His laugh makes me jolt. "I'm fine, Angel. Everything was under control."

"Didn't look like it from where I was standing." I cough, instantly regretting it.

"All those assholes hurt was my pride. They would've been cremated before they took anything more."

My mouth goes dry. It's him. I knew it. My eyes sting as I swallow past the ache in my throat. "I'm sorry... I didn't..."

"Hey now, it's okay."

I turn my face away from him and swipe a tear from my cheek. I'm not a crier. It's just the shock.

"Are you hurt? Do you need a medic shot?"

I shake my head, carefully. "No. I'll be fine."

My heart stops when a massive arm slides around my waist. He moves me like I'm weightless, pulling me back against him as he settles onto the ground behind me. My brain doesn't have time to process what's happening until I'm wrapped in his arms, between his huge thighs, my back against the wall of his chest.

I can't move, or speak, or breath.

"You're cold. I don't want you going into shock on me. I won't hurt you."

My breath comes out in a whoosh. I wonder how crazy he'd think I am if he knew I'm totally fan-girling right now?

"Agent Tarek."

He laughs, and I feel the vibration through my entire body. I am most definitely not cold. I think my skin might actually be on fire.

"So, you do recognize me. Is it because I'm so beautiful?"

I can't help but laugh, even if it hurts. This afternoon I was tripping over myself, literally, to get close to this man. Now, he's snuggling with me to keep me warm.

I tip my head back, resting it on his hard chest. I'll work through the lingering effects of that trauma later. In this moment, it's impossible to feel anything but perfectly safe. And incredibly lucky to be where I am, regardless of how I got here.

"How do you do that? Take the abuse without fighting back?"

I know why they do it, but when you can shift into a dragon and *cremate* your attackers... I wouldn't have that kind of willpower.

"Doing nothing is the best way we can fight these assholes." His body stiffens and his fists clench into deadly weapons. "I couldn't keep it in for much longer. If you hadn't interrupted..."

I hold my breath, but he doesn't continue. It feels like he just confessed something private, but he doesn't even know me.

I turn, shuffling my bum around until I'm sideways so I can look at him. He really is beautiful. His face, like the rest of him, could be carved out of stone. Square jaw, full lips, and thick lashes over those emerald eyes. His hair is falling out of its tie to frame his face with loose strands.

He smells good. Not like anything at all, really. Fresh, but not soapy. I'd think he'd be sweaty after what happened, but I suppose that all disappears when he shifts. I breathe a little deeper, silently geeking out at the fact that I now know what a recently shifted Shifter smells like.

"And I thought you just looked at dragons like that."

I lower my eyes. Busted. "Like what?"

He laughs, but the sound cuts off. When I glance up, his head is tilted, and his eyes are narrowed. "Like a puzzle. Like you might want to take me apart and see how the pieces fit back together."

"I'm sorry." Shit, I'm being weird. The last thing I want to do is take his kindness and turn it into something awkward.

"No. Don't apologize for those baby blues. They can do what they want."

Holy hell. Was that flirting? No way.

His hand moves to my head, his fingers brushing through my short cut and causing the most delicious sensation to ripple across my skin. I hold my breath, watching his expression.

"I always wanted to do that." A boyish grin lights up his face, and I honestly can't tell if he's flirting or just oblivious to personal space.

Either way, I'm game.

I thread my fingers through the loose strands that frame his face, tucking some behind his ear. His playful expression melts into something a little more predatory, and I have to bite my lip to keep from grinning.

I don't care that we're sitting on the ground in the middle of the night. I don't even remember how we got here. All I know is I want more of whatever this is.

I trace my finger over the implant tattoos on his neck. Link and Medic. Just the basics. I drop my hand to his shoulder, then run my fingers down over the exposed curves of his bicep. It's already hard as rock, but he flexes and the muscle turns to steel. His skin is smooth as I follow a vein along the inside of his arm to his wrist. He opens his hand. It's huge compared to mine.

I jolt when his other hand touches my neck, his fingers tracing slowly along my hairline. His eyes are lidded, his lips parted.

Please kiss me.

"Come on, Angel. You need to get home."

He stands, the absence of his body making the night feel cold. What the hell just happened? He holds out a hand, and I let him help me to my feet. I glance around at the vacant lot and the darkened park beyond.

I'm torn between the thrill of what just happened, and the cold reminder of how we got here.

"Are you good to walk home?"

"Yeah. I'm fine." My voice wavers, but it's not because of any lingering fear. It's the feel of his fingers on my skin. Of that moment when I thought...

"Go home and get some sleep. I'll stay above you. No one will hurt you."

COMFORTABLE

"*Y*ou can't be serious?"

"Look, Dawn, I appreciate you care about this so much... but there's nothing we can do."

"They could have-"

"I know. Our Protectors take that risk every day on the job. You're the one who could have been seriously hurt, or worse." Debbie gestures to my neck, a deep frown on her face. "You should have stayed back and called for help."

I clench my teeth to keep from saying something I'll regret. Debbie's a good supervisor. She's always treated me with respect. And Tarek said the same thing; he knew the risks and had it under control. Even six armed people didn't stand a chance if he shifted to his dragon form.

I shiver at the thought, as my mind drifts to the second half of that unexpected encounter. The part I didn't tell my boss and don't plan to. Tarek held me in his arms, touched me, and let me touch him. It was playful, it was fun... it was insanely hot. *Just a big teddy bear*. Yeah, Gideon was exactly right. The mighty dragon likes to snuggle.

"Are you sure you're okay?"

Debbie's deepening concern clues me in that I'm smiling like an idiot. "Yeah, it's just... it was a strange night."

"I imagine it was. Go on up to Ms. Brooks' office and tell her what you told me, okay?"

Oh hell. I don't want to go over all that again. "Yeah, for sure."

"Then go home and get some rest, alright hon? Start your vacation early."

Starting my vacation early sounds pretty damn good. My permanent vacation. They better not ask me to stick around for an investigation or follow-up. The off-world transport leaves Tuesday evening, and I'm not missing it for anything.

After packing up my things and making sure my workstation is tidy and clean, I slip into the elevator.

The floor above the main lobby is full of offices and open areas for cubicles. I rarely have reason to come up here, but I follow the signs to Ms. Brooks' office. Debbie's boss and my manager.

She invites me in after a single knock.

"Ms. Brooks. Do you have a minute?"

"Of course. Dawn Stevens, right? Come in."

I tell her everything I told Debbie.

When I finish, she pushes up from her desk and circles around to perch on the front of it.

"I'm sorry you had to witness that." She pulls her black-framed glasses off, slipping them onto the top of her head. "I can't imagine how unsettling it would have been, but your supervisor was correct; this situation is being dealt with in the best way we can for the moment. Tarek reports to the Elders directly. If there's any information they need from you, I'm sure you'll hear from them."

That's good, I guess. I didn't want them to ask more of me, but I don't like the feeling that nothing's going to come of this. Surely an eyewitness account is useful?

"Do you think something I saw can help?"

She pulls her glasses back off her head, holding them in her hands. "I'm sure Tarek saw as much as you did. If they need you, they'll contact you."

"Yeah. For sure." That's my cue to leave. "Should I type it up and send it to you?"

She sighs like my persistence is boring her. Standing up, she slips her glasses back on and moves around to sit in her high-backed chair. "I can put in a request for Tarek to meet with you on Monday."

My heart skips at the thought of talking with him again. "Um, yeah. If you think that would be helpful."

"I can't guarantee he'll have the time. But I can put in a request if that would help set your mind at ease."

The dull ache in my throat should be a constant reminder of how terrifying last night was, but all I can think about is him.

Shifters have always fascinated me. Getting close to Tarek's dragon form was incredible; a moment I'll never forget. Spending those moments with him in human form was something else.

He's not just a Shifter, but he's more than just a man. He had the power to destroy them, but held it back. He's got the freedom to go anywhere, but he stayed to make sure I was safe.

The thought of seeing him again feels like possibility. The way he looked at me, the way he talked, and touched. I can't get past the thought that if he'd walked me home in human form instead of flying above, I could have invited him in and maybe...

Seeing him again and satisfying this little crush is hardly the most important issue. What I saw last night can't go unpunished. I heard Farmboy's voice, saw his eyes, and got a good chance to size him up. Hell, I deduced that he's been on a farm recently. That's solid intel.

Tarek will give a shit. I'm sure of it.

"That sounds fine, Ms. Brooks. Sorry for the trouble."

"Not at all, Dawn. Thank you for caring."

"WE'LL GET THEM. We just need to be patient."

Fuck. I'm sick of being patient.

I turn my back to the four people that are making my house feel too damn small. Outside my window, the wind is whipping across the short, grassy patch between my cabin and the thick woods.

It's a good day for flying.

The compulsion to shift is getting stronger. The image of that female dragon taunts me to head northward over the mountains. I don't give a shit who she is, or where she comes from, as long as she stays away from the Meadow.

My dragon is far more curious.

"We can't go against the Elders." Whisper's opinion is the same as Gideon's. With those two against me, I've got no chance. "We did what we had to when innocent lives were on the line. We earned our freedom. There won't be another free pass if we go rogue on this."

"I agree with Whisp, brother." Of course he does. The bigger Whisper's belly gets, the more agreeable Damon becomes.

A hand touches my arm, and I don't have to look to know that it's Hope. "I know how badly you want to find them. We all want them stopped."

"The public knows the Terran Defenders are attacking Shifters, yet a Shifter fighting back would make them think less of us." It's bullshit.

Whisper pushes up from the couch, swatting Damon's hand away when he tries to help. "It's proof we still have a long way to go before we're truly on equal ground."

"I'm done with this bullshit. I won't roll over for them again."

Hope nods. "I don't blame you. I wouldn't, either."

"There's a reason we're approaching it this way." Gideon puts an arm around Hope, pulling her close. "If we respond with violence, they'll twist it against us. We need to wait for an opening. A safe opening."

Hope nods, and G kisses the top of her head. A stab of jealousy hits me, and I turn back to the window. I'm not into Hope. I'd never betray G like that, even if the thought crossed my mind, which it hasn't.

I'm not into anyone that way. Never have been. This human form attracts a variety of women, but none of the subtle, or not-so-subtle, propositions ever interest me.

I want a family. A mate by my side. Children.

Whisper's growing belly is a constant reminder of what I'm missing. But the evidence of Hope's clothes fitting a little tighter these last couple weeks hits me even closer to home.

Gideon deserves it. He's going to be a great father.

"Fine. I get it."

They all start talking at once, probably relieved they could talk some sense into me. The conversation moves to other topics, the fridge is raided, and I'm the only one left still dwelling on the facts I can't change.

It's not the safety of Shifters, or the humiliation of taking a beating that has me so worked up. It's *her*.

Those assholes couldn't hurt me. Not in any way my Medic wouldn't heal in less than a day. But Dawn risked everything when she stepped out to rescue me. She's not a Shifter, she's just a decent person who gives a shit. She could have been hurt because of this little dance we're entertaining with the Terran Asshats.

And fuck, the way that woman looked at me. Her smile, and those baby blues that burned right through me.

Back at HQ, she touched my dragon form. She fucking *kissed* my dragon form. Few people have the nerve to get anywhere near that close. Not that I'd want them to. G's the only one I can tolerate putting his hands on me in animal form.

Until her. She can touch me anytime.

In the lot, she touched me again. Put her hand in mine.

"What's up with you and River?"

Hope's whispered question throws me off balance for a moment. "What?"

She rolls her eyes. "Don't be coy. She told me you had a moment, then you stood her up. Are you into her?"

Shit.

She's trying to sound casual, but I can see the excitement bubbling under the surface. Hope's been trying to set me up with someone new every month. She'd probably explode if I said I was chasing her best friend.

I almost wish I could say what she wants to hear. Hell, River's exactly what I want in a mate. At least, I think she is. A couple days ago I could clearly see myself settled down with her and a handful of young at my feet.

I don't have the heart to tell Hope I forgot about River. "We get along." It's a thin response, and Hope's mouth twitches with a restrained smile.

"Then don't stand her up again." She pokes me in the ribs.

It's unlikely I'll be making plans with River again. Between my dragon coaxing me north and my own curiosity with Dawn, there's not much left to offer a potential mate.

This isn't the time to be thinking about any of that shit,

anyway. The Terran Defenders are a bigger problem than anyone wants to admit. I'm certain of it.

Hope makes her way back over to Gideon, and he pulls her into his arms. He's chatting with Damon, drink in hand, while Whisper sits on the kitchen counter eating a toasted sandwich.

They're all so comfortable.

Six months ago, our future as a species was uncertain. We were all willing to give our lives to keep the Meadow safe. Those threats are behind us. In comparison, the Terran Defenders seem like a minor irritation. Maybe they're all just tired of fighting and would rather turn a blind eye to keep the peace they've earned.

It's not good enough. I don't want to watch my back every moment I'm outside of Morwood, wondering when they're going to gain enough strength to knock on our front door. I don't want to start a family with these threats over our heads.

My dragon likes the idea of taking the fight to them. I swear I can feel the fire in my chest even as I stand here.

"Damon." I nod for him to join me away from the others.

"What's up, brother?"

I choose my words carefully. "Do you notice anything different about your dragon form?"

He narrows his eyes, considering my question and no doubt trying to figure out where this is coming from. "In what way?"

"It's temperament. It's... will."

"The dragon's unique." He crosses his arms, staring past me out the window for a moment. "I enjoy it, but I don't spend a lot of idle time in it. It has some instincts I don't really get. Moments where I think I'm on the verge of understanding, but then I lose it."

I nod. It's not just me. I've just been taking that form for a lot longer, and I've certainly spent plenty of idle time in it.

We thought the dragon and phoenix forms were mythical, but Hope's brief time as our Alpha showed us otherwise. These creatures are ones we came into contact with on our home planet. Genetic memories only a few of us can tap into. I don't think the dragons were animals any more than we are.

"It's not like any Terran form."

"No." He answers immediately. "Is it giving you trouble?"

"Nah. Some of those instincts are a pain in the ass, is all."

SUNSET

"Well, that's the last of it."

Rocco thumps his tail on the floor at the sound of my voice, as I tape the last box closed. Three boxes packed and ready for Goodwill. I don't have much stuff, plus I'm leaving whatever's useful for Liam's next roommate. I'll be moving on to my next chapter with everything I need in the pack on my back.

I flop down onto my single bed and stare at the fan rotating silently on my ceiling.

Holy hell. I'm really doing it!

"Come on, boy. Let's go for a walk."

The old man is up and at the door with the agility of a pup, his tail never stopping as I attach his lead and slip on my sneakers. After what happened Thursday night, I don't have the desire to walk alone after dark. But the sunset on the edge is a dream, and I want to see it once more before I go.

I've never had a home. Not really. My parents always traveled for work or fun. My sister and I were just extra baggage. I've never felt connected to any one place.

I guess I inherited some of that wanderlust... only I've been all around this planet already. I want to see something new. New planets, new biomes, new species. I want to be out there, with nothing save for the pack on my back. I want to drift until I run out of credits, then work until I can go again.

A galactic hitchhiker. That sounds perfect.

The door clicks shut behind me as I pull my hood low over my eyes. The street is mostly quiet, though on a Saturday night the traffic never really dies.

As I walk, my mind drifts to Tarek. I should be thinking about my trip, but all I can picture is emerald eyes, sculpted arms, and that heated expression that said maybe, just maybe, he was thinking about kissing me.

Or maybe that's just wishful thinking. Still, I'll take it.

A few blocks from home, a noise makes me pause. Rocco bristles, his stance widening as he focuses intently on a thin gap between buildings that doesn't seem so benign as it did a moment ago. My skin prickles at the image of those assholes from the other night, hiding in the shadows and waiting for me to pass.

For a second, I consider turning back. It's a silly thought. They aren't going to ambush me here. And Rocco is more than just a prop. He might be retired, but he hasn't lost his edge. He won't bark or make a scene, but if anyone threatens us, he'll do what he's trained to do.

I hold his lead with both hands. As good as it is to know he'd protect me, I'd rather us both get home unscathed.

I force my lungs to take in a full breath as I pull out my comm, enter the code for emergency services, and hover my thumb over send.

I'm not taking chances tonight. One glimpse of a black mask and I'm out.

Pulling on Torrent's lead, I urge us both forward.

A shadowed figure comes into view, and my fight-or-flight response kicks in with a rush of adrenaline moments before familiar blond hair and emerald eyes set my mind at ease. My heart's racing a mile a minute and my knees feel like they might give out.

Rocco growls, but a few calming words from Tarek has my four-legged Enforcer squirming against his lead to get closer to his new friend.

"Sorry if I scared you." He crouches down, and I snap out of my surprise enough to give Rocco some slack.

Tarek gives him a thorough rub before turning his attention to me. I jump when he puts his hand on my jaw, tilting my chin and tipping his head to look at my neck. There's no bruise.

"Does it still hurt?"

"No." I lean into his touch. I can't help myself.

He drops his hand. "Where were you going?"

"Just walking Rocco. Thinking."

"Did you tell the Elders what happened?"

"I told my supervisor what I saw, and my manager. They assured me it was being handled and there was nothing I could do."

"That's true."

His gaze holds mine. Or maybe it's the other way around. I don't think I've ever felt this attracted to someone, or this incredibly awkward.

"Ms. Brooks said she would request that you meet with me on Monday."

He huffs out a breath, shaking his head. "Sounds about right. I'll be sure to reassure you we're doing everything we can."

"That's bullshit."

His eyes snap back to mine. I don't mean to offend him. I know it's not his fault, but I keep seeing him as he was the other night. On his knees. It's not right.

"I know it's not you. You could have ended that in a heartbeat. You put up with it because *they* want you to. Because *they're* too afraid to lose what you've gained. And I get that, I do, but it's fucked up, Tarek."

He's standing close already, but he leans even closer. He has that same fresh scent. He shifted recently, and I love knowing that.

"If a video of me putting those fuckers in their place got out, people would use it as a reason to fear Shifters. It would confirm what many are already thinking; that we're animals in human form. Barely in control of our baser instincts."

"You shouldn't have to kneel for anyone. You shouldn't have to pretend to be afraid of them."

Holy hell, I can hardly breathe with him this close. His hand brushes across my cheek as his gaze drops to my mouth. He takes my free hand and presses it against the center of his chest, pinning me between his wide palm and the hard contours of his body. His heart is beating as fast as my own.

"It's not an act." His voice is thick with emotion, his eyes so expressive I can feel his fear and frustration like my own. "If I lose control and give them the so-called proof they're looking for, everyone I care about could be in danger. The life we've earned. Our freedom. I'm terrified I'll be the one to fuck it up."

A shiver runs through me at the intimacy of his confession. Who else has he shared his fears with? Is he always this intense, or am I just the luckiest person on the planet right now?

My hand is still held to his chest. When he releases me, I slide it down just a few inches. Enough to feel the start of hard abs before I pull away.

Holy hell, I want to touch every inch of this man. I need to get a grip. He's being kind, and affectionate, and maybe a little flirty. He's also an Agent. I'm not going to embarrass myself by being next in line to throw myself at him.

"It's bullshit." Focus on the conversation.

He nods. "Yeah. It's bullshit." He takes a step back, then points at Rocco's lead. "Can I walk him?"

"Ah, sure..."

I hand him the lead, and a moment later we're walking side-by-side.

"Where are we headed?" He lets Rocco sniff at the corner of a building, patiently letting the dog set the pace.

"The edge. The sunset's pretty great from there."

"You should see it from the air."

A laugh bursts out of me that sounds a lot like a choking barnyard animal. I can feel Tarek watching me as I struggle to get a grip, but he doesn't comment.

"I'm sorry," I gasp as I get control of my ridiculous outburst. "This is just too surreal."

"How so?" There's no humor in his tone, just curiosity.

I clear my throat. He's been real with me, so the least I can do is be real with him.

"A few days ago, I was pretending to trip just to get the chance to see you up close. Meeting you was a huge moment for me. I was completely geeking out. And now you're walking my dog and we're making small talk and-"

"And you want to ask for my autograph?"

I slap his arm with the back of my hand, and the corner of his mouth curves up in a grin.

"No. I was going to say, now it seems ridiculous. It took me six months to get up the nerve to approach you. Now, here you are. You're sort of just a guy. Until you say something like that, and I remember you're also that dragon, and it's just..."

I let my words trail off, because I'm rambling and even I don't know what I'm getting at. I half expect him to hand over the leash and tap out, but he keeps walking in silence.

Ten minutes later we're at the edge. I thought the vacant lot might trigger some unpleasant emotions, but with Tarek by my side, I don't think it's possible to feel afraid. The sunset is spectacular already. I lean my elbows on the flimsy railing and try to appreciate the natural beauty, but I can't keep my eyes off Tarek for long.

He's not looking at the sky, either. When I catch his eye, he reaches out to touch my cheek again.

"You kissed my dragon." His voice is barely more than a whisper, with the rough edge of a growl.

My throat feels like sandpaper, but I swallow past it and lick my dry lips. "You let me touch you. I wasn't expecting that."

He drops his hand from my face and takes my hand, holding it as his thumb traces circles on my skin. His touch is electric. The sensation crackles over my skin and I can hardly breathe.

"My dragon knew how perfect your skin would feel against mine."

Holy hell. My insides are molten and my heart is mush. I'm putty in this man's hands, and I'm still not even sure if he's trying to flirt.

I look up from our joined hands to find him watching me. He looks like he's about to say something more, but then his eyes drop, his attention turning back to the sunset.

It's a spectacular display of pinks and oranges, as brilliant as any I've witnessed. But it's not the sunset I want to memorize now. The light turns his hair golden and sparks fire in his eyes. He catches me staring, and I snap my attention back to the sky.

I told him I was a fan and admitted what I'd done to get close to him. I don't want him to think I'm a complete stalker, or that I'm only here for the chance to sleep with a Shifter.

But he's the one who stalked me tonight. He's the one still holding my hand, still tracing little circles on my skin and making me imagine his hands in other places.

When the last of the light fades, he lets me go. I want him to step closer, but he backs away, crouching down to praise Rocco.

I don't understand him. With any other man, I'd know exactly what his motives are. He's giving me plenty of signs that he's into me, and I'm not exactly playing hard to get. I don't want to make the first move and risk him thinking that's all I want...

But what do I want? I wanted to meet him, and I did. Getting close to his dragon form, talking to him, *kissing* him. That was everything I'd imagined and more.

I'm leaving in three days. Getting to know Tarek, becoming friends if that's what's happening here... those things aren't on the table. This thing, whatever it is, has a clear expiry date. So why does it matter if he thinks all I want is a casual hookup?

Maybe that's exactly what I want.

I've never been afraid to state the terms in a relationship. I've never pretended like a great first date was destined for anything permanent. One-night stands aren't my thing, but a vacation fling or a summer romance is always nice.

"Can I walk you home?" he asks, like I might actually refuse. Like I could refuse anything he'd ask of me.

"I'd like that."

THOSE EYES.

When Dawn looks at me, those baby blues are full of something I can't define. I want to give it a name; interest, curiosity... lust. But beyond that searing gaze, she doesn't give me any clues. She tolerates my touch, but she admitted to being a fan. Is that all I'm seeing when she looks at me?

I'm not even sure why I care. Why I can't take my eyes off her or stop myself from touching her skin.

She shivers as I take her hand, threading my fingers through hers. It feels like the most natural thing, and she seems completely at ease with the contact.

We chat as we walk, though not as much as we did on the way to the edge. I debated the logic of coming to find her tonight. I stood in that alley for nearly an hour, telling myself it was crazy and completely inappropriate to knock on her door. But then she walked by, and I couldn't walk away.

We reach her door and I hand over the lead as Rocco sits, calm and obedient as ever. Dawn's eyes are on me, and when I meet her gaze, my body heats.

I don't know what this fascination with her is, but she's had me mesmerized since that moment in front of HQ. The moment she faked, apparently, but I don't exactly hate the idea that she wanted to meet me that badly.

"There was no terrorist."

I don't know why I'm saying this. I definitely shouldn't be. There's just something in the way she looks at me that makes me want to tell her all my secrets. All my dreams. I want her to know who I am.

"What do you mean?" Her head tips to the side.

I've already opened up to her more than I meant to. But I keep thinking about the way she thanked Gideon and I for what we did. For the public version. If that's the reason she's interested in my company, I can't let her continue believing a lie.

"The day I broke the Atrium. I didn't do it to take out a Terrorist."

Her brow creases as the corners of her mouth turn down in a frown. "You don't know me. You don't need to-"

"I need you to know. You thanked me for something I didn't do."

She looks for a moment like she might argue, but then her lips press into a thin line and she watches me silently.

"The Elders were corrupt. The Meadow was about to be blown off the map. It was them, or my entire species."

She wraps her arms around herself, her eyes dropping to the

ground. I can see the stiffness in her posture. She's not feeling so comfortable in my presence anymore.

"You killed them?"

"No." She relaxes only slightly. "But I'm just as responsible as the one who did."

She's quiet, looking down at Rocco, or maybe just at the ground so she doesn't have to look at me. "That was the moment that started it all. After that, Shifters were recognized as individuals."

"Not because we were heroes. Tanikka and Tobias are good people. With the corruption weeded out, they could do the right thing."

She nods her head.

I wait for her to ask questions or make a quick exit. When she does neither, I crouch down to give Rocco a final scratch behind the ears.

"Will you come inside?"

I freeze, then rise slowly as if any sudden movement might turn her offer into a rejection. Not that I can accept. I don't have a clue what I'm doing. What do I even want with this woman?

"That's probably not a good idea." It's as close as I can get to the truth.

Her eyes widen and she turns away. Disappointment, or embarrassment that I interpreted her friendly offer as something more? After what I just told her, I'm just glad she's not eager to be rid of me.

"I'll see you on Monday?"

She shakes her head. "There's no need. I think we covered everything tonight. I really appreciate your honesty, about everything."

I reach out, venturing to touch the back of her hand with my fingertips. "Maybe I want the excuse to see you again."

She smiles. That wide, brilliant smile that I can't get enough of. And I know something with absolute certainty. I want to kiss her. I didn't think I'd ever give a shit about that sort of thing, but I want to know what it feels like to have her mouth on mine.

I want to know what she tastes like, and that scares the shit out of me.

INSTINCTS

"Thank you for your assistance, Miss Stevens. And your discretion."

I accept the proffered hand of the robot in a suit, succeeding by sheer force of will not to glance over at Tarek.

"May I escort you to the lobby?"

"I'll take her." It's the most Tarek's spoken since I sat down.

When they directed me to this room, with its casual armchairs and spectacular view, I thought it would be an informal chat. Even though Tarek spent the meeting looking relaxed, the two overpaid lawyers were anything but.

They seemed more concerned about ensuring I wasn't planning to sue, rather than about recording the actual details of that night.

It looks like the suit might object, but when Tarek stands, he backs away with a nod. The Armani twins thank me again with another round of handshakes, then finally leave Tarek and I alone.

"Do you feel like a valued citizen, and that your eyewitness report is being taken with the utmost consideration?"

I glare at him, but I doubt it's very effective considering it's the first chance I've had to openly stare. He's wearing his tactical pants with a button-down shirt. His sleeves are rolled up, exposing powerful forearms.

Holy hell, he's beautiful.

"I felt that way after Saturday night. Now I just feel like dirt under a rug."

"The politics are unavoidable here."

He reaches for my hand, his fingers trailing up the inside of my wrist, up my arm until he reaches the cuff of my short-sleeved blouse. I shudder at the intensity of that gentle touch.

How the hell does he do that? I'm no blushing damsel in distress, but when he touches me like that, I'm ready to swoon and agree to anything he wants from me.

"I want to take you out."

Out? I'm clearly taking that the wrong way. Tarek isn't asking me out on a *date*. He had the chance for far more than a *date* Saturday night and clearly wasn't interested.

"There's a place I like, in Moridian. I think you'll like it."

Oh shit.

This is ridiculous. I'm a grown adult. I need to stop going all doe-eyed around him and say it like it is. There's no point in us dating. Even if that offer is beyond my wildest dreams, it's too late. Getting to spend time with him has been amazing, but there's no point in pursuing this any farther.

"I'm leaving tomorrow. I'm going away. On a trip."

Okay, that's not quite how it is. But it's close. I don't want to tell him I'm never coming back. That sounds too dramatic, even if it is the truth.

"For how long?" His brow is creased, and for a moment I could almost believe he'd miss me.

"A while. I'd really like to explore this." I point from him to me. "But I'm leaving and I..."

What am I doing? Tarek wants to take me out. Why the hell can't I? It's just one night... it'll either be amazing or completely awkward, but if I refuse, I'll never know.

A casual drink and conversation, or a wild night of crazy sex... either way, I can't think of anything I'd rather do with my last night on Earth.

I suck in a breath of courage and step toward him. Mimicking his earlier motion, I reach for his hand and trail my fingers up his arm. His skin is smooth, dusted in soft, blond hair and contrasted by the hard muscle underneath.

He grips the back of my neck and crushes his mouth against mine.

The kiss catches me so off guard, I can't think, let alone reciprocate. As suddenly as it happened, he pulls away.

His eyes are wild, his chest rising and falling with rapid breaths. He looks as surprised by that as I am.

"Was that okay?"

I don't even know how to respond. I don't think there's anything he could do to me I wouldn't be completely okay with. Can't he see that? Can't he tell what he does to me?

"Yeah." It's a pathetic response, but one syllable is all I can manage.

It must be enough, because his smile is absolutely heart-melting.

I can't leave without exploring this.

Deep breath. Courage. Or else I'll regret what could have happened for the rest of my life.

"Are there security cameras in here?"

He shakes his head.

I hold his gaze for a moment more, then slide my hands over his stomach. Holy hell, he's ripped. He's also really, really tall.

"Can we sit?"

He backs up, and I follow, keeping my hands on his body. As

he sits, I slide my knees over his thick thighs to straddle his lap. He grips my hips, and as I lean down to taste his mouth, a growl rumbles low in his chest.

And then I'm kissing Tarek.

It's nothing like the impulsive kiss of a moment ago. I'm in control, and I want to explore his mouth. I kiss him thoroughly, deeply, ignoring the ache between my thighs that's begging for more. There's no rush. I want to savor this moment.

He follows my lead, mirroring my motions but not pressing for more. One hand slides to the small of my back, while the other moves to the back of my neck.

He doesn't break the kiss as he pulls me closer, pressing my body against his. When the unmistakable ridge of his arousal presses against my core, I'm helpless to stop the needy moan that escapes me.

That sound lights him up. He takes control, devouring me with bruising intensity. I'm pinned against his body in arms that could break me, as he grinds against me with a delicious promise of what's to come.

"Tarek, are you-"

A man's voice booms in the silence. We jump in unison as I scramble off his body, smoothing my clothes and no doubt blushing like mad. Tarek lets out a string of curses, adjusting his crotch as he stands. Even with his heavy tactical pants, it's impossible not to notice the outline of his arousal.

Holy hell. I made out with Tarek.

"What the fuck, Mav?" Tarek practically growls at the Agent in the doorway, his voice laced with violence at the interruption.

"I'm so fucking sorry, man."

I recognize Shifter Agent Maverick, and I'm sure he recognizes me when he makes brief eye contact before dropping his eyes to the floor.

"They need you at the Meadow. Now."

"What's happening?"

"Can't say. I just got the message to find you and tell you to haul ass."

"I'll jump in five."

Maverick nods, then leaves us alone. Tarek turns to me with a hardened expression, his jaw set, and fists clenched at his sides.

"I'm sorry, Angel."

"No, don't be. Go."

With one long stride, he's towering over me, pulling me into a tight embrace. I wrap my arms around his waist and breathe in the scent of him. He's solid muscle. So impossibly powerful.

"That was incredible." He speaks against my hair, his voice a low rasp. "I didn't know it was possible to get that turned on."

Holy hell. I grip him tighter, clenching my thighs to stop myself from wrapping them around his waist.

"Tarek..."

"I was so fucking hard. All I could think about was getting your hands on me. Feeling your skin against mine."

He's killing me. I'm going to die of a lust-induced heart attack right here. I push back enough to look up at him, and his emerald eyes are blazing.

He leans down, pressing his forehead against mine. "I don't know if I'll get back before you go. This is new. I've never... I don't know what will happen if you kiss me like that again."

His lips touch my forehead, and I'm still trying to process his words and form my own when he lets me go. He walks out of the room.

That might have been the last time I'll ever see him.

"WHAT'S THE DEAL, BROTHER?"

I'm more pissed off than worried after leaving Dawn like that. I hauled ass to get here in record time, and nothing seems out of the ordinary. The Meadow's bustling with activity on one of the warmest spring days we've had this season.

"There's a fucking dragon on North Mountain."

Shit.

"A female, I think. She's pissed. Won't let me near enough to communicate, and I don't want to risk pissing her off enough to follow me back here."

Fuck. I told exactly no one about the brindle dragon I met last week. The entire fucked up encounter took a back seat to Dawn.

"I'll check it out."

"I don't know. Might be best to let her look and leave. I figured two of us here would change her mind if she's thinking about starting something."

I slap him on the shoulder. "You've lost your touch, old man. I'll reason with her."

I don't want to tell him the whole truth. Not until I have a handle on what happened with my dragon. I have a feeling I'll get some answers now.

Damon punches my shoulder, then nods toward the northern horizon. "Be my guest, brother. Sweet talking is definitely not my department."

The only female I want to be talking to is Dawn. Leaving her after that was so damn hard. *I* was so damn hard. I've never reacted like that to a woman. I've never wanted that. But kissing her, having her body pressed against mine...

I'm going back to her tonight. She dodged my question when I asked her how long she'd be gone, but there's no place on this planet I can't get to. It'll be a hell of a commute, but I don't give a fuck.

I want her. I need to know what comes next.

I circle the windswept, snowy peak of North Mountain as the brindle female watches me with flared wings. My chest burns as that same instinct pulls me toward her.

Here goes nothing.

I land barely twenty feet away, and she crouches. Keeping her head down, she approaches me with slow, deliberate steps.

I dig my claws into the rocky ground, fighting the urge to go to her. To pin her. To dominate her.

Fuck this.

I shift, my heavy boots crunching in the light snow as I rise from a crouch to look up into the yellow, surprised eyes of a dragon. A cold shock of fear slices through me. I've been around Damon in dragon form, but he's a friend. This is what it feels like to face a creature that can kill you multiple ways before your next breath.

I step toward her.

"Shift. We need to talk."

Her eyes are unblinking, nostrils flaring with the rise and fall of her chest.

"That village is under my protection. I can't let you near it. If you have business here, if you need something from us, shift so we can talk."

She growls, long and low. By sheer force of will, I hold my ground as her head dips until one wide eye is level with my face.

"We. Are. Dragon."

Her speech is guttural and halting. Speaking human words in dragon form feels like swallowing shards of glass, but she endures it to avoid shifting.

"I hear you. I feel that, too. But it doesn't control me. I'm in control. Shift, so we can talk."

"Not. Here." She pulls away, flaring her wings and jumping into the air.

Fuck. She didn't roast me, at least. Following her is the last thing I want to do.

I glance over my shoulder toward the Meadow. There's no sign of Damon, but I suspect he's watching.

I slip into dragon form, a rush of anticipation hitting me as I take to the sky. She travels farther north, following the mountain range until the Meadow is far behind us. Farther still, until trees give way to barren brush and even the valleys are white.

She banks suddenly, spiraling downward and straight into a dark crevice etched into the side of a steep cliff. I flare my wings, slowing to perch on the outer ledge.

Inside, areas that have been dug by a dragon's hand offset the jutting stone of a natural cave. She's put a lot of work into this. The word nest comes to mind, but I don't want to dwell on that thought.

She's off to one side, her scales reflecting the dim light that filters in from the overcast day.

She shifts.

Thank fuck.

I join her in human form. She looks my age, but with Shifters that's not always an indication of actual years. She's tall and lean, with thick, red hair. Her eyes are almost the same shade as her dragon's, but maybe more amber than yellow.

"Who are you?"

"I know you feel it. The dragons aren't just forms we take. They *live*." She steps closer, her eyes pleading for me to understand. "I felt it the moment I found her form. I don't want to control her. I want to help her. She needs..." She crosses her arms, chewing on her lower lip. "She needs her own kind. They could thrive here. They could be safe."

"If this is how you want to live, that's your call. Morwood is for all Shifters, and there's plenty of space."

"There is. There's plenty of space for dragons to thrive again."

"Okay, sure. What does this have to do with me? Why were you watching the Meadow?"

She drops her gaze, biting her lip hard enough that I think she might draw blood. "They're a beautiful species. They deserve a chance... but she can't do that alone."

"Oh, fuck no."

Her head jerks up at my instant refusal.

"If you're looking for a sperm donor, that is not my kink."

She shakes her head. "The black dragon is mated. She could smell it on him. You're the first male she's found. You're powerful, intelligent... beautiful."

She blushes at the last word. What the hell dimension did I fall into?

"How can you say that with a straight face?"

"Don't you feel it? The dragon is her own creature. I have no interest in you, but she feels a connection to your dragon. This is bigger than us."

"All I'm hearing is that you want to mate in animal form to procreate a potentially dangerous alien species and-"

She slaps my face so hard I stumble back a step. I feel the growl in my chest, but my ears are ringing with rage.

"I'm not an animal and neither is she!"

"Hit me again, female. You won't get another free pass."

She slips into her dragon form, splitting the air with a shrill roar as her teeth gnash mere feet from my face.

I rise to the challenge without thought. Dragon instincts take over as I lunge, maneuvering into a solid grip on her slender neck. She knows she's no match for my bulk. Her body relaxes as she submits.

I pin her beneath me, denying the leverage to struggle out of my grasp. My tail curls around hers, restraining her further as my claws anchor into her shoulders. She arches her back, fitting her hips against mine.

I release her as quickly as I pinned her, skidding on the rough cave floor to put some distance between us. She stays where I put her, ribcage heaving as she watches me retreat.

I don't waste a second. I get the fuck out of there and fly like my ass is on fire.

CHARADE

I suck in a breath, pull my hood over my head, and step onto the waiting tram.

It's packed with people this time of day. Pointless to look for a seat. I squeeze between a woman who looks like she's ready for the clubs and a ruffled suit who might take a nap where he stands. The railing's still warm from the last hands that gripped it. As the tram glides forward, I lean over just enough to see what I'm leaving behind.

Afternoon sun reflects off the polished sides of a small shuttle as it detaches from the roof of the terminal. The shuttle that would have taken me to the Launch Pad, and my transport off-world. It dips out of sight to begin its route, the lineup for the next one already reaching out the door.

I thought I would feel something. The tram pulls away from the squat little building on the edge of the Solar, and I wait for the regret to hit.

Still nothing.

It's only one more month. Considering how long I've been waiting for this day, one more month is nothing, really.

It's not like I could leave now. Not yet. Not after what happened with Tarek yesterday.

I kissed him. He kissed me. I don't know what would have happened if we weren't interrupted; how far that would have gone. I'd never fault him for doing his job, but holy hell, that was terrible timing.

I can't leave without knowing what comes next. Maybe that's crazy. I'm pausing my life to have a fling with a man I barely know.

One more month, then I'll catch the next transport off-world. We'll have an entire month to explore this crazy new... whatever this is. By then, I'll have him out of my system. And, hopefully, some sexy memories to keep me warm at night.

I step off the tram just outside HQ. For one fraction of a second, I think about going inside to ask if I can swap my vacation time. An extra month's work would cushion my digital wallet a little more. Buy me more time before I have to stop somewhere to find work.

I push that thought away. Liam hasn't found a new roommate yet, so I won't be homeless. I'll enjoy my two weeks off, hopefully with Tarek, then work until next month's launch day.

I turn toward my flat as strong hands grip my arms and a hard body presses against my back. Heat blooms in my belly as my heart races.

I freeze, smiling from ear to ear.

"Hello, Blue."

Hot anticipation turns to terror in an instant. It's him. That voice. The asshole in the mask.

I turn and the world keeps spinning.

"Agent Thomas." I squeak out his name with the last of the air in my lungs.

It's him. They're the same person.

The image of Tarek being beaten hits me and I sway. He grips my shoulders. I can't process this. He's a Protector.

"Are you okay?"

I take a step back, out of his grasp. Maybe he doesn't know I've connected the dots.

"I just... you took me by surprise."

"Hmm." He hums a satisfied sound as he steps closer, tipping his face to mine. He smells good, like mint and soap. "You took me by surprise, too."

Oh, shit. I swallow past the lump in my throat. "When?"

I hold my breath for his answer, but he gives a low chuckle and makes me wait. His eyes flicker from mine, studying my face, reading the involuntary cues in my expression.

He's trained to spot a lie, but I haven't lied yet.

"I've wanted to catch you off-duty, but our shifts don't line up. Now here I am with a few days off, and the first person I see is you."

I let out a shaky breath.

"What's wrong, Blue?"

"Nothing."

That answer was too fast. I need to calm down. Think.

Daniel Thomas is an Agent. He transferred up from Moridian about five months ago, so he's clearly good at what he does. Someone upstairs trusts him.

He's also a Terran Defender. He might be the reason they always know where to strike and who to target. Tarek never shifts in public, but Daniel would know his face.

He's watching me still. Patiently waiting while I figure out how to get a violent terrorist to trust me.

I need to get him to admit who he is. The sound of his voice and a nickname won't be enough to convince anyone. Even if I'm the only one who hears his confession, Tarek will believe me. I can take a polygraph to prove I'm telling the truth.

"I'm sorry." I take a deep breath, forcing myself to relax. I'm the one playing him, now. Not the other way around. "You caught me with a lot on my mind.

"Talk to me. I'm a good listener."

He eases back, giving me space to breathe.

I'm perfectly safe. We're in a public place.

"What do you think about the Terran Defenders?"

His posture stiffens as his blue eyes turn icy. My resolve wavers, but only for a moment. After working the front desk for two years, I can bullshit my way through any conversation.

"I'm sorry." I drop my gaze. "That was unprofessional."

"No." He gestures for me to walk with him. "We're both off the clock. What's on your mind?"

Every step takes us farther away from HQ, but the street is far from empty. It's not like I'm following him into a dark alley. This is perfectly safe. I pull my hood off, hoping for a clearer eyewitness description if I'm tossed into an unmarked vehicle.

"I'm tired of the charade. You heard me the other day, giving my lines to that woman."

"That didn't sound like a script, Blue. You sounded pretty pissed off."

"Yeah, pissed off that I have to pretend to- Nevermind. I really shouldn't be talking like this. I'm just tired."

He stops. When I risk a glance, he's watching my face with renewed intensity. He leans in, and my stomach twists.

"Pissed that you have to pretend they're people, and not just animals walking around on two legs."

Holy hell. I wish someone could hear this.

"Does that make me a terrible person?"

"No, Blue." His eyes search mine. I wish I could know what he sees there. "You might be the only person who makes any sense in this place."

We stand in silence while a group of people walk past.

They're chatting loudly, but the words are a blur of noise as my brain scrambles to come up with the next thing to say to him.

"What do you think about it all?"

He glances around before answering. "I think we should talk more. But not here."

Walking down the street was one thing, but I'm not stupid enough to go anywhere with him. Not without Tarek, or someone, knowing what I'm doing.

"My roommate's expecting me. We have a dog who can't stay alone. I..." Holy hell. I can't believe I'm about to say this. "Can I see you again?"

A slow grin spreads across his face. "Absolutely."

I cross my arms over my chest, trying to hide the shake in my hands.

"Tomorrow?"

"Tomorrow." His eyes dance as he gives a low chuckle. "I look forward to it."

THE MOMENT the door closes behind me, I sink to the floor and suck in air like I've been holding my breath for the entire six blocks. Maybe I have been.

What the hell just happened? One minute I'm basking in all the possibilities of another month with Tarek, and the next I've got a date with the asshole Agent who also happens to be a Terran Defender.

Tomorrow morning at nine. Breakfast at the outdoor café a few blocks from HQ. I think I might be sick.

But there's no reason to freak out. I won't be anywhere near that café tomorrow. I'm going to be at HQ first thing in the morning to tell them everything.

Rocco's furry head burrows under my arm, snuffing and pushing until his wet nose finds my face. I wrap my arms around him, vowing to never leave the flat without him ever again.

"Whoa, what happened to you?" Liam's bare feet come into view, as he crouches down to my level.

A heavy knock at the door has me jumping to my feet. Shit. He followed me. Why didn't I have the sense to just go back into HQ instead of leading him right to my place? Not that he wouldn't be able to find me if he wanted to.

"Talk to me, Dawn. What's wrong?"

"I'm sorry. I'll explain everything."

I stiffen my spine and paste on a smile. Hiding won't do me any good now. I wait for another knock, then swing the door open.

"Tarek?" It comes out sounding like a question, but I can hardly believe my eyes. "Come in."

The moment he's past the threshold, I close and lock the door. I've never been so happy to see another person.

When I turn, the men are staring at each other. Tarek with his arms crossed, putting his immense biceps on full display. Liam with narrowed eyes, his jaw tight.

"Liam, this is Tarek. Liam's my roommate."

The testosterone-laced silence drags on for another moment before Tarek looks to me. His expression is hard, maybe even a little pissed off.

"I thought you had a plane to catch?" The accusation in his voice is thick. Is he pissed off that I *didn't* go?

"I was waiting for you. I thought I could put my trip off for a few weeks..." Hell, that sounds so lame now.

He raises an eyebrow, scepticism written all over his face. Because of Liam? I told him I had a roommate.

"I came to see you off, but it was a little crowded."

What is he...

"Shifter Agent Tarek." Liam holds out a hand as he puts the pieces together. Tarek accepts the gesture with a quick shake.

Liam's eyes are dancing when he looks at me. He knows I'm fascinated by Shifters. He's heard me mention the green dragon on more than one occasion.

"It's a long story," I say to Liam, hoping he'll get the hint to not embarrass me right now. I turn back to Tarek. "What do you mean?"

"You seemed to enjoy Agent Thomas's company. I didn't want to interrupt."

My chest constricts at the thought of Tarek coming to say goodbye, only to find me cozied up to another man.

"That wasn't what it looked like."

"Wow." Liam claps his hands together. "I definitely need to take Rocco for a walk."

"Liam, I'm sorry."

"No, no. We're good." He gives me a wink. "You two take all the time you need. Rocco's got a lot of pent up energy to burn."

I slap his arm as he walks by, knowing full well that's a dig aimed directly at my sex life.

"Thanks, Liam." The fact that he's joking about this is a huge relief.

Neither of us speak until the door closes. I don't even know where to start. What if Tarek doesn't believe me? What if he-

"I have no right to be jealous. Who you see is none of my business."

Holy hell. How can he think I'd want to *see* anyone else? After the way we kissed... but I suppose women falling over him is hardly a rare occurrence. He's not jealous, because he wasn't reading anything deeper into it. I'm the one who postponed my flight. He didn't ask me to.

But that's hardly the most important part of this conversation.

"It was him, Tarek."

His brow knits in confusion.

"That asshole from the night you... the night we met. It was him."

"He told you that?"

"Not exactly." Doubt flickers across the memories, but I know what I heard. "It was him. I'm sure of it."

He walks past me, crossing the sitting room with three long strides. As he sits on the sofa, I instantly flash back to yesterday. To his kisses, his arms, the feel of his body against mine.

Holy hell. I kissed Tarek.

Heat washes over me like I just stepped out into the sun.

"Tell me everything he said. The first night, and today."

I cross the floor to sit beside him on the sofa, as much distance between us as I can get. I repeat everything, word for word, but I can't look at him as I do. The only thing my story tells him is that I'm a good liar when I want to be.

"I know it sounds ridiculous. I can't prove any of it."

Silence stretches on, but I still can't bring myself to look at him.

"You postponed your trip to meet with him?"

"I had already deferred my ticket." It feels silly to say it now. But I need him to know I didn't choose to stay because of a fake date with Agent Asshole. "I was going to tell you when you came back."

"I thought you had to go?"

"I do. I will."

He leans back, stretching one arm over the back of the sofa, his hand resting just inches from my face. "Why didn't you?"

I swallow. This shouldn't feel so terrifying. "I wanted more time with you."

His hand moves, his fingers brushing through my hair, over my cheek. The rough pad of his thumb traces my mouth.

I don't dare move. I can't even breath.

"I want to kiss you again."

I'm not shy. I'm certainly not conflicted about whether I want to kiss Tarek again. Hell, I want to do far more than that. But when I meet his eyes, something in them keeps me frozen to the spot. There's more than just heat, there's a vulnerability. Like he honestly doesn't know how I'll react.

I tip my face to his hand, brushing a soft kiss against his palm. My legs uncurl from beneath me as I move toward him, and he takes me in his arms, guiding me to slide a leg over his lap to straddle his hips.

"Angel." His voice is rough, like he's on the edge of control. I wish he'd let go. "I've never wanted this with anyone."

I slide my hands up his arms and over his shoulders. My fingers linger on the soft skin of his neck, then trace the outline of the course stubble covering his jaw.

"What do you want?"

I shiver at the thought of learning this about him. What does he want? What does he like? I want to know everything.

"You." His answer is so simple, so damn sweet, I swear my heart's going to burst.

Deep breath. Ignore that pesky organ. I focus on the molten heat pooling where our bodies are moulded together. Tarek's not my boyfriend. This isn't some fairy-tale beginning of a happily ever after. This is the start of the most incredible, mind-blowing sexual adventure I've ever been on.

He needs to know that. He needs to know I'm not reading more into this than what's here. I want him. For the next month, my only goal is to make as many filthy memories as I can to fuel my daydreams for decades to come.

"You can have me, Tarek. Any way you want me. I'm down for whatever you like, no strings attached."

He grips my hips, his fingers digging into me as a low growl rumbles in his chest. His breathing is unsteady, his eyes blazing, and it takes all my restraint to wait. Wait for this god of a man to combust and take what he wants.

"What if I don't know what I like?"

The idea that maybe Tarek isn't a player makes that heart of mine jolt to life again. I'm sure he's had an endless parade of men and women, eager to be the focus of his carnal desires. But maybe he doesn't play that way. Maybe he's not usually into casual trysts.

I lean slowly, brushing my mouth against his. He doesn't relax his grip on my hips, keeping me tight against him as I kiss his perfect lips. He lets me taste him, exploring his mouth with unhurried movements as my hands explore the contoured expanse of his chest, down the ridges of his abs.

I can feel him harden beneath me, and I roll my hips just enough to let him know.

He takes control of the kiss. His mouth claims mine, the contrast of soft lips, rough stubble and the wet heat of his tongue driving me wild.

I pull his shirt up, desperate to feel the heat of his bare flesh against mine. My fingers explore the landscape of his stomach as he nips a fiery path along my jaw, down my neck. I find soft hair dusting his chest, then rake my fingernails down the trail that disappears beneath his belt.

His hips buck against me, and I can't help but moan at the dirty promise.

I reach between us, finding the thick length of him through his pants. Holy hell, he's big.

The sound of keys rattle in the lock.

He jumps as I scramble to the opposite side of the sofa. My

heart's pounding as Liam steps inside with Rocco at his heels. He looks from me to Tarek and back again, as the corners of his mouth twitch with a restrained grin.

I smooth my hair, not daring to glance at Tarek.

Rocco crosses the room, jumping onto the sofa between us. He settles onto his belly, head on Tarek's thigh.

"I've got work to catch up on. I'll be in my room." Liam gives me an obvious wink before heading down the short hallway to his room.

When I hear the door close, I hazard a glance at Tarek.

His face lights up with a smile, and I can't help but grin back. I almost had him in my hands. If Liam hadn't interrupted, maybe I would have unzipped him. Felt the weight of his arousal as I learned the pressure and speed he needs.

I shudder at the prospect of knowing him that intimately. I've never fantasized about giving someone a hand job, but the thought of holding his pleasure in my hands, of watching him come undone... holy hell.

Tarek takes a deep breath, clearing his throat as he strokes Rocco's shoulder. "Agent Thomas. You're certain he's the one from that night?"

Right. Back to business. Of course.

"Yes. I know it was him."

He nods. "I believe you."

"Thank you. Should we go to the Elders?" Maybe Tarek will want to go alone first. Call me in after as a witness. Maybe they won't care about what I have to say, and Tarek's word will be enough.

"No." His hand strokes along Rocco's big body. His eyes are unfocused. "It's not enough. All we have is a hunch, and an Agent looking for a date. That's all they'll see. He hasn't confessed to anything."

"But he's-"

"If we take this to the Elders now, they'll pull him in for a chat and then he'll be in the wind. Best-case scenario, they put surveillance on him. But the TD seems to smell our eyes and ears a mile away. You'll miss your date, and he'll put two and two together."

Shit. But Tarek doesn't look concerned. His jaw is tight, his eyes following the path of his hand as he continues to stroke Rocco.

"What are you going to do?"

"You need to keep your date." He says it so casually, I assume there's more to the ridiculous statement. Until his eyes meet mine, and there's nothing but seriousness there.

"I'm not going on anything resembling a date with that asshole." When Tarek's stare doesn't waver, I stand up. "No fucking way. I'll end up with a roofie in my drink. He'll find the wire. You won't get any more usable information, and I'll wake up dead!"

"You can't wear a wire. It's too risky."

What is happening right now?

"Tarek..."

"I'll be with you. He won't hurt you. You can get him to talk, and when we take it to the Elders, I'll be able to give them first-hand intel."

"How?"

He pats Rocco, making his tail thump with appreciation. "You can take him."

"That won't..." I clue in to what he's suggesting, and it's ten times worse than roofies or being buried in a swamp. I lower my voice to a whisper. "You can't be my dog! I can't put you on a leash and treat you like-"

He stands, making Rocco grumble at losing his attention. He steps close, taking my face in his hands and pinning me with his intense, green eyes.

"You were there. You saw me on my knees. I was lucky, thanks to you, but others haven't been. We can't have a life here. We can't have families here. Not until those assholes are stopped. The thought of getting you involved makes me sick. But if you can do this, I can play my role, too. We can nail this fucker. But I can't do it without you."

DATE

*T*his was a stupid idea.

Dawn's laugh sounds genuine, as Agent Thomas entertains her with stories of botched missions and slippery marks. Hell, I've got a million stories I could tell her from my years with Gideon. I've been doing this job twice as long as this asshole has.

Sure, there's been fewer hands-on missions and more patrolling since we moved up to Elite status, but I've still got far more experience than this little asshole.

I reach a hind leg up to scratch at the leather collar, and Dawn's hand brushes the top of my head.

Fuck, this is rough. I'd take a week of recon in a swamp any day over this shit.

Yesterday, Dawn was in my arms. I've been taking human form for a while now, but that's the first time I've felt like a man. Like this body has a purpose beyond being a meat shield.

I can't get enough of kissing her. The taste of her skin, the feel of her under my lips and my teeth.

What would have happened if we were somewhere else? If Liam hadn't interrupted? She reached between us and gripped me, and in that moment so many wicked, carnal images flashed through my mind. My cock was so fucking hard. I was ready for all of it.

I've never cared about sex. I considered myself asexual, and that suited me just fine. I want to find a mate and have a family, but it's never been about sexual attraction.

It's different with Dawn. I don't want to jerk off, and I don't want to marry her. But I sure as hell want to get my hands on her again.

"Tell me about your problems at work."

That question perks my ears up. This is the reason we're here, not all that small talk that sounds a little too much like a real date.

"Oh, I'm sorry. I really shouldn't have said that. I was frustrated and you were a friendly face. It was inappropriate."

"Don't say that. Don't even think it."

They're quiet as a server tops up his coffee and offers Dawn a refill on her latte.

"Thank you. I'm good."

"My pleasure. That's a well behaved pup you have there. He's beautiful."

"Thank you. He's a retired Enforcer dog. He doesn't like to be left behind. Still thinks he's on duty, I suppose."

"What a sweetheart." The young woman looks at me with a hand over her heart.

"And I thought you brought him to make sure I stayed at arm's length." Daniel's all smiles when the server moves on.

"Oh, no. My roommate and I share him, but Liam's been swamped with work lately. When I'm not at HQ, Rocco's with me."

She's good at this. Even though we practiced lines and prepped as much as we could, it surprises me how naturally she's able to deliver them. She appears shy, maybe a little intimidated, but not suspicious.

"That's good of you to give him a home. Taking on a dog like that's a big commitment."

She shrugs. "He deserves it."

I settle down onto my belly on the smooth ground, watching the cars and people passing by.

"So, you have a soft spot for dogs, but not Shifters."

Silence follows his statement. I swear I can feel her tension kick up a notch. I repeat the lines we practiced in my head, wishing I had the Link connection with her that I do with Gideon. No matter how much stealth the mission requires, or how far undercover we are, we can always talk without fear of being overheard.

"It's not that I have a problem with Shifters. They're fascinating creatures. It's just..." She lets her voice trail off, as if she's thinking this through on the spot. "They had their place. But now, they could be anyone. They're made to be weapons, but they can live like people without anyone around them knowing the strength they possess."

"I hear you. I do. It happened too fast. One moment a Shifter is demolishing the Atrium. The next, they're people and no one can say shit."

"Exactly!"

"The Terran Defenders get that. They know this can't work, and they want to make sure people see the truth."

"Do you think so? Their methods seem unnecessarily cruel."

"Maybe that's necessary. My Shifter never hesitated to draw blood to take down a mark. He never gave a second thought to the humanity of his targets."

It's not enough. Secretly sympathizing with terrorists is cause for concern, but it's not enough to charge him with anything other than being an asshole.

"I feel like I should do something."

"Like what?"

"I met them. Some of them. The Terran Defenders."

With a brief squeal of metal on metal, torture to my canine ears, Daniel pulls his chair in closer to the table. While I can't see above it, I can tell that he's leaning in closer, eager to hear what she says.

"How?"

"I didn't know it was them. I saw some thugs ganging up on a guy, and I tried to help. It was stupid."

"Did they hurt you?"

I can't help it. I look up at Dawn, watching her face as a small grin plays at the corner of her mouth. Her hand moves from the table, up to her neck.

"He took control. He did what he had to do."

"Did he hurt you?" Thomas's voice has an edge of concern that's almost convincing.

"No." Dawn drops her hand, bringing her mug to her lips and closing her eyes as she sips. "I think he's the reason all this has been bothering me so much lately. I wish I could talk to him."

A mix of anger and jealousy surges in my chest. She's too good at this.

"What would you say to him?" His voice is lower than it was. Rougher.

There's a scuffing sound on top of the table, and Dawn sucks in a breath. What the fuck is he doing?

"It's silly."

"No. I want to know."

"I'd just ask him to explain it to me. Show me what's behind the curtain, you know? Tell me what I'm missing."

"He would. He'd want you to understand."

"I HEAR YOU, Tarek. But there's no usable intel here."

"Goddamnit!"

I clasp my hands a little tighter in my lap, keeping my eyes down as Tarek argues with Elder Tanikka. I expected saluting, some *at ease, Agent*, and a whole lot of *yes, ma'am*ing.

This private meeting in her personal office has been anything but formal. He's debating with her like they're equals. Like formalities and chain of command are concepts that don't apply to him. Maybe they don't.

It's insanely sexy.

He's in his tactical pants and shit-kickers, with a white t-shirt that accentuates his bulk. He'd look like sex on a stick no matter what he was wearing.

And now I'm imagining him wearing nothing at all...

I hate Liam so much. Why did I think it was a good idea to have a roommate? Something about limited rental options and saving credits, but I can't remember anymore. I can't stop thinking about what might have happened if we hadn't been interrupted.

Elder Tanikka's in a long, slender dress that gives her legs for days. Her hair is piled on the top of her head in a complicated design that must have taken a team of stylists. Her makeup is perfect, her lips a shameless crimson. I feel like the extreme femininity should come across as showy, but as she sits on the edge of her desk and argues with Tarek, I get the impression this detailed look is exactly how she feels most comfortable.

"Miss Stevens can see him again. Get him to admit something specifically incriminating."

No way.

"No fucking way." Tarek stops barely a foot away from her, staring down with a glare that would make a grown man cower.

She reaches out and touches his arm. "We need more proof than this. You know I'm right."

"And you know I'm right. That asshole works for you. And he

works for them. Doesn't that piss you off enough to do something about it?"

She doesn't flinch. Doesn't look away or even raise an eyebrow.

"The question is, does it piss Miss Stevens off?" She turns to me, and I want to disappear.

"She's not going to date him to get intel. She's not going anywhere near him."

"I think she can speak for herself." Elder Tanikka straightens, moving past Tarek to sit on the velvety chair beside mine. "Dawn, you've done so much already. The night you stepped up to help Tarek took a lot of courage."

"Thank you, ma'am." I hold her stare. I'm so far out of my league here. The last thing I want to do is get more involved than I already am.

"You met with Agent Thomas when you suspected he was one of the assailants from that night. That took an entirely different kind of courage."

Meeting with Daniel had nothing to do with courage. I did it because Tarek asked me to. Because I don't want him, or any other Shifter, to be treated like they're less than human.

As nerve-wracking as it was, Daniel was actually nice. He seemed genuine in his interest in what I had to say, and I got the impression he wanted to tell me more. Not that I feel anything less than hatred for the man. Talking to him wasn't that much of a hardship, though. It certainly wasn't an act of bravery.

"Would you do that again?" Elder Tanikka reaches over and takes my hand. "You've already laid the groundwork to have Tarek by your side as your dog. Would you lead him on a little longer?"

Tarek growls, but she ignores him.

"I don't think he just wants to talk."

I don't miss the fire in Tarek's eyes at my statement.

"I don't doubt your instincts. I'd never suggest nor expect you to sleep with him for the sake of a mission. But can you stomach the flirting? Can you keep up the ruse of attraction?"

"Maybe." It's the only honest answer I can give.

"If he forces himself on you, Tarek will pull the plug. You'll have a safe word, and it will be over."

"This conversation is over." Tarek grabs me by the arm, pulling me up to my feet like I'm weightless.

Elder Tanikka springs to her feet, her eyes wide as she looks at Tarek's possessive grip on my arm. He pulls me toward the door. I might be pissed off if his dominance wasn't so damn sexy.

"What if they target Tarek again?"

I dig my feet in, and Tarek stops as I turn back to the Elder. She plants her hands on her hips, her eyes dark and knowing.

"What if they tire of the baiting routine and go back to bullets? What if this is our only opening?"

"She's manipulating you. Let's go."

"Tarek, think. This could be exactly what you've been pushing for. A chance to get closer. Dawn is our way in."

I look back at him, and while he's still radiating anger, there's something new in his expression. He's torn. He knows what she's saying is true, but he doesn't want to put me in danger.

"From your description, Agent Daniel Thomas sounds a lot like the man I used to call my husband. I know what a man like that is capable of; what he'll do for his cause."

I turn away from Tarek's pained expression. How can I refuse what she's asking?

She reaches over her desk, retrieving a tablet and swiping the screen. A few gestures later, she holds it out to me.

"What's this?"

"It's our standard non-disclosure agreement for civilian operatives. If you do this, you're under our protection. You'll have to keep everything you see and hear absolutely confidential."

"Don't sign that." Tarek's voice is calmer, but no less commanding. His fists are balled at his sides, the veins in his forearms popping. "We'll use what we've learned to catch that asshole. You don't need to risk anything else."

But I do. If I don't do this, I'm turning a blind eye to a person who might be capable of murder.

To a person who might hurt Tarek.

It's not a choice.

CLASSIFIED

he moment my door closes, Tarek hooks a paw in his collar and twists free. His body immediately reshapes into a very pissed off man. Everything from his jaw to his fists are clenched.

"Are you okay?"

His green eyes are blazing as he looks at me like I must be crazy. "This was a stupid fucking idea."

"It worked."

"That is not what I wanted to happen. One meeting. One conversation. That was supposed to be it. I never would have started it if I'd thought this is where it would lead."

"You didn't start it. I did."

"Everything okay?" Liam and Rocco emerge from his room, and I greet the dog with a good scratch.

It's strange, considering a moment ago it was Tarek in this form.

"Everything's good. It's classified." I widen my eyes and wiggle my fingers, telling the truth while keeping it light.

Liam nods, looking between us a few times before backing away. "I'll be working in my room if you need me."

"Thanks."

When Liam's out of sight, I motion to Tarek.

"Come on. We can talk in my room."

Once we're closed in, I lean against the door and press my fingers to my temples.

"I hated treating you like that. The leash, the commands..."

He's silent for so long, I half expect him to be gone when I open my eyes.

Far from it. He's standing in the middle of my bedroom, arms crossed, staring at my bed.

Heat surges through me, becoming an inferno when he turns toward me and holds my gaze. In one long stride, he braces his arms on either side of my head, caging me in with his body.

"Why the fuck did you sign that contract?"

"What else was I supposed to do?"

"How about staying the fuck out of it? You're not an Agent."

"No. I'm the person who has a date with a Terran Defender."

I swear there's fire in his eyes.

"We'll get the evidence, then it'll be over."

"If he puts his hands on you, there won't be any evidence left."

I shudder at the deadly threat. Tarek might be a big teddy bear, but I don't envy anyone who gets on his bad side.

"I know you won't let anything happen to me."

He leans even closer, his arms dropping. I hold my breath as his hand brushes my hair and his warm breath caresses my ear.

"I don't want him to know what it feels like to be this close to you. I don't want him to know that your hair smells like honeyed oranges," he dips his head and I feel his nose brush the sensitive skin behind my ear. "And your skin smells like strawberries. Or that you hold your breath when you're nervous."

Holy hell.

I let my breath out slowly.

I can feel the heat from his body. His breath is on my cheek as his fingers trail down the side of my neck.

I turn my head, inhaling his smoky scent as I brush my lips against his. He sucks in a breath, and when he doesn't move, I trail the tip of my tongue along the seam of his mouth.

He growls, a low rumble that starts deep in his chest and moves upward until I feel the vibration on my lips.

"You shouldn't do that."

"Why not?"

His eyes meet mine, the emerald flashing. "I'm a Shifter."

My chest constricts. It couldn't have been easy for him to hear that conversation with Daniel. I know I'm a good liar. It's part of the job, really. Carrying on conversations about topics I have no interest in, pretending to like sports teams I've never heard of or movies I've never watched. I've never considered it dishonest. I like to make people feel comfortable.

"I know you're a Shifter." I reach up and touch my fingertips to his lips, brushing them along his stubbled jaw and down his neck. "You're incredible."

His lids drift shut as he rests his forehead against mine. He is incredible. He's also beautiful, kind, and the sexiest man I've ever laid eyes on.

"I've never wanted a female like this before."

I shudder at his words. The way he whispers them, like a confession. The way he uses the word *female*. It's so raw, so pure.

"I want you, too."

He pulls his head back, meeting my eyes.

Then his mouth is on mine. His kiss starts with a sweetness that makes me melt into him, then turns demanding. He grips my hips, pulling me tight against him as he presses me to the wall. The thick length of his arousal presses into my stomach, and I practically claw at his shirt, desperate to see more of him, to feel more of him.

My comm buzzes in my pocket. I'm more than happy to ignore it, but Tarek freezes. He grips my wrists, stopping my fumbling attempt to get his clothes off.

"You should see who it is."

"I don't care who it is."

He grins, tipping his head. "If it's Tanikka, ignoring her will have an Agent at your door in five minutes."

I groan, but he releases my hands and I check the screen. My stomach drops.

"It's him." I hate to even say the words.

Tarek growls, his hands turning to fists. "You don't need to do this."

I slide my thumb across the screen and put the comm to my ear. Because I have to do this. I am doing this.

"Hello?"

"Hey, Blue. It's Daniel."

"Hey. How did you..."

"Sorry, I should have asked for permission to look up your number. I couldn't wait to run into you at work."

I laugh, hoping it sounds genuine enough. "Or you could have just asked for it."

"Can you tell I don't date much?"

I don't know how to respond to that. I fumble for a reasonable response that doesn't shut him down entirely, but also doesn't imply I'm actually interested.

Daniel doesn't wait for me to find my words. "I've been thinking a lot about our conversation."

"Oh?"

"There's something I want you to see. Will you come with me tonight?"

I grab Tarek's hand, and he laces his fingers through mine.

"I should probably say no, considering I barely know you." Can't be too easy.

"That's smart." He's quiet for a moment, but I doubt he's going to give up that easily. "I'll be honest, I can't think of any way to reassure you without making myself sound more like a predator."

This time, my laugh is genuine. He's got charm, that's for sure.

I take a deep breath, releasing it slowly and letting him hear my nervousness.

"Can I bring Rocco?"

"Yes. For sure. Absolutely. He can even sit in the middle."

"He might be retired, but he still knows how to take down a perp."

"I'm sure he does. I'll pick you up at seven?"

When I end the call, I can't bring myself to look at Tarek. He doesn't let the awkwardness last, as he slides his arms around my waist. He pulls me tight against him, surrounding me with his heat and impossible strength.

I burrow against him, loving the contact.

"I don't like that you're doing this. But I swear I'll keep you safe."

"I know." I push back enough to look him in the eyes, so he can see how much I trust him.

His expression is so serious. I trace my fingers across the worried lines on his forehead, then rest my palm against his cheek. When I kiss him, it's soft and tender, and I feel it in my chest as much as I do between my legs.

He cups the back of my head, matching my gentle pace while threading his fingers through my hair. All too soon, he pulls away to rest his forehead against mine.

"I want to take you to the Meadow."

My heart stops. Everything stops.

Morwood is a vast, dense forest. Six months ago, it became

official Shifter territory. And the Meadow... I've only heard rumours.

"It's a real place?"

Tarek laughs, the vibration shaking my whole body.

"It's where I live. Where most of the Shifters I know live."

My entire life I searched for evidence that Shifters were more than they seemed. The thought of going there. With him.

"I don't know what to say."

He kisses me, then whispers with his lips against mine. "I built my house there, with a fireplace for warmth and a view of the forest. My bed is far bigger than yours." He nips my lower lip, sending a shiver down my spine. "And definitely no roommate."

Holy hell.

"I'd like to see that."

He chuckles, and I'm definitely blushing because hell yeah, I'd like to see the Meadow. But seeing Tarek's bed... seeing Tarek in his bed... yeah. I'd like to see that.

"We need to get out of here."

"Oh. Why? Daniel's picking me up at-"

He covers my mouth with a rough, brief kiss.

"I can't take you home today. But there is some place closer we can go. Someone I think you might like to meet."

TANNER

"*W*here are we?"

I scratch the door and stare at a panel set into the wall. A moment later, it opens a crack and a wary eye peers out at the two of us.

"Can I help you?" He looks at Dawn for a moment, then focuses on me.

"Hi, ah... my name's Dawn Stevens."

I shoulder my way through the door, pulling Dawn along behind me. Once inside, I claw out of the collar and shift to my human form.

"Well, shit. Tarek on a leash..."

"Don't you fucking say a word." Tanner holds out his hand, but I pull him in for a quick half-hug. "This is Dawn. Dawn, Tanner."

"Ah yes. The woman holding said leash." He gives her a welcoming smile, and she accepts his handshake. "I'm certain this is a story I want to hear."

"Long story. We need a place to chill for the afternoon."

"Of course. Hungry?"

Tanner won't press for details. He trusts I'll tell him what he needs to know. He also loves to talk, and since Dawn's obviously curious about Shifters, it's the perfect place to kill the afternoon.

"Fuck yes," I answer, because I'm starving and Tanner's kitchen is always stocked.

He looks at Dawn and gives an exaggerated eye-roll. "Not sure why I bothered to ask. Coffee or Tea, Dawn?"

"Coffee, thank you." Dawn's smiling, already at ease with Tanner.

I didn't tell her anything about where we were going. I insisted on using the dog form when we went out, just in case her place is being watched. After an hour of walking a meandering path and doing my best dog impersonation, I was confident we weren't being followed.

Tanner leads us to a cozy sitting room, with as many sofas as can possibly fit in the modest space. When he leaves us to get snacks, I kick off my boots and get comfortable in my usual spot.

Dawn's standing in the doorway, looking around, and when I pat the cushion beside me, she takes a seat and tucks her feet under her.

I had to get out of her flat. I've been dancing around these new emotions that surface whenever I'm close to her. Trying to figure out how they fit with the way I see myself. The way I think of sex. Not anymore. It was crystal clear... I want her. And she wanted me, too.

My arm's draped across the back of the sofa, my hand just inches from her shoulder. When I reach to touch her cheek, her lips part as she sucks in a breath. Fuck, I love that. The way she reacts every time I get close. The way she seems to forget how to breathe as her baby blues turn stormy.

She does the same damn thing to me.

"Okay, here we go."

At the sound of Tanner's voice, I pull my hand away and Dawn sits up a little straighter. He sets a tray of food on the low table, and I dig in. Meats, cheeses, and other appetizers are piled high. Dawn thanks him as she samples a few items. We all eat in silence for a few minutes before Tanner speaks.

"So, Dawn, tell me about yourself?"

I listen as she tells him the basics; where she lives and where she works. She tells him she grew up 'a little bit of everywhere', and I make a mental note to ask her about that later.

She's being vague, probably not knowing if she can trust him. That's good. I'd trust Tanner with my life, but Dawn doesn't know him yet.

He doesn't pry for too long, and instead he launches into his own life story. Dawn's eyes are wide when he reveals he's a Shifter, and she keeps that look of awe as he tells her about his twenty-plus years working undercover at BioSol, helping to smuggle supplies and the occasional Shifter to the Meadow as needed.

"That's all behind me now. These days I'm head of security for World Bank. Gives me the freedom to work remotely, and the excuse to travel."

"That's amazing. It must be such a relief not to have to hide anymore."

"I still keep it need to know. Old habits die hard, I suppose. When Fury was murdered, well, I figure it's not quite time to show all our cards just yet."

Dawn gets quiet, looking down at her hands. "I don't know how humans can be so cruel. How they can still deny Shifters are people."

"It's human nature. It's still a struggle for human women to get equal treatment in some areas. For people like that, accepting an entirely different species is out of the question."

"It's not fair."

"No, it isn't. When did you realize the truth?"

Her eyes flicker between Tanner and I, then settle back down at her hands. It's strange to think that not that long ago, Dawn would have looked at me like any other animal. Hell, I've seen her at HQ for years, and never gave it a second thought.

"When I was seven."

"Seriously?" That was not the answer I was expecting.

She looks at me with worry in her eyes and nods. "I was with my family at a fair. I can't remember much, but I ended up alone, hiding in a corner of a parking lot. A cheetah walked by and noticed me. I knew I wasn't supposed to stare, but I couldn't help myself. He walked right up to me, pushed his head against my shoulder, and started to purr.

I don't remember finding my parents, but I remember him. I remember how safe I felt."

Her eyes are unfocused as she tells the story. Her mouth curved down in a frown. She's known, or at least suspected, the truth about us for longer than I've been alive. It's not fucking fair. How many people knew? How many people suspected what we were and never did a damn thing about it?

"I tried to talk to someone about it. I tried for years to find someone who knew, or some proof that I was right. It became kind of an obsession."

"Is that why you wanted to work at HQ?"

Dawn nods at Tanner's question, but she's looking at me with a wary expression. Maybe she thinks I'll judge her for knowing and doing nothing to change it. She couldn't have done anything if she'd tried. It took a hell of a lot more than words to fix that shit.

"I wanted more proof. I wanted to meet someone who saw what I saw."

"Did you?" I ask.

"No. Not once."

"I can't say I'm surprised. When did you meet Tarek?"

She glances at me, her cheeks flushing the slightest pink. "I saw him at work often, but it took a while to get up the nerve to talk to him."

"She introduced herself to my dragon." I laugh, and her blush deepens.

"I'm impressed. Most humans give our dragons wide berth."

"I've never been afraid of Shifters. Certainly not Tarek."

I don't know why that makes my chest swell with pride, but it does. She's small and fragile, but she wanted a closer look, so she made it happen. Just like she's doing now with Thomas. She wants his confession, so she's doing what it takes to get it.

I stand to clear the empty tray and mugs. Tanner stands as well, taking the dishes from my hands and insisting I sit back down.

He gives me a wink as he excuses himself and heads for the kitchen. I look over at Dawn, and she's staring at my arm where it's draped over the back of the couch.

Her eyes drop back to her hands, and an almost sad expression crosses her face.

"Are you okay?"

"Yeah." She tips her chin up, schooling her expression as if she didn't mean for me to see it. "I'm nervous about tonight."

"No one can hurt you unless they go through me first."

Her baby blues are glassy as she avoids my eyes. I don't want her to be afraid of anything while she's with me. There's nothing I wouldn't do to keep her safe. That thought should probably be alarming, but it feels too right.

"I'll fucking burn it to the ground before I let anyone touch you."

She snaps her gaze to mine. My reminder of the destruction I can wreak makes her eyes dance, and a smile tug at the corners of her mouth. My animal side doesn't turn her off, not for a second.

"I'd like to see that," she says as a smile lights up her face.

I can't help myself. I cup my hand around the back of her

head, threading my fingers in her short hair. She doesn't resist as I pull her toward me.

"Anyone have a sweet tooth?" Fucking Tanner takes that exact moment for re-entry. I immediately drop my hand and lean back.

I glare at him, hoping he'll get the hint and back off again. He does the opposite, laying out a platter of sweets and more coffee before making himself comfortable.

He launches into more stories from his years at BioSol, captivating Dawn's attention with every detail. Every Shifter he mentions has her eyes lighting up.

The afternoon slips by with endless stories and easy conversation. Tanner feeds us supper, then it's time for us to head back to Dawn's place and wait for Thomas.

Dawn excuses herself to the washroom, and Tanner clamps a firm hand on my shoulder.

"You like her."

It's not a question, so I don't bother responding.

"She likes you, too."

INITIATION

I can't stop replaying every detail about this afternoon. Sitting with two Shifters, eating, sipping coffee and listening to Tanner's never-ending stories. I learned more about Shifters today than I have in my entire life.

"That's him."

Tarek's voice brings me out of my thoughts, and my stomach turns to stone at the sight of a black SUV pulling up to the curb. It's not the same one from the night Tarek was attacked, but it's a similar make.

I grab Tarek's hand, threading my fingers through his. He pulls me into his arms, wrapping me in a tight hug. I burrow into him, soaking up his heat and his scent.

"Don't be too quick to step in." I pull back enough to look him in the eyes. To make sure he hears me. "I know what you're capable of, but if you show yourself, all this is for nothing. Please, no matter how uncomfortable it gets... don't pull the plug unless you have no other choice."

"I won't let him touch you."

I stretch up on my toes and press a kiss to his mouth. "Promise me you won't step in unless I use your name?"

"Dawn..."

"Promise me."

His jaw clenches. His eyes go dark. He understands what I can't bring myself to say. I don't care if Daniel touches me. I'll deal. I've come this far, I'm not blowing it that easily.

He nods. That'll have to be enough.

I slip into my sneakers as he slips into his Rocco form. The real Rocco's locked in with Liam. We let him know the dog had to be kept out of sight for the evening, and thankfully he agreed without asking too many questions.

When we step out into the cool evening, Daniel jumps out of the truck and comes around to open the door. I grip Tarek's leash like a lifeline.

I'm so far out of my league here. I can smile and nod behind a desk, but pretending to want to join a criminal organization in the fight against Shifters? There's no way I can pull this off.

"Are you alright, Blue?" Daniel's smile twists with concern.

Tarek's warm, wet tongue slides over my clenched fist. I pull him closer, reaching down to run my hand over the top of his head and around his soft ears. He leans his shoulder against me, and I wish we could talk. I want to hear him say it again; *I'll burn it to the ground before I let anyone hurt you.*

There's no point in pretending not to be scared shitless. Daniel's an Agent. He's not stupid, and he knows how to read my body language.

I straighten my spine and walk up to him, ignoring the open truck door and instead stepping toe-to-toe and looking up into his eyes.

"This isn't a date."

He raises one eyebrow, the last of his smile fading.

"What is it then?"

"I thought I knew. I thought I was reading between the lines and had you figured out. But now you're here, and I'm second guessing everything, including my sanity." I take a deep breath. "Especially my sanity."

"I think you have good instincts."

"I'm not so sure."

"Say it."

I shake my head, but when I look away, he grips my chin and pulls me back to look at him. Tarek growls, but Daniel doesn't acknowledge him.

"I can't."

"Say what's on your mind, so we can move on without the games."

His eyes search mine, and even though his grip on my face is bordering on painful, I'm not afraid of him.

And it's not just because I have a dragon on a four-foot lead.

There's something soft in Daniel's eyes. Something hopeful.

"It was you that night."

His eyes close as his grip relaxes. When he looks at me again, his expression is almost sad.

"I hurt you. I'm sorry. I was amped up; ready for a fight. I... there's no excuse. I could have scared you without hurting you."

"You opened my eyes."

He nods. "What do you want from me, Blue?"

I take a moment to consider my answer, but the best lie is an honest one. "I want to understand the Terran Defenders. Who they are. Why they do what they do. I want to see inside."

For a few long minutes, he doesn't speak. His face is a mask as his blue eyes scan my face. He admitted to being there that night. He was the one who threatened me. He's a Terran Defender.

"If you come with me, I'm going to be the friendliest face you meet tonight. I'll make sure they know you're with me, but they won't trust you without testing your loyalty."

He steps back, gesturing to the open truck door. He's giving me the option to back out. Agent Daniel Thomas might just be a decent guy, despite being a violent criminal.

I hesitate for only a moment, then coax Tarek onto the front seat ahead of me. With him sitting tall in the middle, I take the opportunity to lean into his warmth, wrapping an arm around his waist and kneading my fingers into his thick fur.

It looks like I'm keeping him calm, but the truth is he's the only thing keeping me from going into full panic mode.

I'm so far out of my depth here. They're going to see right through me. I left my ticket by my bed. My disappearance might not surprise anyone else, even if it is sudden. But Liam will know I wouldn't leave without that ticket.

The city passes by in a blur. I hope Tarek's paying attention to our route, because I'm too deep in my own head to keep up.

Why did I agree to this? What can I possibly offer these people to make them trust me?

It's not long before we pull up to a darkened restaurant, the delivery door at the side sliding open with the screech of rusty hinges. When we're sealed inside, lights flicker on to illuminate a big, open loading area.

"When we get out of the truck, do exactly what you're told."

I climb out, keeping Tarek on a short leash. It's quiet. There's no sign of anyone else, and now I'm thinking this was all a trap and Daniel just brought me here to dispose of my body with the restaurant waste.

One of the many unmarked doors around the room swings open. A man in a mask walks through, wearing the same fake tactical gear as the other night.

"Shit, D, you let her see your face. It must be love."

There's an edge to the teasing that makes my skin crawl. When I glance at Daniel, he's not smiling. I shorten Tarek's lead, gripping it with both hands as if that could stop him.

"Let's skip the bullshit, shall we? She won't be leaving my side."

"No can do, boss. The old man wants proof. Whether she's putting out has nothing to do with it."

Instead of focusing on the last part of that, I zero in on one word; boss. Daniel isn't just a member, he's someone important. Someone higher in the ranks. But the old man. Daniel's father? Could this all be a twisted family business?

Daniel's a successful Agent. He would have had his own Shifter partner for years before the truth came out. How did he go from that to the Terran Defenders? If he's a high-ranking member, or even if it's a family thing... why risk staying in the Protectors?

He catches me staring out of the corner of my eye and attempts an unconvincing half-smile.

"Let's get on with it then."

"What's up with the mutt?"

"It's not a problem."

I keep pace with Daniel as we follow through the door.

"What's your skill set?" The masked man calls back over his shoulder as we make our way through a narrow hallway. "You don't look like much of a fighter."

"I'm not." Might as well kill that idea right away. "I know tech. Programming."

He doesn't respond. Instead, he stops abruptly, opening a door and gesturing for me to go inside ahead of him.

I look to Daniel for confirmation, but his face is grim when he nods.

"Light switch is on your left."

I stand in the doorway, keeping one foot out so I don't get locked in a broom closet. Just as I find the switch, Tarek growls. Light floods the white room, empty save for a rusted metal dog crate in the back corner. A huge husky sits inside. It eyes us warily, but barely has the strength to hold its own head up.

"How does that make you feel?"

I close my eyes and loosen Tarek's lead. He doesn't move, but I can feel the tension in his body as he presses against my leg.

"We picked that one up a couple nights ago. Takes a hell of a lot to keep them quiet, but with enough broken bones, they learn their place."

I don't bother to swipe the tear that escapes down my cheek. Tarek's braced, the fur on his shoulders and rump standing on end. He's staring at the Shifter, ears forward. He looks every bit like an Enforcer dog, focused on a target and waiting for his command.

"What if I told you to shoot it to prove your loyalty?"

I can't do this. I can't pretend to be okay with this.

Daniel's face is expressionless. I search his eyes for some hint of compassion, but there's nothing.

"I shouldn't have come here."

"I figured as much. Your girls got a soft spot for Shifters, D. What are you going to do about that?"

"I'm not..."

"What's that, sweetheart?"

I take a deep breath and turn my back on the poor creature in the cage. They can't do this. They can't treat Shifters like this and get away with it. But that's exactly what's been happening.

"I'm not a killer." I ignore the masked asshole and keep my eyes on Daniel's. "If that's why you brought me here... I thought I wanted to help, but that doesn't mean I want to kill. Human or animal, I can't do what you're suggesting. I won't."

"You think Shifters deserve to live?"

"Yes." My answer is immediate, and his neutral expression breaks into one of surprise.

"The Terran Defenders don't kill Shifters. The one time you did, so many of you were arrested, the organization all but vanished. Disagreeing with the laws that make them equals and wanting to draw some attention to change that... that's one thing. But out right murder, it's-"

Daniel's arm wraps around my shoulders, pulling me abruptly into an embrace. I'm stunned into silence when he plants a kiss on the top of my head.

"It's alright, babe. You're good."

I'm not sure what's happening. The asshole with the mask reaches up and pulls it off, revealing a messy shock of bleach blond and brilliant pink hair. He's got tattoos covering his neck to his chin, and more piercings than I've ever seen on one person's face.

He can't be older than twenty.

"That was a brilliant answer, *babe*." The exaggerated endearment is clearly meant as a jab at Daniel. He holds out a fist for bumping, which neither of us acknowledge. "I'm Gareth. Welcome to the Terran Defenders."

"What..."

"You're absolutely right. We don't kill Shifters. And the last thing we need is a new recruit who's too eager for violence. We want to show people they are the violent ones, not us."

Daniel's arm is still around my shoulders as he pulls me away from the room. I crane my neck to see the Shifter one more time, but he's not even looking our way.

"What's going to happen to it?"

Gareth chuckles as he turns off the room light, leaving the poor creature in darkness. "He's going to sleep off the sedative, then go home."

"He's not hurt?"

Daniel gives me a slight squeeze. "He's fine. He's not even a Shifter."

"It's a friend's dog," Gareth admits with a smirk. "Had to make it convincing."

Daniel laughs, releasing me from his grip. "Convincing, not theatrical, dickhead."

Gareth shrugs.

"Is this where you operate out of?"

"Hell no. This is all for you, Blue. If you'd failed, or we smelled trouble, we'd clear out of here in minutes."

Shit.

"Let's go for a drive."

THE FARM

reathe in.

Tarek's fur between my fingers. The drone of tires on pavement. The sickening scent of a fruity air freshener.

Breathe out.

Tarek's solid body between my knees. The crunch of tires leaving the smooth highway. The dusty scent of fields.

Breath in.

"Almost there." Daniel's voice is light and holds a hint of excitement. Like we're going somewhere fun, and I'm not blindfolded in the backseat. The knowledge that Tarek is paying close attention to our route is the only thing keeping me from freaking out.

"Okay, you can take it off."

I don't waste a second pulling off the length of course material, blinking as my eyes adjust to the sudden, unexpected light. I'm not surprised to find that we're on the ground, but I am a little taken aback at the sight outside.

We're parked in the centre of a wide, dirt courtyard. A pale farmhouse fills the front window. A pair of wooden rocking chairs sit on its wide, covered porch and little hearts are carved into delicate shutters at every window.

Daniel and Gareth get out of the truck, and I let Tarek out ahead of me before jumping down. I swing my backpack over my shoulder. Daniel insisted on stopping at my flat to pack, but I didn't know for how long, so I just packed everything that would fit.

I squint against the glare of flood lights mounted at the apex of two looming, red barns. They enclose us in a dome of light, along with the shadowed facades of various outbuildings, tractors, and other farm equipment.

Behind us, the driveway is a dark, endless tunnel through thick cornfields.

"Welcome to the farm."

Daniel's voice is proud. I recall that first night, when I nicknamed him 'Farmboy'. Now it makes sense. This is an actual farm.

"Not what I was expecting."

I pull Tarek closer. He's sniffing the air and wagging his tail like he's loving the smells of a functioning farm. The metallic creak of a gate grabs his attention, and I nearly lose my grip on the lead as he makes a lunge in its direction.

"Come on." Daniel puts his arm around my shoulder, guiding me toward the house.

Instead of climbing the well-worn stairs to the covered porch, we skirt around to a path that leads behind the house. Here, the lighting is far dimmer. Just enough to illuminate the space between a row of small, unpainted cabins.

"These are for the farm hands. If anyone asks, you're here on contract to update the security system."

I don't know what I expected. A dingy warehouse; an underground lair; a metal tower. Something that screams *bad guy hideout.*

If this is where the Terran Defenders are operating out of, it's no wonder we haven't found them. The land between Moridian and Fentondale is covered in farmland. Huge ranches that stretch from Morwood to the ocean. The expression needle in a haystack feels very appropriate, but now that we know which haystack to look in...

He leads me with quiet footsteps into the first cabin. There's a kitchenette with a sink full of dirty dishes, and a tiny nook with a worn sofa and ancient flat-screen tv.

There's a narrow hall with two closed doors on either side, and a small bathroom at the end. Daniel carefully opens the farthest door on the left, and steps aside.

It's a tiny bedroom. Barely big enough for the single bed, crooked bureau, and a little table with one chair. The walls are covered in a floral wallpaper that's faded and peeling, and the floor is rough chipboard.

I step inside and shrug off my pack. The room looks old, but clean. There's a faint floral smell in the air. I let go of Tarek's lead, and he lowers his head to sniff around the bed.

Daniel hovers in the narrow doorway, his tall frame dominating the small space. "It's clean and comfortable enough. Ma makes sure of that."

Ma? Protector. Terrorist. Mama's boy?

I nod. "What am I doing here?"

He smiles, the corners of his eyes crinkling. He crosses one ankle over the other, leaning his hip against the door frame. "You're here because I like you. That's a good enough reason for now. Once you're done with the security system, we'll see what the vote is."

"I'm actually updating the security system?"

He shrugs. "It's pretty much plug and play. That's what the box says, anyway. You know tech shit better than I do."

Okay, then.

I fold my arms, glancing around the room and pretending like I don't notice he's staring at me. Tarek's still sniffing every nook and cranny, snorting and growling when he finds a particularly interesting spot.

"This is your room while you're here. No one will step through this door without your permission."

I look up at him, then drop my gaze to his feet. His boots are on the threshold. Half inside, half outside.

"You can stay here, but I'd rather have you in my room."

I don't look at him. I can't shut him down outright.

"I should sleep. It's been a day and I..." I risk a glance up at him, but he looks neither hopeful nor disappointed. Maybe it's another test. I offer what I hope is a friendly, but not too encouraging, smile.

He responds with a quick nod, as his gaze flicks briefly to my mouth. "I suppose that's a good excuse for tonight."

I'm not sure if his wink is flirty or creepy, but I don't breathe until he closes the door and I confirm the deadbolt works.

I nearly jump out of my skin when hands slide around me, but then I turn to wrap my arms around Tarek's firm, warm waist. Just being close to him, the feel of his body and that freshly-shifted scent, it's impossible to feel anything but safe.

"There're no wires here. But we need to stay quiet."

His warning is barely whispered, his lips brushing my ear. I respond with a nod of my head against his chest.

I want so badly to talk about everything we've seen and heard so far. Daniel, Gareth, the farm itself.

"Have we seen enough?"

He's quiet, but he doesn't need to answer. I wouldn't leave now even if he wanted to. We're here, and no matter how much we've already learned, I can't pass up the chance to learn even more.

"Whatever they've got for a security system, I'll figure it out. I'll prove I want to be a part of this."

I feel Tarek nod, but he pulls away. The lack of his arms around me makes the tiny room feel much too big.

"You should sleep. I'll be fine on the floor."

"No." I don't want him to spend one more moment than necessary as that dog. "We can share the bed."

He raises a skeptical eyebrow as he looks from me to the single mattress. "Are you sure about that?"

I nod, blinking away the sting behind my eyes. It's more than just not wanting him to take Rocco's form. Maybe I'm being selfish. We barely know each other... "I want to be close to you."

I half expect him to shift when he realizes how needy I sound. Instead, he makes quick work of the clasps and velcro of his tactical pants, and pushes them down over his hips.

Holy hell.

Tarek's legs are like tree trunks. Long, muscular, sexy as hell tree trunks. And his boxers... they're clinging tightly to his hips and his massive thighs. His huge-

His hand on my face makes me tear my eyes away from all my daydreams coming to life. I snap my mouth closed just as his lips brush mine, trailing along my cheek to smile against my ear.

"I'm not trying to start anything." Even in a whisper, I can hear the rough edge to his voice. "I'm just getting comfortable so I can sleep."

All I can do is nod.

"I'll stay on top of the blankets. I won't-"

His words cut off when I grip the hem of his shirt, pushing it up over his ripped stomach. He helps me get it over his head, and then my hands are on his bare chest.

Holy hell, he's beautiful. I press a kiss over his heart, feeling its powerful rhythm as a light dusting of hair tickles my face. I run my hands over his broad, round shoulders. Down his arms to trace the veins back up again. Over his chest. Down his carved abs.

I've been touching him all evening. Burying my hands in his fur or rubbing his ears, needing the contact to remind myself that he's here and I'm safe. I want more of that. I want skin against skin.

I reach out and turn off the light. As my eyes adjust to the soft, silver moonlight seeping through the edges of the curtain, I pull my shirt over my head. My jeans join my shirt on the floor, and I grasp Tarek's hand as I pull back the heavy quilt and crawl between cool, smooth sheets.

He doesn't hesitate to climb in with me, and after some slow, careful adjustments we settle with him on his back, and me nestled against his side. I wrap my arm around his waist and drape my leg over his huge thigh. His shoulder is my pillow, as I watch the rise and fall of his broad chest and listen to the steady sound of his breathing.

I don't care where we are. I don't care what's outside that door or what I have to face in the morning. This is exactly where I want to be. I'll deal with whatever role I need to play during the day, if this is how my nights can be.

I swear I can feel the courage soaking into my body from his. I hug him a little tighter. I can do anything with Tarek by my side.

His hand moves, his fingers trailing up my side to my shoulder, then down and over the curve of my hip. He repeats the motion, up and down, raising goosebumps and shivers even as he heats me way past boiling.

It doesn't take long for my focus do drift away from the comfort of his skin on mine, and toward much less innocent thoughts. Of all the things I imagined happening when we reached the lair of the Terran Defenders, getting Tarek nearly naked in my bed wasn't one of them.

Now that we're here, with a locked door and hardly anything

between us, I want to do so much more than cuddle. I know exactly which fantasy I want to enact tonight, and I don't think Tarek will have any objections.

~

I SHOULD REVIEW everything I saw and heard today. Commit the details to memory and work through the possible scenarios we'll face tomorrow.

Fuck that.

Dawn's offer to share the bed seemed practical enough. But watching her strip down to a black sports bra and lacy blue underwear... Sweet fuck, those curves. Her body is sheer perfection, and laying like this, with her skin against mine, I can't think of anything other than this woman.

She's still in my arms, but only for a moment. Her hand moves over my skin, tracing my chest and sliding over my stomach. I'm done for. My cock is rock hard, and the only thing keeping it hidden is the heavy quilt over us. If her hand goes much lower, she's going to know exactly what she's doing to me.

She moves to prop herself up on her elbow, her face in shadow as the pale moonlight casts a soft halo around her head. Her hand keeps moving in lazy circles, drifting lower over my stomach as her eyes follow.

Her fingers trace along the top of my boxers, and I can't take it anymore. I grab her wrist, pulling it up to my chest.

"I love your hands on me." I pull it to my mouth to kiss her palm. "If you keep touching me like that, I'm going to lose my mind."

A smile spreads across her face. She looks at me, and her eyes are as playful as her grin.

"Can you lose it quietly?"

"What do you..."

She leans down to brush her mouth across my chest, then bites my nipple. The sudden, sharp pain makes me stifle a growl, as I grip her ass hard enough to make her gasp.

I can feel her smile against my skin, as she continues to nip my flesh, working her way down my stomach.

Fuck, I've never felt anything like this. Not even close. I want her so damn bad, but we can't, not here. Can we?

When her lips hover just under my navel, her hand slides down. She doesn't even hesitate as she reaches under the quilt and finds me hard and straining against my boxers. We groan at the same moment as she grips me through the thin fabric. I grab fist-fuls of blanket, grinding my teeth to keep quiet and fighting to stay still.

She lifts herself up, straddling one of my thighs and staring down at the evidence of what she does to me. I can feel the heat between her legs, and I don't give a fuck where we are, I need to be inside her.

She braces a hand on my chest. "Don't move."

Her eyes are wild as she traces her fingers over my stomach, then over a scar on my thigh. The one injury my Medic couldn't fully heal. Concern flashes in her eyes as she looks up at me, but the expression melts into heat as her hand finds the button on my boxers.

A moment later, she's gripping my length and all I can do is watch. Her small hand is wrapped around me, and my entire body's on fire as she strokes me with slow, deliberate movements.

"Dawn." Her name's the only word I can manage.

"Shh."

Her tongue darts out to moisten her lips, then she lowers her head and takes my cock in her mouth.

Fire burns through my veins as I watch her perfect lips stretch around me, her tongue driving me nearly insane with want. I grip the headboard and the edge of the mattress, hissing through my teeth to keep from roaring with the pleasure of what she's doing to me.

I fight to stay still as she takes me deep into her mouth, then lets me go again. It's all I can do not to grip the back of her head and drive myself back into her heat.

I've never felt anything like this. Never imagined such a simple act could light me up and fucking slay me in the same instant.

"Fuck, Angel. You're killing me."

She smiles, radiant and wicked as her eyes dance. She dips her head, her eyes holding mine as her tongue darts out to lick me from base to tip. I shudder and close my eyes as she explores and plays with my cock until I can't take it anymore.

"Stop. I can't." Fuck, I can hardly breathe, let alone speak.

"Please," she whispers, her lips brushing the tip of me. "Let me taste you."

She takes me in her mouth again, sucking me so fucking perfect and deep that I lose it. My orgasm barrels down my spine and I'm fighting to keep quiet as I empty myself inside her perfect mouth. I can feel her stifled moans as she drinks me down, sucking every last drop before she releases me to kiss her way up my body and into my arms.

HUNTER

$\mathscr{I}$ wake with a jolt, barely processing where I am or how I got here. My eyes land on Tarek with his arms over his head as he pulls his shirt on, the gorgeous expanse of his abs on full display.

Holy hell. I gave Tarek a blow job.

There's a knock at the door, and then I'm the one scrambling for my clothes.

"Good morning, sleeping beauty." Daniel's voice is bright and cheery from the other side of the door.

"One second!"

I rake my fingers through my hair, hoping for a stylishly tousled look. Tarek's already in Rocco form, but when his dark eyes meet mine, all I can think about is last night.

I can't believe I did that. Oral isn't exactly my idea of a fun night, and I certainly didn't plan to do anything like that here. I just couldn't resist getting my hands on him.

Holy hell, his cock is gorgeous. Every inch of this man is perfection. And his reactions; the intensity and awe in his expressions.

I lean in and nuzzle my face against his cheek, then plant a kiss on his velvety muzzle.

"You're beautiful."

He pushes against me, then nuzzles his warm nose against my cheek.

It's not the greeting I would have chosen for this morning, but it'll have to do.

I pull the door open a few inches, and I'm immediately greeted with a steaming mug of coffee. I swing the door open and grip his offering with both hands. I really want to hate this guy, but morning coffee earns some serious brownie points.

"Sorry, I'm not used to farm time." I inhale the glorious scent as the steaming liquid bites my lip. A small price to pay for the first sip of the day. "Can I meet you outside in five?"

"Don't take too long, or you'll miss Ma's breakfast." He flashes me a smile, raising his own mug in a toast to the day ahead.

After a quick trip to the surprisingly clean bathroom, I fasten Tarek's lead and meet Daniel outside the cabin. There's no sign of anyone else around, but I suppose the day starts early in a place like this.

I shield my eyes against the sun, breathing in the scents of earth and fresh air. The Solar smells nothing like this. I missed the ground. The breeze picks up, bringing with it the faint scent of farm animals.

"Over five thousand acres of cattle and crops," Daniel says, his eyes watching my reactions.

The rich scent of freshly baked bread greets us when we step inside the big farmhouse. The front room is bright and clean, decorated in countless little knick-knacks lovingly arranged on every available surface. We take off our footwear at the door as an older woman scurries down the hall toward us, a wide smile on her weathered face.

"Good morning, handsome." She pulls Daniel down for a firm kiss on the cheek before turning her bright eyes to me. "Hello, dear. Aren't you a pretty little thing!"

"This is Ma. Everyone calls her Ma. She owns the place, and keeps the farm hands fed."

"It's lovely to meet you." I hold out my hand, but she swats it away and wraps her strong arms around me.

"None of that, now. If you're here, you're family." She pulls back, sweeping her eyes over my hair before she turns her attention to Tarek. "And who is this beauty?"

Tarek bristles, but when Ma crouches down and pats her knee, he steps forward with his head and tail down.

"That's Rocco. He sticks pretty close to me... we both get separation anxiety, I think."

She reaches out to pet him, and I stiffen. He knows I like to pet him in any form, but watching someone else do it is a different story. Tarek stays in character, shying away from her hands for only a moment before leaning into her touch. She gives him a gentle pat on the head, but doesn't linger.

"What a sweetie. Will the two of you be staying long?"

"Oh, I-"

"Dawn's here to update the security system. Not sure how long that will take."

"Oh, that silly thing. I've lived here all my life, and we've never had to worry about security. Pa and I had a few good dogs," she nods to Tarek. "That was all we needed to feel secure."

"Bosses orders."

"Oh, I don't doubt that. My boy has his own ideas."

Even as she rolls her eyes, the affection for 'her boy' is obvious. I glance down at Tarek, knowing he's making a mental note of the connections, too.

Tarek reluctantly stays at the door as Ma leads us into a huge, modern kitchen.

"I've got ham and eggs, or pancakes if you prefer a sweet breakfast?"

"Eggs would be perfect. Thank you."

She bustles around for a moment, then takes my empty mug and hands me a plate piled high with scrambled eggs, glazed ham, and thick, buttered toast.

"Oh. Thank you. This is too much..."

"Don't be silly. The boys have all eaten, so you have your fill and share the rest with your pup."

Tarek will be happy to hear that. Daniel sits at the end of a long, wooden table to dig into his breakfast. I excuse myself and return to the front room. After picking out a piece of egg and both slices of toast, I set the plate on the floor and turn my back to give him some privacy while he eats.

Daniel strides out of the kitchen fifteen minutes later, patting his flat stomach and thanking Ma for the meal. We make our exit after many more thanks and promises not to be late for lunch.

"Ma seems sweet," I say once we're out on the dusty ground.

"She's a machine, keeping up with all of us. We're all spoiled with homemade meals three times a day, and she won't even agree to take on an assistant." He shakes his head, but his affection for her is obvious. "Come on. I'll show you the barn."

I follow Daniel across the farmyard. The bustle of life on a farm replaces the stillness of our late-night arrival. It looks straight out of a postcard, with the classic farmhouse and assortment of red barns. There's farm equipment of every sort parked or being driven by men that look nothing like terrorists, and very much like authentic cowboys.

The barn is a huge, red building that appears to serve more as a garage. He leads me past a dissected tractor and shelves of tools, into an office that looks like a set from an old movie. The laptop on the desk is hooked up to six monitors, all showing multiple images from around the farm. Animals, vehicles, entrance gates. Nothing that looks like the living quarters, thankfully.

"Have a seat." He pulls out the chair. It's dusty and frayed, probably older than the computer system.

I do as he asks, wiping the dust off the keyboard. Wires snake between everything, and an ethernet cable runs from the laptop to the wall. Daniel reaches past me to open a cupboard and pulls out a flat box.

"We've been overdue for an upgrade." He opens the box, revealing a sleek, black tablet. "Take the day to get everything switched over. Dinner's in the main house at five."

"Okay. Should be simple enough. Can I go out to walk Rocco when he needs it?"

"Of course." He crouches down, earning a growl from Tarek. "As long as you're with me, no one here will give you trouble."

He puts his rough hand over mine, and I fight the urge to pull it away.

"Why are you vouching for me? You don't really know me."

"You're adorably innocent, Blue."

"What do you-"

"I don't want you to get the wrong idea. I'm not looking for a girlfriend. But I like you. Any other woman would have fallen for my advances months ago, but you barely noticed me."

His *advances* were hardly unique. As the first face Agents see in the morning, or after a mission, flirting and propositions are basically part of the job description. One of the perks, if I'm being honest.

"It was nothing personal. I don't date Agents, or coworkers."

His laugh is one part charming, one part predatory. His hand drifts up to my elbow, then back down to my wrist, raising goose-bumps in its path.

"Last night I offered for you to come to my bunk. I plan to get you there."

Make that two parts predatory. I pull my hand away from his, and he rises to brace his hands on the chair arms. His sleeves are rolled up to reveal muscular forearms, and as he leans toward me, I get a glimpse of a carved chest under his button-down.

It's impossible not to notice how attractive he is, but I'm pretty certain Tarek has ruined me for other men. No one could come close to what he's got going on.

I close my eyes for a moment, letting flashes of last night warm my skin. Tarek stripping off his clothes, joining me in bed, letting me touch him. Letting me taste him.

Deep breath.

"This is all... a lot."

"Don't worry." He shifts his weight to one arm as he reaches up to draw a finger along my jaw. "I'm patient."

I shiver at his touch, recalling those same hands gripping my neck. At least he's not insisting we hook up now. If he's happy with the illusion that we might, eventually, then I can stomach going along with that.

He seems satisfied with the exchange, pushing up from the chair and leaving me alone in the dingy room.

I look down at Tarek, wishing I could speak to him but not naïve enough to think we have privacy here. As if reading my thoughts, he pushes his head against my thigh so I can rub his ears. Then he settles down onto his belly and fixes his eyes on the door.

I guess the security system upgrade makes sense. They brought me here, but it's not like they're going to make me part of their secret club on day one. A test. A simple task to prove I have some skills to offer. They *are* clearly overdue for an upgrade.

I dig in. Swapping out the laptop, installing programs, transferring files, updating, and testing. We venture out twice so I can find a washroom and let Tarek off-leash to do his business privately in the fields. By the time five o'clock nears, they've got a new security system, and I'm bored out of my mind from the simple task that mainly involved waiting for programs to load.

Supper and conversation sound pretty damn good, even if it means spending time with Daniel. And when that's done, I can make an excuse to get to bed early and have Tarek all to myself again.

THE MAIN HOUSE is busier than a restaurant and smells just as good. My stomach rumbles in anticipation of the home-cooked meal, even if I am stuck eating in dog form.

Dawn loops my lead around the porch railing, and I growl a warning. No way she's leaving me out here. I don't want her out of my site for a minute. My hearing is good, but I'll lose her in this crowd. At least two dozen farm hands have gathered for the meal. Most of them male. Most of them a little too curious about the new little female in their midst.

I bite at the leash, twisting my head. Letting her know I'm not okay with this in the most dog-like way I can.

"Easy. I'll get food, then I'll be back out."

She pats me on the head, her fingers lingering on the sensitive spot under my ears. I hate being treated like an animal, but Dawn touching me is pretty damn good in any form.

I growl again, but she holds my stare. She can't take me inside or avoid the meal. Either would look suspicious. Fuck. I lower my rump, conceding to wait. Ready to tear out of this damn collar if I hear so much as a gasp through the din of conversation and bouts of laughter.

She disappears inside, and the minutes tick by like hours. I growl a warning to anyone who stops to look at me, and lucky for them they give me a wide berth.

My canine sense of smell filters through the mouth-watering

scent of meats, roasted vegetables and sweets. My stomach is begging for food, even though I can easily go days without it in this form. I just really like food.

A new smell registers, its subtle note barely noticeable in the heavy mixture of food, sweat and farm. Subtle, but familiar. I turn to find a woman standing at the bottom of the stairs. She's wearing a dusty t-shirt and mud-caked boots, her red hair pulled back in a tie under a tattered cowboy hat.

It's too late to look away. She knows what I am just as surely as I know who she is.

Her amber eyes dart to the field beside the house, then back to mine. I watch her as she moves with an unhurried gait away from the crowd and disappears into the swaying corn.

A few twists of my neck, and I'm free of the collar. Bodies try to block me, but I weave between them and give chase to an unfortunate chicken. I hate to abandon Dawn, but I need to know why there's another Shifter at the Terran Defender's ranch.

A few laps around the farmyard and the stupid bird finally leads me into the cover of the corn. I abandon the chase immediately to make a wide circle back to the place where I lost sight of the red haired woman.

She doesn't make me search for long. Her scent marks a clear trail, and when I find her, she crosses her arms and raises an eyebrow.

"What are you doing here, Shifter?"

She doesn't recognize me in this form, but I need to know why she's here.

"Whatever form you take when you're not playing dog, I guarantee mine's bigger. I suggest you shift and convince me I shouldn't haul your ass to the boss right now."

Idle threats. Has to be. There's no way she works for them.

I shake out my fur and stand on human legs, watching her eyes widen in recognition.

"I think we both know mine's bigger."

"Holy fuck." She pulls the hat off her head, running a hand over her equally dusty hair.

"Exactly my thoughts."

"What the hell are you doing here? Did you track me?"

She's more curious than pissed. I'll take that as a good thing.

"I was wondering the same thing about you."

"Nice try." She steps toward me, and I brace for an attack. "Why are you here? I need to know you're not a threat."

"Why are you anywhere near these people?"

"I don't spend all my time indulging my dragon's whims." She grins and crosses her arms. "I enjoy hard work, a roof over my head, and a home cooked meal. The farm gives me all that, and it's close to Morwood for when I want to fly."

"And I assume you know nothing about terrorists who want Shifter's rights taken away?"

Her jaw twitches, but she doesn't look surprised by my accusation.

"You don't know the whole story."

"Tell me. Then I'll know."

"You haven't met the boss yet. When you do, he'll explain."

"How about you explain why you're betraying your entire species?"

She presses her lips into a tight line, but doesn't take the bait. I step in close and she doesn't shy away. She's tall, but still has to look up to keep eye contact.

"You're a dragon. Don't tell me you've let yourself become someone's pet?"

"Says the dog on a leash."

"Who are you?"

"That depends on who's asking." She presses a finger to the centre of my chest, trailing it downward until I take a half step back.

I like this woman. She's bat shit crazy, but I like her. The way I see it, I have two options. Trust her and come clean, or risk her exposing us.

"My name's Tarek. I'm a Protector."

Her eyes widen, but then she nods. "I'm Hunter."

"You're a Shifter. There's no way you're with those people."

"You don't know anything about me."

"Give us one more day. You don't let on you saw me, and I won't mention you in my report."

"Or, I can tell my boss about you, and there won't be any report."

"I think you know I won't be that easy to get rid of."

"Maybe not, but I suspect your little friend is a bit more delicate."

I clench my fists and stifle a growl. "How can you be loyal to them?"

"You don't know the full story."

"I just need the day. If you have any loyalty at all to your own kind, give me that."

"Don't patronize me. You know what I want. Give it to me, and I'll keep my mouth shut. You can stay as long as you like."

"I won't have sex-"

"I told you already. This isn't about sex." She lets out a string of creative curses under her breath. "Just fly with me. Tonight. Let your dragon take the lead and don't fight him. Don't over-think it. Just let nature take its course."

"It's not that simple. I have a... I'm with someone." I nearly called Dawn my mate. I can imagine the look on her face if she knew I staked that kind of claim on her.

Hunter rolls her eyes. "Think of the cave, when your dragon took over. Did you feel aroused? Did you have a raging hard-on when you shifted back?"

"Fuck no."

"Exactly. I felt nothing like that, either. It's procreation. Instinctual. It's not lovemaking. From the way my dragon braced, I'm expecting it's not even a pleasant experience."

I take a deep breath, forcing myself to be calm even though I want nothing more than to shake some sense into this woman.

"I don't have any interest in helping you breed dragons."

She holds my stare as we both will the other to back down. The noise of conversation from the farmhouse reaches my ears, along with male laughter and the sound of scraping dishes. My patience is just about expired when something like sadness breaks through her resolve.

"I know who you are, and I know who your girlfriend is. I also know where the Meadow is. You can be my sperm donor, or you can challenge me now in dragon form. Otherwise, I give all of that information to the boss."

A challenge in dragon form sounds fucking perfect. I want nothing more than to show her who she's dealing with. I can feel it under my skin; talons and teeth begging to break free. Problem is, I'm not sure it's a fight he's looking for. The damn creature might give her what she wants, regardless of my own opinions.

"Stop fighting it. Your hands are tied. No one would blame you for making the smart choice."

I can't believe I'm fucking doing this. "I'll meet you here at midnight."

HOLLOW

"$\mathscr{H}$e went after the chickens."

I spare a glance over my shoulder to find the tattooed man from last night, Gareth, eating his supper in a rocking chair. He sweeps his eyes over me, and I return my focus to Tarek.

He's sitting exactly where I left him, but his collar's laying at his feet. My heart's pounding in my chest and I jump when Gareth appears at my side.

"I wouldn't worry. He's obviously trained enough to come back. Shit at catching chickens, but well trained."

"Yeah. I guess so." I give him a smile, even though something about the way he's grinning at me gives me the creeps.

"Seems a little odd that Daniel gave you your own bunk. Thought you'd be sticking close to him."

Oh, hell. "I wanted to get settled in first. Figure out how I fit in here."

His grin widens. "I'm curious to see how long Dan's patience lasts with that."

What is this guy's problem? Thankfully, he laughs at his own joke and walks away. I glance around to find a few more eyes on me.

Balancing my heaping plate on one hand, I untie the lead with the other. I guess Tarek's off leash now. What the heck was so important he had to fake a chicken chase?

"You're welcome to eat inside." Daniel's smooth voice is in my ear as he takes my plate, freeing up my hand so I can work the knot a little easier.

"Thank you." I take my plate back after draping the leash around my neck. "I think I'll just head back to my room. That chair needs an upgrade more than the computer did."

He laughs. "You're right about that. I'll walk you back."

His offer's not unwelcome, after that odd exchange with Gareth. I know I'm perfectly safe with Tarek here, but I'd rather not get myself into a position where he has to intervene and blow his cover.

We walk in silence with Tarek following obediently at my side. As much as I hate the leash, I liked the security of being attached to him. As if sensing my thoughts, he moves a little closer, so I can feel the brush of his shoulder with each step.

"Boss wants to meet you tomorrow morning."

I stop, turning to look at his expression. It's been one day. I've proven nothing beyond the fact that I can do basic software maintenance. Why would their boss show his face so soon?

"Is that a good thing?"

He smiles, reaching up to tuck my hair behind my ear even though the gesture is wasted on my short cut.

"It's definitely a good thing." There's a flicker of uncertainty in his perpetually cocky expression, but it passes as quickly as it came. "Come for a walk with me tonight. I'll show you more of the farm."

I'm uncertain if it's a request, or a condition. Does the boss's invitation mean I'm in, or is my presence still dependent on keeping Daniel on the hook? He's actually not so terrible to spend time with, even though I'm sure it's an act meant to get my guard down. I hate to admit, but as much as I hate the man, I'm also curious about him.

"I'd like that. I'd like to see more of the farm."

He leans close, and I turn my head as his lips brush my cheek.

"I'll be back to get you in an hour."

He backs off, walking away without looking back. I can't even glance at Tarek. This is so fucked up. I get it. I get why I need to do this, and as much as I want to pull the plug and stay as far away from *the boss* as possible... how can I pass up the chance to see his face?

I don't know why Daniel wants me to take a walk with him, but I'm assuming it's for more of that kiss he just tried to land. How the hell am I going to keep blocking him, while staying on his good side? What if Daniel demands more later, and that's the price for meeting the boss?

When we enter our little cabin, there's a farm hand draped over the small couch watching a ball game. He does a double-take as I walk by, but I don't linger to explain. As I reach my room, the washroom door swings open and a big man in a tiny towel steps out.

I duck into my room and close the door.

After a few calming breaths, I turn around and lean my back against the wood.

Tarek's standing there, wearing what he always wears and looking like he always looks. Holy hell, I've got it bad. There's no amount of Daniel's practiced flirting that could come anywhere near the way I feel when this man looks at me. There's no naked, freshly showered cowboy that could hold my gaze for a second after seeing Tarek's body.

I've never wanted to sink into someone's arms the way I do right now. But his eyes keep me in place. The way his jaw ticks and his fists stay clenched at his sides. I set the plate of food on the small table, then shove my hands in my pockets to keep from reaching for him.

"Where did you go?" I'm only curious, but his eyes narrow at my whispered question.

"We're leaving. Tonight."

I let out a long breath, feeling some weight lift off my shoulders.

"Do you have enough information?"

"It's the closest anyone has gotten to them. We'll find whatever they're hiding when we start looking in closets and ripping up floorboards." He looks away for a breath. "I can't do this shit anymore. I can't stand by and watch him touch you one more fucking time."

Even in a whisper, his words are rough with emotion. I throw my arms around his waist and bury my face in his chest. He jumps at my sudden attack, but then his arms are around me.

"You should eat." His voice is all softness and warmth. None of the hard edges of a moment ago.

"Go ahead, if you want it. I'm not really hungry."

"Eat. You'll need the energy when you're riding your getaway dragon."

My heart stops. I can't breathe. I push out of his arms because I need to see his face right now. "Are you serious? I can…" I can't even say the words, it sounds too surreal.

His face splits into a grin, a silent laugh shaking his wide shoulders. "Angel, if you wanted to ride me, all you had to do was ask."

I can't even begin to think of a clever comeback for that. I just stare at him like he's speaking in tongues, then I grab a thick slice of cold turkey off the plate. He doesn't protest when I hand him the rest.

Holy hell. I'm going to ride a dragon. This man is incredible.

I've never considered eating to be a sexy sort of activity, but watching as Tarek devours the cold food with obvious appreciation does dirty things to my mind. The way he chews, the way his neck moves with each swallow. I was devouring him not that long ago. Just the memory of his body, the way he tasted, the stifled sounds of pleasure my mouth pulled from him…

"When will we go?" I force my mind off all the delicious things I want to do to his body. The man deserves to finish his supper before I jump him, and there are certainly more important things to think about than his perfect cock in my mouth.

"I'll wake you well before dawn. By the time they notice you're gone, the Elders will already have a team mobilized."

He sets the empty plate aside and breathes a contented sigh. That's all the invitation I can wait for, and his arms welcome me as I crawl onto his lap. Sliding one knee on either side of his thighs, I straddle his hips and wrap my arms around his neck. I kiss his mouth, and he pulls me close with one big hand on my lower back. His other hand grips the back of my neck, holding me in place while massaging the tension out of my muscles.

"I'm so ready to take you home." His words whispered against my lips between kisses cause a full-body shiver. He moves his hips just a little, letting me feel the proof of just how ready he is.

Two can play that game.

"I can't wait to make you come again." His breath hitches, his hands gripping me even tighter. "I want to see your face. I want to hear the sounds you make when you're so deep inside me you can't hold it back anymore."

"Fuck, Angel. You're killing me."

"Then let me taste you again."

His head jerks back, his eyes finding mine with a look that's one part hopeful, one part questioning my sanity. There's nothing sane about the way I feel about him. I want to own his pleasure.

I slide my hands down his body, finding the ridge of his cock through his pants. His entire body tenses at my touch.

A soft knock at the door shatters the moment. I grip fistfuls of his shirt as he grips my hips, both of us hissing our frustration through clenched teeth. He presses his forehead against mine for a brief moment before lifting me off his lap like I weigh nothing.

He brushes a soft kiss across my mouth, then slides his lips to my ear. "My turn next, Angel. You're the one who'll be squirming under *my* tongue."

Holy hell.

Another knock at the door. "Blue?"

I straighten my clothes as Tarek shifts back into that damn dog.

∾

"IT'S A BEAUTIFUL PLACE."

"It is."

The affection in Daniel's voice is clear as he leads me along the edge of a grassy paddock. Tarek's off-leash, alternating between following obediently at my side, and exploring the path ahead.

The stalks of corn at our left tower above my head. Somewhere beyond them is Morwood Forest, and I'm jealous of the setting sun as it dips toward the horizon.

Tarek's going to take me there. A community of Shifters. It's going to be amazing to see their culture first hand, but after a lifetime of obsession, I don't think it's them I'm so curious about anymore. It's only him. Shifters aren't this mysterious concept anymore, they're just people. Tarek thinks I'm looking forward to a tour of the Meadow, and I suppose I still am. But it's his life I want to see. The home he built with his own hands.

Daniel's watching me. I reach out and brush my fingers over a papery corn leaf, as if it's the cause of my wandering attention. It's dry and faded with age. "I don't know a lot about farming, but how is this so old already? It's not even summer."

"Only the smaller farms rely on the seasons."

He reaches between the stalks and pulls out a thick corn pod. Peeling back the protective layers of husk, he uncovers a cob of dull, almost grey corn.

"Centaurian tech?"

"Yep. It's not edible for humans, but livestock do just fine on it. It needs barely any nitrogen or phosphorus. Not a bit of potassium. We fertilize all our fields right after the last frost, with a grey mineral sludge. We plant the seeds, and by the time we need to plant our own crops, this stuff is done. Doesn't touch the minerals our native crops require, so the soil can be turned and planted immediately."

"That's amazing. I knew the off-world tech was used in farming, but I didn't picture this."

He huffs, like he's not impressed. "Alien crops are one thing, but we start raising blue cattle or chickens the size of elephants and I'll be keeping my ass on the Solar."

I laugh, but I get his point. It's a little troubling to think that our own industry isn't good enough; that we need Centaurian tech to keep up with demand.

He turns his back to the corn, and gives a quick, low whistle. With a snort and the dull thud of hoofs on soft ground, a grey dappled horse answers his call.

I lean against the rough wood of the fence, running my hands over the soft, powerful neck.

"It's been years since I've been around horses."

I take a deep breath through my nose, letting the familiar scent take me back to the summer we rented a house beside a stable. I think I spent every day on horseback. One older mare would happily go about her day with me lounging on her wide, bare back. Those were good days.

I lean in, nuzzling my face against her and wishing I could bottle the smell.

"We could go for a ride tomorrow night." Daniel's hand slides around my waist, pulling me against him as his lips brush the back of my neck.

We're leaving tonight. I don't need to play along this much.

I lean away, pulling out of his grip. Something flashes in his eyes that makes my pulse race, but it's gone as quickly as it came.

"Why don't you have a girlfriend?"

His eyebrows shoot up, the corner of his mouth twitching into a smile. "Are you offering?"

"You seem nice. Intense, maybe. But strong and passionate. You're certainly easy on the eyes." I hope my blunt compliments make it clear I'm being friendly, not flirty.

His expression darkens. I went too far.

"I'm not interested in a girlfriend. People come and go. That's life. If I got attached to everyone I felt a connection with, it would only make the inevitable disappointment harder."

His words echo from a conversation I had with Liam a lifetime ago. I glance over at Tarek, who's abandoned his explorations to watch me.

"Sometimes getting attached just happens. You don't choose it, but you can't take it back, either."

Tarek's ears droop just a little, his brown eyes leaving mine as his head dips to sniff at something on the ground. I am attached. My body craves him. Something in my heart does, too. Something I've never felt before. And I wouldn't take it back, even if I could.

Getting to know Tarek has been amazing. Not just because he's a Shifter, that's barely even on the top ten reasons I'm crazy about him. He's funny, kind, affectionate, and intense. He's gorgeous, and sexy, and somehow adorably innocent.

I shake my head. What the heck am I thinking about this for? Daniel's watching my face with rapt attention, with no idea that my thoughts have nothing at all to do with him.

He puts a warm palm on my cheek, angling my face so I'm looking directly at him.

"When I find a woman I want, I get her. I don't lead her on. I don't pretend there's something there that isn't."

His thumb ventures to brush the edge of my mouth, and I stiffen. I know better than to pull away. I can't piss him off. But I won't encourage him, either.

"I like you. I want you in my bed, Dawn. Preferably tonight. I'll make it good for you, that I guarantee. But we're both adults and I don't need to pretend I'm in love to get what I want." He leans down. I close my eyes and clench my jaw. He presses a soft, almost affectionate kiss to my lips. "What about you?"

His question takes a moment to sink in, through the haze of alarm bells and fight-or-flight instincts. "What about me?"

He chuckles, stepping back out of my personal space to lean against the fence, one hand lazily stroking the horse's back.

"How the hell is a woman like you single?" His eyes make a deliberate run over me. "You're all kinds of sexy. You're smart, funny, independent. If I were in the market, you're definitely girl-friend material."

He's too good at this. Pushing my boundaries, then backing off and getting as comfortable as an old friend. Too good.

"Honestly, I've never seen proof that it lasts." I can't resist looking over at Tarek. He's sitting now, watching me openly. "Commitment. Love. It's fun until it isn't. It's convenient, until it isn't."

I swear I see disappointment on Tarek's face. But it's a reminder I needed to hear, even from my own mouth. I'm madly in lust with this man, but it can't last. It's going to hurt like hell when I leave him, but that'll be a hell of a lot better than sticking around to watch whatever we have die a slow, natural death. He'll always be this perfect in my mind. It'll never have to fade.

"We might just be perfect for each other, Blue."

I'd probably laugh at that, if I could take a full breath. The thought of ripping Tarek out of my life like a band-aid should be reassuring. Knowing I won't have to suffer through the slow death of our affection should be freeing.

I don't want to leave him.

"I thought I wanted to stay that way. I thought it wasn't possible to like someone enough to want to keep them. I couldn't imagine..."

"Past tense? Are you trying to tell me you're not so single after all?"

"No. It's just... I can imagine it, you know? What it would feel like to..."

"To be in love?" He looks amused, like he's stifling a laugh at my expense. Hell, I can't blame him. I sound pathetic, and the truth is even more pathetic than reality. I'm using the man I'm pretending to like as a therapist to work through my feelings about the man I actually like.

"To have someone who feels like home."

"Yeah. I'll pass. The one good thing my parents gave me was the sense to realize that people can't be trusted. Family is an evolutionary illusion. Just because someone has a blood relation-ship to you, or signs a paper vowing to stay by your side, doesn't make them magically become something they're not."

What a sad way to live. Never trusting that anyone really cares. But I guess that's been me, hasn't it? The image of myself on a nameless starship, with nothing but a backpack and endless potential... it's a daydream I've had so many times and for so long it feels more like a memory than imagination. It feels cold now.

Hollow. Is it Tarek, or just the idea of having someone who's mine?

I press my fingers against my temples. I can't keep thinking about this. With Tarek looking at me like that and Daniel holding back his laughter.

"I hope you find someone who proves you wrong." I give him a gentle punch on the arm, to make sure he isn't thinking I'm offering to be that someone.

"I suspect that'll be the first heart I break." He puts a hand on my shoulder, giving a firm but gentle squeeze. "Come on. Let's get you back. I'll be waking you early to meet the boss."

Oh hell. I forgot to ask about that. I'd be terrified if I were actually sticking around to meet the *boss* of the Terran Defenders.

"What should I expect? How should I act?"

"For starters, I wouldn't act like you're thinking about turning me down." His eyes darken and he grips my hips, spinning me around to pull me against him.

So much for friendly conversation.

I keep my eyes locked on Tarek's as a wide hand slides around to splay across my stomach. His breath is hot against my neck.

Tarek's ears flatten, a low growl peeling his lips back in a canine warning.

"I won't lie to him, so if you're thinking about turning me down, tell me now." His breath becomes a kiss on the sensitive skin below my ear, and I shiver despite myself. "I'm ok with a chase, but I'm not okay with being used. I want you in my bed. Tonight. Tell me now if you'd rather go home."

So that's it. All out on the table now. Tarek's barely holding himself back, but I can't ruin this. I doubt turning him down would end with a handshake and a free ride home.

I place my hand over Daniel's. "I'm not trying to play games.

I'm just scared. What if I meet him and realize I don't want to be a part of this?"

"You'll get answers tomorrow. There's no way you won't be all in once you know the full story."

The full story. "What's he going to tell me?"

He answers with a low chuckle against the back of my neck, but it's not the brush of his lips that makes me shudder. When Tarek suggested leaving tonight, I jumped at the chance. How can we leave now? Tomorrow morning, I can meet their leader. I'll see his face, hear their story from his own mouth.

I can only imagine the look on Elder Tanikka's face if I tell her I was this close and walked away.

"Give me tonight. Let me meet him and understand what I've gotten myself into. Then I'll be able to relax."

"I can wait one more night."

DRAGONS

I crouch low to the ground, barely daring to breathe. Through the narrow gaps in the rough corn stalks, I watch as a gorgeous, red-haired woman smiles down at Tarek.

He shifts, and when he stands on human legs, she steps in close.

"I was beginning to think you weren't coming." Her voice is timid as she smooths the front of her sleeveless shirt, the neckline swooping low. She seems impervious to the midnight chill.

"I told you I would."

His voice is low and even. I can't see his face, and I don't dare move for a better vantage. I swallow a wave of guilt at my sneakiness. I'll feel guilty later. For now, I watch in silence as she puts a hand on his bicep. He doesn't even flinch.

After the talk with Daniel, I told Tarek I wanted to stay for the meeting. He was pissed, but logic won him over and he eventually agreed it was an opportunity we couldn't pass up.

Once the decision was made, he pulled me onto the small bed. He held me close while we talked about all the scenarios that might play out during the meeting with the boss. We talked about after; flying to Morwood and meeting his family. We talked about all the dirty things we'll do when we're alone in his house.

We couldn't keep our hands from exploring while we talked, but neither of us made a move to do more.

I was just drifting off when he slipped out of bed, reassuring my drowsy confusion with promises that he'd be back soon. He wouldn't look me in the eye when he said it. I couldn't shake the feeling that something was wrong.

I had to follow.

"There's a clearing not far into Morwood. We'll have privacy there." She lowers her hand from his arm. Her gaze moves to the sky, and she tightens her long ponytail as she steps a few paces back.

In one fluid motion, her body reshapes into a dragon. Coppery and slender, she crouches below the height of the corn as I flatten to my stomach and pray she can't smell me. In the next moment, Tarek's green body looms above.

Even the crickets are quiet, the only sound the deep breathing of these two incredible creatures. The woman slinks forward, her nose pressing into Tarek's chest, her cheek gliding along the silken skin of his bunched shoulder.

Familiar. Affectionate.

Something pinches in my chest. Then it twists as acid rises into the back of my throat. How did this happen? I know better. I swore I'd never feel this.

I let him in, and now my heart is breaking.

She backs away, spreading her wings as Tarek does the same. With a gust of air that hits me like a cresting wave, they're both gone into the sky.

I'm left muddy and shivering, wondering what the hell just happened. As I pick myself up, anger sears in my chest. How stupid could I be? Those two beautiful creatures were utter perfection together, and yet my heart aches at the image. My eyes sting with childish tears.

Fooling around with Tarek was fun, but somewhere over this last few days I let it become something more. I let myself believe in a possible future. I don't even know when it happened. I certainly didn't want it.

It fucking hurts.

Even under the warm, weak spray of the shower, I can't stop the tremble in my jaw. The shiver in my bones. I knew better than to let those attachments take hold. I knew better than to trust those emotions.

He never made promises, or fed me lines. He was casual and playful from the start. I twisted it. I made it mean something more.

I should never have postponed my flight.

But that thought's just as pathetic and self-serving as the rest. I dry off with a hand towel, pulling my clothes on over damp skin and cursing the humidity.

I'm not here because I had a crush on Tarek. Daniel had the poor judgement to think I could be trusted. Tanikka inspired me to take a risk and do something meaningful before I leave this rock in my dust.

I'm also here because of my cheetah, and because of what I just saw in the cornfield. Two Shifters. Two dragons with the sky and the earth at their fingertips. They deserve to live without fear. They deserve this planet far more than humans do.

Flirting with Daniel is a small price to pay for their freedom. Knowing that Tarek has someone, that he's not actually hoping to keep me around, sets me free to do what needs to be done. I'll play my role. I'll get all the information I can before I put this behind me.

∾

THE AIR IS STILL within the shelter of the forest, and as I fold my wings, the only sound is the rustle of the wind in the trees above. Hunter watches me from as far away as she can get in the small space, the yellow of her eyes a thin ring around her dilated pupils. Her wings are folded high on her back, her breathing deep and measured. She's afraid.

Maybe I am, too.

I shouldn't be here. I shouldn't have left Dawn alone. I gave her some vague excuse about needing to go look around, but the suspicion in her eyes cut to the bone. She's never looked at me with anything but trust in those baby blues.

But she was right. Leaving tonight is not an option. Missing the opportunity to uncover their leader's identity would be unforgivably selfish.

There's no way I can tell Dawn, or anyone, the truth about this. Whatever happens here, I won't tell another soul. Maybe I can forget about it. Go back to being a man and not an animal rutting in the woods.

I close my eyes, shake my head, and dig down. Like Hunter said, I need to take a backseat and let my Dragon free. If I don't give her what she wants, she can blow our cover. She can lead the Terran Defenders to the Meadow. I don't even truly believe she would go that far, but I could never risk it no matter the cost.

I'm a Protector. I won't risk innocent lives because of emotion. Hell, Gideon once lived with a mark for a month to get the intel he needed.

She was sadistic as fuck. He barely left her bedroom the entire time. He kept her happy, earned her trust, and in the end she got what she deserved; death by lethal injection. I'm sure G would have gladly delivered her punishment personally. The bitch had murdered her son and kidnapped her two grandchildren. If she'd felt threatened in any way, she could have just kept her mouth shut and those babies would have never been found.

I've got no excuse to be tucking my tail between my legs with the task in front of me. Hunter is far from an aging socialite with homicidal tendencies.

Fire burns in my chest as I approach, and she cowers against the treeline. I take a deep breath, try to take a backseat, but my dragon instincts aren't kicking in. Focusing on the female in front of me is impossible when Dawn's alone and vulnerable in that place. I need to get this over with. I can't back down.

Fuck it.

Flames lick at the back of my throat as I lunge. She tries to dodge, but I secure the back of her neck and pin her with my weight. This fucking reptile needs to take over, because I sure as hell haven't given enough thought to dragon reproduction to know how it works.

There's nothing. Not a damn bit of the compulsion that gripped me in that cave. Nothing but the heat of anger and the overwhelming urge to break her skin with my teeth.

I push away.

She shifts, looking as pissed off as I feel.

"Shift. Now!"

I do as she demands. If my dragon won't put out, I don't know how the fuck I'm going to keep her quiet.

"What the hell? Are you still fighting him? Just let go!"

She stalks toward me, fists clenched like she might just take a swing. I keep my palms open, stance relaxed.

"I'm not. I'm doing exactly what you said, but it's just pissing him off. It's nothing like it was in the-"

"It's her."

I don't move a muscle, giving nothing away with my eyes or my body language.

"You fell in love with her."

It's not a question. I stay neutral, ready to give her a free shot before I put her to the ground. Instead of breaking my nose, the fight drains out of her. Her shoulders slump and her eyelids drift closed.

"I can force it. I can keep my end of the deal."

"No. You can't."

She jumps when I grip her shoulders, but there's no anger in her eyes.

"Please. Don't blow our cover." I don't want to think about my other option; silencing her permanently so she can't follow through with her threats. Just the thought makes me sick. Anything is better than that. "I'll try again. If he won't, we can do it in this form."

Her eyes widen as her lip curls back in disgust. She swats my hands away.

"Stop. I won't turn you in."

I really want to believe that. "Why not?"

She takes a deep breath, crossing her arms over her chest. "I was a weapon for many years. I swore I wouldn't hurt innocent people ever again."

"Then why are you here?"

Shame crosses her features as clear as day. She hugs herself a little tighter.

"My bondmate wasn't a good person. It took me a long while to accept that maybe he never was. I could have walked away after our bond was broken. But I'm female... I shouldn't have even been alive. He saved me from that fate, so there has to be some good in him. I thought maybe... it seems foolish now."

"Do you love him?"

"No. It was never like that. He's my family."

"Who is he? Is it Thomas?" But I know it can't be. I remember the wolf he was paired with, and he definitely wasn't female.

She shakes her head and swipes at her cheeks. I can't feel

anything but compassion. She still feels that loyalty, and it's keeping her apart from her own kind.

If Dawn wasn't waiting for me, I'd take this woman to the Meadow right now. I'd show her what family looks like.

"Turn them in. Go to the Elders with everything you know."

She shakes her head.

"You owe him nothing. End this and set yourself free."

"It's not that simple. Even if they trusted me, I don't know enough details to make any difference."

"If you won't stop him, and you don't agree with him. Why stay?"

"Because it's going to get worse before it gets better. I need to stay close. I need to be there if he has doubts, if there's any chance of changing his mind."

"He hates Shifters. He won't have a change of heart."

"He doesn't... it's not what you think." She presses her lips into a thin line. She knows more than she's saying.

"What does that mean? What aren't you telling me?"

"I can't."

"Tell me what to do to end this!"

"I'm sorry. I can't."

I take a step toward her, then another. This conversation has gone as far as it can, and I need her to fucking talk now.

She plants a hand on my chest. "Don't bother. I've said all I can. He's meeting her tomorrow. You'll probably know more than I do by the end of that conversation."

"Why would he trust her?"

"Because Daniel wants her. Because he thinks he's invincible and knows it's too late to stop him anyway."

"No. There's more to this. Letting her in was a risk."

Her eyes drift off to the side, her gaze turning inward. "I don't know for sure."

I growl and her eyes snap back to mine, a spark of fight returning to her posture.

"I'm not lying to you!" She lets out her own growl of frustration, pressing her middle fingers to her temples. "He doesn't tell me everything. I'm not... I'm still just the muscle."

Fuck, that's sad.

"Prove him wrong. I'm not asking what you know. Tell me what you think."

She sucks in a breath, her expression saying she's never been asked to have an independent thought. Never been required to have an opinion.

"I think something was missing. I think he got ahead of himself and made promises he couldn't keep. Whatever he needs, she has access to it. I just don't know what that is."

"Thank you."

I turn to leave. I've been away for far too long as it is.

Hunter grabs my arm.

"Tarek." She chews her bottom lip, her expression conflicted. I stay quiet, hoping she'll decide to say what's on her mind. "Just be careful, okay?"

REGRETS

*H*oly hell.

I can't form any words, let alone thoughts.

"Good morning, Miss Stevens. I trust you're enjoying your stay?"

Isaac Durant holds out his hand. I take it, but he doesn't shake. He just grips my hand and watches my expression. Daniel's light touch on my lower back is suddenly not so unwelcome.

What dimension did I just fall into?

Isaac Durant was a well-known politician before he was implicated in the Horizon Zero scandal. His father was one of five Elders who stepped down because of it. He was also Elder Tanikka's husband, though she never talks publicly about him other than to say the divorce was a mutual decision.

"Everything okay, Dawn?"

"Sorry, Sir, I... this is unexpected."

My mouth feels too dry to swallow. When Daniel led me up the narrow, plywood stairs to the loft above the barn's security room, I expected a shadowy figure hidden among the bales of hay.

I certainly didn't expect this clean, modern office or the man in front of me.

"This farm's been in my family for many generations. I hope you've gotten a chance to explore." He crouches, turning his assessing gaze on Tarek. "Beautiful animal."

"Thank you. His name's Rocco."

Isaac reaches out as if to pet him, and Tarek jerks his head away with a growl.

"He's protective."

"That's fine. I love dogs." He reaches into his pocket and pulls out a bone-shaped dog biscuit. "Here, buddy."

Tarek hesitates, but he's sniffing the air. His ears perk up. His tail thumps against my leg. Isaac moves closer, hand outstretched with the treat on his palm. I close my eyes as Tarek goes for it, struggling to keep my stomach contents down as I hear his crunching.

It's not the treat itself... anyone who had a dog as a kid knows milk bones don't taste so bad. It's the degradation of it. Tarek doesn't deserve to be treated like a dog.

I open my eyes to see him sitting tall, seemingly loving the attention he's receiving as Isaac rubs him all over the face and neck.

"See? We're buddies now."

I force my fists to unclench. Tarek's playing his role, and I can play mine. I picture him in dragon form with that woman, and I ignore the pain in my chest at the memory. That's why I'm here. They deserve to live in the open, without fear.

"He recognizes a dog person." I attempt a laugh, but I can hear the nervous edge in my voice.

"They usually do." He turns away from Tarek, wiping his hands on his jeans. His clothes hardly scream farmer, but they look nothing like the suits he wore anytime I saw him at HQ. "Why do you want to join the Terran Defenders?"

Whew. Okay. I practiced for this. After scrubbing away the mud and embarrassment last night, I practiced for every possible line of questioning.

"I heard the stories, saw the news and read the memos from HQ. I didn't really give a... I didn't think about it much until recently."

"So, what took you from indifferent, to here?"

I look at my feet. "Something didn't feel right, but I said my lines, regardless. The night at the edge... I got scared."

"Of my men?" That's the first confirmation he's given that he's the one in charge here.

"No. The Shifter wasn't fighting back, just like the reports said. He wasn't giving them the footage they wanted, no matter what they did to him." I pause, letting the very real emotions of that night sink into my very fake story. "I saw how smart it was. He wasn't worried about getting hurt, because most of them have Medic implants. They can shift into whatever they want. It doesn't matter how many of them appear non-violent, because if just one of them gets pissed off enough, they could do unthinkable damage."

"You realized our cause might have a point, after all."

I nod. "I couldn't actually do what your men do. But if I can help in other ways..."

When I glance up at him, there's a warm smile on his face.

"You're right. One Shifter could do a lot of damage. A group of them, even more. But they're not a violent species by nature. Protective, yes. But not overtly violent."

"Then why-"

"My grandfather was there the day we struck an official deal with the Centaurians. In the years since, we've only become more dependent on their technology. People trust them, but they don't see the truth."

Daniel's watching me, his mouth pressed into a grim line. Isaac waits with a patient smile.

"What's the truth?"

"They want our planet. They gave us the tools and instructions, and so we terraform the land, skies and oceans. BioSol has locations around the world, stocked with Centauri tech. We take it. We use it. We think we need it. Now, the planet's almost ready. When they come, they'll eliminate humans and Shifters. There won't be anything we can do about it."

I don't know what to say. I've never heard anything like this before. Never seen any hint that what he's saying is true... yet his words are accurate. Centauri tech is everywhere.

"Why aren't the Elders doing something about it?"

He laughs, stepping a little closer. "The Elders were preparing, but they're gone now. My ex-wife never took it seriously, and those dim-witted fools sitting with her are just as blind. Making peace with Shifters is their pet project, and the entire world hangs on their every word."

"Why do you kill Shifters?"

"We don't. Not since I took over. The Terran Defenders were nothing more than criminals with a grudge, but they had the reach I needed. It's not about Shifters. It's about making people doubt the Elders. Making them scared so they'll think for themselves."

"But they're not. You're considered terrorists."

"We may not be winning that particular battle, I admit. We've expanded our network and used the Shifter distraction to accomplish more important things under the radar."

I don't want to ask more questions. I just want to leave and get as far away from this as possible. We've seen his face. We know where the farm is. It's enough.

But I'm also curious. I never suspected there was more to this than a personal vendetta against Shifters.

"More important things?"

"People need to wake up. Soon, they'll have no choice. We're taking down Solar One."

I suck in a breath, and my lungs forget how to exhale. My heart races, the sound of it beating loud in my ears. I look at Tarek, and while he hasn't moved, his dark eyes are locked on mine.

"Taking it down?" That could mean so many things. My imagination's going in a thousand different directions. "How?"

"We're going to show them the Centauri tech can't be trusted."

"Like a blackout?"

He smiles. "Like a nuke."

My knees turn to rubber. Hands grip my waist.

Hell no. I'm not going along with this bullshit for another second. We've heard enough. Tarek must have enough information.

I try to pull out of Daniel's grip, but it only tightens. He can't let me go. He can't let me walk out of here with this information.

"Why are you telling me this?"

"I'm a powerful man, Miss. Stevens. I plan to save the world."

Holy fuck. I turn to Daniel. His face is etched with concern as he looks down at me. "You can't possibly be okay with this."

"It's already in motion. You can't stop it." His grip on me softens, his eyes imploring me to accept this and move on. "You're safe with me, Dawn."

"Where is it?" The question's a long shot, but I hold my breath that he'll lay it all on the table. And that Tarek will have the sense to leave me and take the info to the Elders as fast as his wings can carry him.

Daniel doesn't answer, he just looks to Isaac.

"I wasn't looking to recruit. Another set of hands is useless to me at this point. But Daniel's got a soft spot for you, and so here you are."

I close my eyes. Blocking out Daniel's searching gaze and trying without success to wrap my mind around all of this.

Daniel's hands move to my shoulders, then rub up and down my arms. It's almost comforting. He doesn't need to say the rest for me to understand the score. I'm not welcome to stay unless it's in his bed, and they certainly can't let me leave with what I know.

THE MOMENT THE DOOR CLOSES, I'm on my feet. I make sure it's locked, then wrap my arms around Dawn as she sways. She clings to me, grabbing fistfuls of my shirt and burying her face in my chest.

I run my hands through her hair, over her arms, her hips.

"We're done. We're getting the fuck out of here."

I'm still reeling from everything I just heard. Still vibrating from the effort of sitting there and watching Dawn deal with it alone, while Daniel's hands never left her body.

And I'm pissed off. All this time, fucking around with the illusion that we were dealing with one problem, when all along there was a ticking clock no one could hear. A fucking *bomb*.

Her hands relax their hold on my shirt. She tips her head back to look at me, her baby blues swimming in unshed tears.

When I returned last night, she'd already given up waiting. I slept in dog form on the doorstep and didn't see her until Daniel came to get her just after daybreak. It feels good to have her in my arms again. It feels fucking perfect.

I slide a hand up her spine to grip the back of her neck as I lean down. She stiffens, but I don't want her to think about everything she just heard. Not now. I kiss her, and I swear I can feel my dragon purr. Her mouth opens for me, and I taste her sweetness in a whole new way.

This woman is mine.

The thought hits me, and I've never felt anything so right. I lift her off her feet and lay her back on the bed.

Her baby blues are wide as I climb over her, never breaking eye contact as she welcomes me between her thighs. I shudder as I press my hips to hers, grinding my cock against her core. She answers with a breathy moan as she wraps her legs around me, trapping my body against hers.

I kiss her again, then brace my forehead against hers as I try to form coherent thoughts.

"He won't touch you again."

"Tarek-"

"No one touches you but me." I move my hips, reminding her what I've got to offer; what already belongs to her, whether she realizes it or not. She gasps and grips me tighter.

I don't know where this possessiveness is coming from. I've got no right to claim ownership of her, but she's not arguing and I'm not taking it back. Then she nods. She fucking nods. I want to take her right here, right now. I've never crossed this line with anyone, but I know exactly how I want her body.

Last night with Hunter made me realize a few things. I'm lucky to have people I can trust; to have a family I chose, and who chose me. And I love this woman. I fucking love her.

But I can't confess that. Not yet. Dawn's fiercely independent and I don't think she's too eager to trust. Words won't mean much to her. But I can be patient. I'll show her.

"We're leaving. Now."

Her eyes change. The heat frosting over as her jaw tightens and her soft lips press into a stern line. She unwinds her legs from around my hips and pushes against my chest. I reluctantly obey, rolling off her body and onto my back.

"No, Tarek. I'm not leaving." She sits, keeping her back to me. "You heard what he said. You need to go tell Tanikka everything, but I need to stay. I need to convince him to tell me where it is."

She leans forward, resting her arms on her thighs as she cradles her head in her hands. I wish I'd never gotten her involved in this, but we'd never have gotten this far without her.

"I didn't want to do this. I didn't want to be anywhere near this."

"I know, and I'm sorry. But it's done now. You don't need to worry about him, or any of it."

She shakes her head. "It doesn't matter what I want. If there's any chance he'll give me more information..."

"He made it perfectly clear what he wants from you."

"It's not your decision to make. You need to tell Elder Tanikka about all this. If I walk away and he commits mass murder that I could have stopped..."

"No. You're not going near him again. He's not having you. Not as long as I breathe." Even though we can't speak above a whisper, I make sure my words are laced with a growl. I want her to remember that I stood back and watched by choice, not because I didn't have the means to stop this charade at any moment.

She pushes up from the bed to pace the tiny room. I reach to pull her back down into my arms, but she halts me with a glare.

"Angel, please."

"Dammit! I'm not your mate!"

Her words are hissed through clenched teeth. The chill in her eyes is glacial now. She's angry, but I won't let on how much her words cut. She's not my mate. Not yet.

"I don't belong to you, Tarek. Any more than you belong to me. If I choose to let that asshole touch me so I can get what I want, that's none of your fucking business."

I stand up from the bed, and she shrinks back. I unclench my fists, forcing a breath into my lungs. "I won't let you-"

She hits me square in the chest with both hands. She's too small to move me, but the look in her eyes as she does it makes me take a step back.

"Don't you dare pretend like you own me."

I fight the urge to grab her body and pull it to mine. I don't want to own her. Not the way she says it, like some kind of forced captivity. I rub my chest where she hit me. It fucking hurts. Not from the blow itself, but from the look on her face as she did it. The hatred in her baby blues.

I think back over everything... the way she looks at me, the way she touches me. I thought she... but who am I kidding. I don't know a damn thing about females.

I look toward the curtained window. "I need to go. I can't keep this intel to myself."

When I look back at her, she wraps her arms around herself. Her eyes are glassy, and I'd give anything to know what she's thinking in this moment.

She nods in agreement, not even glancing in my direction. "I'll try to have more information by the time you come back."

Fuck, I hate the sound of that. I hate everything about this.

I try to do what's right, even when it doesn't serve me personally. I've never done something I regret, but that's about to change. There's no doubt I'm making the wrong call. I'm going to regret leaving her here. The problem is that taking away her right to choose would be just as wrong.

There's nothing I can do besides physically force her, and she'd never forgive me for that.

"I want you to come with me. Please. Come with me."

I can hear the ragged edge in my voice, even at a whisper. I hope that tells her more than my words can. No trace of warmth returns to her eyes.

"I'm staying."

PLAYING ALONG

I clutch the faded, pink throw pillow against my chest and sink farther down into the plush sofa.

"He might come back in the morning." Daniel's voice is soft. Comforting.

I fight the urge to stiffen as he sits beside me, resting his hand on my thigh.

The warm cup of camomile tea Ma made for me serves as a distraction for my hands. It's a mild flavor, and the warmth soothes my raw throat. Since *Rocco* took off, I've been yelling his name into the cornfields. It might have been a fake name, but the feeling of loss didn't need to be faked.

I still can't believe he's gone, and I'm on my own. He clearly didn't want to leave me here, but there was no denying he had to go. I know it's what needed to happen, but that doesn't stop me from feeling a completely irrational surge of betrayal.

Maybe that's just my emotions from last night coming back to haunt me.

I all but told him I didn't have real feelings for him. That I'd be giving Daniel whatever he wants if it gets the information I need.

No one touches you but me.

A shiver ghosts across my skin at the memory of his posses-sive words. There was ownership in the way he said them, and the way he held me to him and kissed me like he was staking a claim.

How does that fit with the Shifter woman from last night? The level of deceit it would take to keep us both on the hook just doesn't fit with the man I've gotten to know. But maybe I haven't gotten to know him as well as I thought.

My plans haven't changed because of him. I might have taken an unexpected detour that's left me with my first broken heart, but I've still got my ticket. As soon as I've gotten the information I need here, I'll be moving on with my life.

The only way to get that information is through Daniel... and he's got a very uncomplicated price.

"Have you thought about everything Isaac told you?" Daniel's voice is low. Ma's working in the kitchen, and I get the impres-sion she doesn't know her family's farm has become a front for her son's criminal organization.

But they don't see themselves that way. The crusade against Shifters is a distraction; a tool to get people questioning their government. The Terran Defenders are working to prevent a Centaurian invasion, and they will use any means necessary to defend our planet from that fate.

It's crazy even to think it. The Elders wouldn't be blind to this. They would have a plan; one that didn't involve a disgraced ex-politician ordering Shifters to be beaten in the streets.

And no matter how I spin it, no matter how I shape the words to make them fit, nothing excuses a bomb that will kill millions. Solar One and Moridian spread out below. The docks. Would the fallout reach Fentondale? How much of Morwood would burn? Even this farm. I don't know much about explosives or nuclear weapons, but I can imagine the devastation and it's not an accept-able sacrifice in any fight.

"I don't want people to get hurt. If there's another way..." I let my voice trail off, hoping he'll give me a lead. Something I can work with. He squeezes my thigh a little tighter.

"People are going to get hurt, Dawn." Isaac speaks up from his seat across the room. His voice is low, but not as cautious as Daniel's. "When the Centaurians get what they want, no one will be safe. No one believed my father. No one believed me. I thought once I became Elder... but my wife has that title now. She won't acknowledge the truth if it means proving me right. If there was a chance that appealing to the current government would work, I'd do it. I'm not a violent man, but these are desperate times."

His forehead is creased, the corners of his mouth drawn down in what looks like a genuine frown. My heart sinks to my stomach. What if he's being honest?

"You really think the Centaurians will invade?" It sounds silly even saying it out loud. But he looks at me, and this conversation is anything but silly.

I'd already decided Isaac was the enemy. This is the first time I've considered something different.

Maybe there is no bad guy here. Tarek's the purest person I've ever met, and yet he's capable of deceiving someone he claims to care about. Maybe there is no good or evil, only people doing what they think is best in their own misguided way.

Daniel's watching me closely. He's no saint, that's for sure. But I can't reconcile what I know of him with the kind of personality it would take to commit mass murder.

"They're coming." Isaac's voice is as grim as his expression. "It's a dark side of the universe, but it happens. More often than you know. Humans did it, as the more technologically advanced cultures spread across the continents. This is no different."

I push up from the couch, moving to the window to look out over the dusty yard and alien cornfields beyond. I don't trust this man. Not for one second. But what if? Would the Elders really bury something like this?

Hands grip my arms as a warm body presses against my back. "I know it's a lot to take in."

I turn, and he steps back a few inches. "I want to understand all of this. I want to trust you."

His hand cups my cheek, and I lean into it. He'll believe my actions far more than my words. I glance up at him, and there's a soft smile on his lips.

"Are you sure about her?" Isaac asks.

"She wouldn't be here if I wasn't."

A look passes between them. Something private. Isaac rises, placing a hand on Daniel's shoulder for a brief moment.

He yells a thank you to his mother and leaves without a backward glance. The creaky screen door swings shut with a bang. Out the window, a flock of chickens scatter as a huge, green tractor rolls through the yard.

"What are you thinking?"

I return to the sofa and my cooling tea. Daniel settles beside me, his thigh lightly touching mine.

"I'm still trying to absorb all of this. And I'm worried about Rocco."

"He'll be back. I'm sure." A shadow flickers across his eyes, and when he catches me watching, he leans back on the sofa. "I had a Shifter, before they woke up."

"A brown wolf. I remember the two of you at HQ."

"He was a good companion. Never left my side."

"Where is he now?"

"He took human form, like they all did. Broke the bond and never looked back. Taking care of him for five years didn't earn me a minute of gratitude once he had somewhere better to go."

"That must have hurt."

He waves his hand like it's no big deal, but I can see it in his eyes. "I was dumb enough to give a shit about him."

"That night on the edge, you seemed to be enjoying yourself. Isaac said you have no problems with Shifters, but you didn't seem to mind faking it..."

"Shifter rights are bullshit. I meant every word I said about that. Isaac doesn't agree, but that's because his Shifter stuck around. I was one of the original Terran Defenders, back when it wasn't just a show. Back when we actually gave a shit about the invasion that already happened."

"You mean Shifters."

"Yeah, I mean Shifters. Shipped in from the same fuckers that want our planet. We grow them, train them, and now we've given them land and equal rights."

"What's Isaac say about that?"

He shrugs, but the motion is forced. "He says it doesn't matter. His bomb will get people to wake up. The ones that survive."

"Is it really worth all those innocent lives?"

The way he flinches at my words tells me plenty. He doesn't support Isaac's plan, not really. But does he oppose it enough to do something about it? And if so, why hasn't he already tried to stop him?

"It doesn't matter what I think."

"It matters to me."

He meets my gaze, and for the first time I don't feel like I'm looking at an enemy. I set my hand on top of his where it rests on my thigh. His eyebrows lift and a smirk plays at the corner of his mouth.

"Isaac's a powerful man. This is happening whether or not I support it. I might as well be on the winning side." He leans forward, his elbows resting on his knees. "I became a Protector to protect. But at the end of the day, no one really gives a shit unless they have something to gain."

I set my half-empty mug aside and stand. He follows my lead.

"This isn't what I thought it was."

"I know. And I'm sorry I couldn't be more upfront about what you were getting into."

I need to know where that bomb is. That's the one thing I know with absolute certainty.

SACRIFICE

"*R*elax, brother. You're stressing me out."

I stop by the window, crossing my arms to keep from pulling my hair out. "It doesn't make any fucking sense."

It took four days to get a team on the ground. They went in as food production inspection, and that should have been the end of it. Isaac should have been busted, and Dawn should be here. With me.

"There's nothing there. It's a ranch."

"It's a front."

"I believe you, but anything we could use to prove your intel isn't at that location. We need more information, and unless we can go in there and start questioning-"

"No. We can't spook them."

Gideon's hands are on his hips as he follows my gaze through the window to the edge of the forest. He's got a nice place here. A little cabin he built with Hope. Cozy, warm, and just big enough for the family they're planning.

"Dawn will get more information." Fuck, I hate that this rides on her getting that asshat to trust her.

If it were simply the attacks on Shifters, this mission would be done. My report was plenty to justify pressing charges. But with that bomb in play, everything changes.

Our team scanned every inch of that place. There's nothing there. All we can do is monitor for any outgoing signals, keep eyes on anyone who leaves, and hope Dawn learns something concrete.

Every evening I go there, and she meets me in the cornfield. She tells me the same damn thing every night; give me a little more time. Daniel's not so bad, she says. He's respecting her space and they're *comfortable*.

She won't even let me touch her anymore, but she's getting *comfortable* with the man who beats Shifters for kicks.

But her eyes don't back up her words. Those baby blues are full of fear, guilt, and mistrust. When I step close, she sways toward me like her body can't resist the pull of mine. When I hold her gaze, her chin trembles.

It's fucking breaking me. But the last thing she needs is another voice telling her what to do. I tell her I hate everything about this. I tell her I need her in my arms like I need oxygen. I tell her I'm sorry.

Last night, a single tear traced down her cheek.

Gideon runs a hand through his hair. "I know you want to trust her with this, but you saw the same video feed I did."

Yeah, I did. Thomas and Dawn, hand in hand. They were only caught on camera for a moment. I was the only one who could see the way she stiffened when he put his arm around her.

"She's giving him what he wants, so she can get the intel we need."

"She's not trained for that kind of-"

"I know she's not trained!" I get in his face, but even with my bigger size, he doesn't back off. "You think I wanted to leave her there? I don't give a fuck if they vaporize the Solar and turn Moridian into a fucking crater. None of those people are worth..."

Gideon's eyebrows lift, and I want to punch the smirk off his face. "You like her."

I step off, heading for the exit.

"Tarek. Wait."

I stop with my hand on the door. I don't want to get into this with him.

"She's a good woman, I get why you have a thing for her. I've just never seen you... like this."

"She's a civilian, and I put her in a situation she's not trained for. I'm responsible for her safety."

Gideon doesn't look convinced. I almost want to tell him how I feel about her. He'd get it. But it's the part where she doesn't love me back I can't bring myself to put into words.

I don't want to talk about this anymore.

I need a drink.

∿

"HEY HONEY, what's on your mind?"

Kelsey slides onto the stool beside me, two open bottles in her hands. She's the one who got me into beer. I could never understand the appeal of that shit Gideon drinks, but a craft brew is the perfect way to end any day. Even a day as shit as this.

I thank her and take a long pull. I don't give a shit about the label or the flavor tonight. My Medic won't let me get much of a buzz, but I can take the edge off for a moment before it's time to meet Dawn. Calm my nerves before I have to watch her push me away again.

I look over at Kelsey, as she reads my expression with a practiced skill honed over years of being a bar stool therapist. Her crystal blue eyes miss nothing.

"Your hair's different." I gesture to the new purple tips. "It's cute."

"Aw, thanks." She brushes the ends with her fingers. "You've got a couple curious ones eyeing this seat. If you want to avoid crushing their dirty dreams, a few of the boys are watching the game out back."

I turn, slowly, in my seat. It's a typical Tuesday night at Kelsey's, but the scant crowd of young people is a blur of faces and color. I can't tell who she's talking about, but she always spots them. She's like my anti-wingman.

I like to sit out here. The pounding music, the din of conversation and laughter, the lights reflecting off mirrors and bottles behind the counter. It's the opposite of the calm and quiet at the Meadow, but it's energizing in its own way.

But I hate the drunk, flirting girls. Maybe it's my size, but they seem to need a few drinks before they work up the nerve to approach me. By then, it's hardly flattering. Kelsey mostly keeps them off me, but now and then one slips through.

"I'm not staying long."

I take another drink, and she does the same. Kelsey might be the only person who really gets me. She knows when I need someone to listen to my shit, and she knows when I need someone to talk some sense into me.

"My dragon's got a mind of its own, and it came damn close to making some dragon babies with a crazy female who thinks we need to bring back the species. The only reason it didn't was because it knows I'm in love with Dawn. It's monogamous, apparently."

I watch her in my periphery as she takes a long drink, then sets the bottle down slowly. She turns in her stool, angling her body toward me and leaning in closer.

"Are you serious? Did you really meet someone?"

Her brow furrows, but her eyes are hopeful. Of course Kelsey would ignore the potentially rogue dragon and zero in on that other detail.

"Yeah, but I don't think she feels the same."

"Are you sure? This is all so new for you. Are you sure it's love, and not just a strong, physical connection?"

"It's both. It's definitely both."

Kelsey's face lights up, and it's impossible not to smile along with her. "She must be something, if she's earned that whole package. I can't believe the first woman to get a taste of you would willingly let you go. What happened?"

I wish I fucking knew. But maybe I do. "She doesn't do relationships. She made that clear from the start. And it's complicated now. She's in a tough spot."

Kelsey's lost in thought for a few long moments, biting her lower lip as she works on my problem.

"What did it feel like to you? Was she just into the physical parts, or did she linger on the quiet moments? The kisses and the touching and just staring into each other's eyes. Did you have any doubt that she felt the same?"

I've got a lot of fucking doubts now. We had all that, I thought. Until she didn't want any of it anymore. "I thought so."

"Then what's stopping you?"

She makes it sound like I didn't try hard enough, but I laid it all out for Dawn. She knows I want her.

"I can't carry her back to Morwood and force her to stay."

Kelsey snorts. "Oh. Now I get it."

She takes a drink, tapping her fingers on the countertop like she's bored with the conversation. Her eyes scan the room as she waves to someone further down the bar.

"What the fuck is that supposed to mean?"

She looks at me, one eyebrow raised. "Do you really want to know what I think?"

I growl at her cocky attitude, but I want her insight more than I want my next breath. "Please, Kelsey."

She puts a hand on my arm. "No matter how much you care

about someone, you can't throw away parts of your heart to make them fit. It won't last. Maybe she's sacrificed her goals for someone in the past, or maybe she's watched it happen to someone else. Maybe she's just wiser than the rest of us. If you love her, show her you fit in *her* life. If that's not possible, maybe it's best you're here."

Fuck.

"She knows I want to settle down in the Meadow, have a family, live a quiet life."

"And what does she want? What was her plan before she met you?"

Fuck, fuck.

"I don't know. She's got a ticket. A trip she delayed, but she doesn't want to miss."

"Where's she going?"

"I don't know."

"Why is it so important to her?"

"I don't know."

"Is she coming back?"

"I don't fucking know."

She slides her hand into mine, giving my palm a squeeze. "You're a good man, Tarek. The best I've ever known. Any person would be lucky to have your heart."

That's the problem, isn't it? I feel all these things for her, things I've never experienced with anyone. I gave her my heart and decided that should be enough. I didn't bother to ask her what she wanted, not really.

"You can love her and still let her go. You don't have to sacrifice your dreams any more than she has to sacrifice hers. It's ok to enjoy a moment, make some beautiful memories, and feel the hurt when it's over."

TRUST

*T*he moon is still lingering through the open curtains as the sun lights the early morning sky. I've barely slept, but that's become my new normal.

It's not that I'm having such a terrible time here. Far from it. Hanging out with Daniel, helping with basic chores and meal-times with Ma... it's kind of nice, if I'm being honest. We've gone horseback riding, he's been teaching me some basic self-defence, I learned how to drive a tractor, and I even assisted the on-call vet with a goat birth.

I can't really claim that I haven't been enjoying my stay, and that makes the nights even harder.

Every evening after sunset, I go for a walk. I tell Daniel I want to be alone, so I can call for Rocco and listen for his answer, and so I can think. I meet Tarek deep in the cornfield, and it's breaking me a little more each night.

I can't touch him. I can't let him pull me into his arms and kiss me. He's not mine, and I was never planning to be his. I thought I could do casual with him, but I fucked up. I was stupid enough to think he was different. That we could be different.

Every night I tell him the same thing; I don't know anything more, but I need more time. The bomb is always 'soon', but I don't know what that means. It's been five nights, and I still don't know a damn thing more.

"Hey, sleeping beauty. I've got something that'll help you wake up."

The suggestive lilt in Daniel's voice earns him a pillow to the head. He never misses an opportunity to throw out a thinly veiled offer for sex. I know him well enough now that I don't take it personally. He's just a hopeless flirt.

"Seriously. Coffee's ready. Isaac wants to meet in twenty."

I groan as I crawl out from under the warm covers. I moved into Daniel's cabin the day Tarek left, but he's slept on the couch without complaint every night. As far as anyone here knows, we're a couple. He doesn't confirm or deny it, though he holds my hand and keeps me close when anyone is looking.

A quick shower later, and I'm scooping cold scrambled eggs onto a plate and downing black coffee like it's my only hope of staying upright. Which is probably true.

I sit at the small table and look at Daniel for the first time this morning. He's in his usual jeans and button-down shirt, leaning against the wall and watching me apparently check him out. Maybe it's the lack of sleep, but I feel the urge to be blunt.

"You said I could only stay if we slept together."

His eyes dance with mischief, and I'm rolling my eyes before he even responds.

"I said I wanted you in my bed. Seems to me like I accomplished that."

I snort as I shovel some eggs into my mouth. "No. I'm pretty sure this isn't what you were planning. What is this? What are we?"

He smiles, reaching for the coffee pot to refill my mug. It pisses me off. I don't want him to be nice. I don't want to like him.

"I like women."

"Oh, really? I hadn't noticed."

He leans back against the wall and levels me with a serious stare. "I like cute, sexy women who resist me just enough to make it interesting."

I swallow, then set my fork down. "You like the hunt."

"Exactly. I'd noticed you plenty of times. Cute. Sexy. But so fucking polite." He mimes a gag, and I can't help but laugh. "Until I saw you freak out on that woman. That's when I thought the good girl might be one hell of a catch in bed."

I grip my coffee mug and take a sip, hoping it hides the flush I feel in my face. The coffee's too hot, so I switch to water. I've definitely lost my appetite for eggs.

"And now you've changed your mind?"

"Nah. I still think you'd be one hell of a fuck."

I choke on my water, taking a moment to recover and breathe normally again. The only thing stopping me from making a quick exit is the fact that he's still relaxed against the wall, a goofy grin on his face like he's having a little too much fun with this.

"You resisted my charms." He sighs as he pushes off the wall, moving to sit in the chair across from me. "And now I've gotten to know you."

"Oh. That's a deal breaker?"

"It is. I like you. You're fun to be around and easy to talk to. If I try to mix sex with that, things will get all emotional and awkward." He scrunches up his face like someone just suggested olives on pizza. "I don't do relationships. I can find someone else to fuck. The friend zone works for me."

"Well, I suppose I should be honored." Even I'm grinning now. As easy as it's been to be around him these last few days, I've still been waiting for the other shoe to drop. Wondering when he's going to try to collect on this implied condition of my being here.

He shrugs. "You should be disappointed. I would have ruined you."

"That sounds..." I'm not even sure how to reply to that.

He throws his head back and laughs, and when he recovers, I quickly change the subject.

"What's Isaac want with me this morning?"

His expression turns serious. "You're not only here because I wanted you around. He needs something done, and you're in a unique position to do it."

"Oh?" I take a careful drink of water. I knew there had to be something more. "You mean other than the security system?"

"That was overdue, but no, that wasn't his reason for bringing you in."

"What does he need?"

"Not my place to fill you in. He's waiting for us when you're ready."

I'm more than ready to have this all make a little more sense.

I stand and clear the dishes, ignoring the queasiness in my stomach at the thought of talking with Isaac again. I've seen him occasionally and exchanged generic greetings. Daniel makes this place feel comfortable, but Isaac has the opposite effect. It might be his family's farm, but everything about *him* feels out of place.

As we head to the meeting, I'm not at all reluctant to take Daniel's hand.

We meet Isaac outside the farmhouse, and he asks how I'm feeling about all of this now that I've had a few days to settle in.

"I'm having trouble accepting the loss of life, but I understand. You're doing what needs to be done."

I can feel Daniel's stare. He knows I'm not as accepting of this as I sound.

"I'm pleased to hear you see it that way." Isaac holds out a tiny, metallic flash drive. "This is our plan B."

I'm hesitant to take it, feeling like just touching the thing will make me part of something I'd rather stay far away from. "What is it?"

"It's a virus. It will misdirect the Centaurians warp drives when they come, sending them far from our solar system. Their fleet will be stranded, delaying their plans by years. It will give us time to find another way."

"You won't have to destroy the Solar?"

"Exactly."

The tiny drive in my palm suddenly feels a lot heavier. Isaac's smiling like he's waiting for me to absorb the brilliance of his plan. It's too simple. Why would he acquire a bomb, if all he needed was a code?

"How does it work?"

He waves a hand like the details are unimportant. "It needs to be uploaded to the servers at Solar One HQ. It will stay dormant until the Centaurians lock on to our end of the warp, then it will do its thing."

"Are you sure?"

"I don't know a damn thing about code or hacking, but I trust the team who designed this for me. I'm not an evil man, Dawn. Killing innocents was never my first choice, but saving our planet has to come first."

I suppose his train of thought makes sense. Kind of. A few days ago, he was talking about a nuke. Now all that's needed is a virus. I want to believe what he's telling me, but it feels too convenient.

"What do you need me to do?"

"I need this uploaded at HQ."

"I took two weeks off. I'm scheduled to be back to work on Monday."

"Good. Take the weekend to relax. Maybe go visit your lovely sister and those adorable nephews over in Fentondale."

The tone of his voice sends a chill down my spine. The

corners of his eyes crease as he watches the veiled threat sink in. He steps closer, the intensity of his stare making it impossible for me to look away.

"No harm will come to you or your loved ones if you do as I'm asking. But I need to be honest with you, Dawn. This is a critical step. It will save many lives. I want to trust you, but I need a guarantee."

Holy hell. This just got a lot more personal. I'm not exactly close with my sister, but I never considered that this would put her and the boys in danger.

"I wouldn't..."

"I want you to know, deep down, that if you breathe a word of this to anyone, I'll make sure your family meets a very slow end."

Deep breath. He's going to see right through me. He's going to find out that this was one big setup right from the start.

"Boss, that's not-"

Daniel's protest is cut off with a raise of Isaac's hand, even though his steely eyes never leave mine.

"I can ensure you live the rest of your life regretting the moment you betrayed me. Do you understand? Do you truly believe that I will go to any length required to save us?"

I nod, but he waits for more. I swallow past the lump in my throat.

"I understand. You can trust me."

STILL A MAN

$\mathcal{M}$y eardrums nearly burst from the high-pitched scream as my sister throws her arms around my neck in a choking hug. I return her enthusiasm, as we do our usual dance. Celebrating finally getting to see each other after all this time, even though we live less than two hours apart and could make time for visiting if we really wanted to.

"It's so good to see you, little sis."

"You too, big sis."

"Did mom tell you about Renee?"

"She did. She called."

Cassie nods. "The boys are thrilled you're here."

She wraps her arm around my shoulders and leads me into the cute little split entry she's lived in for the last ten years. It hasn't changed much since I last visited, but the boys sure have.

Aiden's nearly twelve now, so he greets me with a quick hug and some updates on his school and budding cadet career. Riley's a couple years younger, and far chattier. He fills me in on every game he's played since the last time we talked. I bought the boys their first console, and while Aiden never had more than a fleeting interest, Riley's my gaming buddy.

Cassie rolls her eyes and shoos the boys into the kitchen. "Come on you three, lunch is ready."

I only gave Cass a few hours warning I was coming, but I could smell the home-cooked meal the moment I stepped in the door.

It was strange to leave the Farm, and even stranger to come here. Isaac was insistent that I remind myself what I've got to lose. As if I wouldn't take his threat seriously otherwise. As if a man who can commit mass murder might hesitate to harm one family.

Daniel drove me to the edge of Fentondale, but we barely spoke along the way. He's barely talked to me at all since that chat with Isaac yesterday, and I get the feeling he didn't know about this *plan B* that's burning a hole in my pocket. He's not used to being out of the loop.

There was really nothing to discuss, anyway. Isaac made it pretty black and white with his *do this or else* speech.

I don't get it. All the prep and expense of attaining a bomb, then he has a virus coded that avoids the need for destruction altogether. It's too convenient.

"It's good to have you here," Cassie says, once we're all seated with heaping plates that look more like a Christmas dinner than an unplanned drop-in. "Trevor's been working out of town a lot, so it's usually just the boys and I."

"This is amazing, Cass. You didn't need to go to all this trouble."

She swats the air like it's nothing. "Maybe you'll visit more often if the hospitality is good enough. Wouldn't you like that, boys? If Aunt Dawn visited more often?"

The boys agree, of course. Especially Riley, who starts listing off all the couch co-op games we need to play. It's sweet. It almost makes me feel guilty for not spending more time here. Except Cassie hasn't once visited me, not that I'm keeping score.

Or that every time I'm here she bends over backward to prove what a great homemaker she is, and how she made all the right decisions when she got knocked up at sixteen and married at seventeen.

We both know the truth. Since she settled here, she's barely seen anything beyond these four walls. She and Trevor are hardly even friends, and she takes every chance she can to pawn off the boys on family or sitters. She's not happy, she's resigned. For her, any home is better than the constant upheaval we grew up with.

Of course, I don't say any of that. I put a hand over my heart and prepare to deliver my usual line about how I'll try to get away from work more often. I can't do it this time, though. The bomb, the invasion, this drive in my pocket...

I grab my sister's hand and look back and forth between the boys. "I love you guys. I might not be any good at being an Aunt, but I do love you, okay?"

Aiden blushes and mumbles, but a grin tugs at the corners of his mouth. Riley beams and says he loves me, too. Cass just sits in silence, her fork hovering above her plate.

The chime of a doorbell breaks the spell, though it still takes Cass a minute to jump up from the table. After a few moments of silence, she calls my name from the entryway.

Time moves in slow motion as I imagine Daniel, or Isaac, standing in the doorway. Here to prove they can get to my family. I might have left the Farm, but I'm far from out of their reach.

I brace for anything, but when I round the corner from the dining room and see Tarek looming in the doorway, I nearly jump out of my skin.

"Tarek?" I say his name like a question, as if my brain might just be playing tricks on me.

"Hey, Dawn."

"So, you do know him?" My sister's eyes are wide, but her

mouth curves into a smile as she looks from me to Tarek. "Please, come in."

She moves aside, and he steps through the door. My heart kicks up a gear, but I take a deep breath to calm it.

"What are you doing here?"

"I'll give you two a moment." Cassie winks at me, then turns her attention back to Tarek. "We were just sitting down to an early dinner. If you like chicken and potatoes, you're welcome to join us?"

I open my mouth to protest, but the look on Tarek's face stops me. Cassie scurries by, shooing my curious nephews back into the dining room.

Tarek doesn't move, but his eyes are bright as he waits for me to talk first. I hate how awkward this feels. How awkward it's felt every night since he left the Farm. I start toward him, but then second-guess myself and stop. I guess that's all the encouragement he needed, because he closes the distance and wraps me in a hug.

I'm not prepared for the emotion that hits me. The feel of his arms around me, his scent, his heart beating wildly against my ear. I slide my hands around his waist, squeezing him as tight as I can while breathing him deep into my lungs.

"Fuck, I missed you." His words have a rough edge as he buries his face in my hair.

"You just saw me last night." My voice sounds as rough as his.

"Seeing you isn't enough." His hands knead into my back as he nuzzles against my ear.

What am I doing? I can't do this. I push out of his arms, and he growls as he lets me go.

"Are you with him?"

The question takes me by surprise, and my hesitation makes his eyes darken as his jaw clenches.

"Of course not." I hear the defensiveness in my tone, and anger clenches in my gut. Why the hell is he pretending like it matters? He's clearly fine having multiple playthings. Why shouldn't I do the same?

I cross my arms. I haven't even hinted at what I saw that night, because it's none of my business what he does or who he does it with. But if he wants to pretend like he's jealous of me being with someone else, it's time we levelled the playing field and dropped the act.

"Come on, you two. Dinner's getting cold!" My sister calls to us in a sing-song voice that takes me right back to when we were kids and our mother called us home.

I hold Tarek's gaze for a moment longer, then lead the way into the dining room, where my sister is waiting with an all-too-eager expression on her face.

"So, how do you two know each other?" She starts her questions as soon as we sit. There's a place made up for Tarek like it was always there, his plate piled high with a bit of everything.

"We work together." I offer, hoping that will satisfy her curiosity enough.

"Are you a Protector?" She asks, her eyes lighting up as she openly admires his arms.

"Yep. I'm a Shifter." He states the fact as he takes his first bite of chicken. "This is amazing. Is that tarragon?"

My sister's eyes fly wide, the boy's faces matching her look of surprise.

"Yeah, wow, uh, it is." Cassie stammers over her words, and I'm not sure if she's more taken aback by his nonchalant admission that he's a Shifter, or his apparent knack for detecting seasoning.

"Seriously?" Aiden asks, and Cassie gives him a warning stare that he ignores.

Tarek doesn't seem to notice he's the only one still eating.

"What can you turn into?" Riley speaks up, leaning over his plate.

Cass shushes him, but it doesn't deter the excitement etched on his face.

"Whatever I want to."

Tarek's clearly impressing the boys as they fire questions at him like he's the coolest thing they've ever seen. Even Aiden has dropped the chill, almost-a-teenager persona to assuage his own curiosity.

Cassie appears less impressed. Now that the initial shock has passed, she keeps her eyes on mine. I can see the gears turning, as she works out who Tarek is and why he's here at her table. After listening for years to my incessant infatuation with Shifters, here we are.

"Okay, boys. That's enough. Let our guest eat in peace."

The boys keep their eyes on Tarek as the rest of the meal passes in relative calm, punctuated by the occasional question one of the boys can't hold back, and Cassie's somewhat awkward attempts at small talk.

Tarek seems genuinely at ease with all of it. I try not to stare like the rest of them, but I can't help catching his eye now and then. Each time, he gives me a smile that sends my heart skittering.

"That was perfection. Thank you, Cassie." Tarek sets his fork down, the first to finish even though he was the last to start. "You boys help me clean up dinner, and I'll show you what I can do."

"No, that's not-" Cassie's protest dies in her throat as Aiden and Riley jump to their feet, grabbing dishes and grinning like fools.

"Don't worry, I won't go full dragon on them." Tarek winks at Cass, and her jaw hits the floor. "That was an amazing meal. You two go relax. We'll take care of this."

"I don't think my boys know how to wash a dish..."

"Well, miss, they're about to learn."

Tarek practically pushes her out of the kitchen, and I know my expression must look nearly as dumbfounded as hers as I follow.

"What just happened?" Cassie asks once we're out of earshot in the sitting room.

"I'm not sure." It's an honest answer. This is a side of Tarek I certainly didn't expect. So... domestic.

"He's a natural with the boys. I don't think Trevor's ever offered to help clean up after a meal, let alone kicked me out of the room."

We sit in stunned silence for a while, listening to the sounds of dishes, water, the boy's laughter, and Tarek's deep, rumbling voice. This feels so... I don't know what I'm feeling right now.

"He's a Shifter." Cassie doesn't attempt to hide the accusation in her voice. She's probably having a field day with the implications of Tarek following me here.

We both startle at the sound of a screen door slamming, then jump up to investigate.

The kitchen is spotless. The table's cleared, the floor swept, and the sink empty and shining. The dishes are even put away, instead of left to air dry... who does that? Cassie just stares, and I swear her eyes are misty.

When she peeks out the window, her hand flies to her chest with a gasp. "Holy shit."

I rush to her side to see what she's looking at. Holy hell. Is this really happening?

Riley and Aiden are looking a little pale as they cautiously approach a massive grizzly. Thankfully, their back yard is fenced in. I'm sure the neighbors would freak out if they could see what's going on.

He's huge. Tarek stays still, head lowered, as they inch close enough to touch his shaggy fur. He pushes with his front legs, rising off the ground to stand on sturdy hind legs. He's twice the height of the boys. His paws are bigger than their heads and tipped with deadly, black claws.

Cassie lunges for the door, but I grab her arm. "He's safe," I assure her. "He'd never hurt them."

My assurance doesn't calm the maternal fear in her eyes. I can't blame her, but I hold her in place as we watch without interrupting.

The boys quickly lose their apprehensions as he plays with them. He lets them climb on his back and even shows them a few other forms as we watch from inside. The boys look years younger as they laugh and roughhouse, and Tarek looks like he's having just as much fun.

When he shifts back to human form, I push the door open and walk out into the warm spring sun. His eyes light up when he sees me, and I feel a stab of something in my chest. Why does he look at me like that? What does he see?

"Did you see that, Mom!" Aiden's voice is a high-pitched squeal.

"I haven't seen them play like that for a long time," Cassie says when Tarek gets close. "At their age, it's all about comms and VR."

"They're good boys." Tarek's compliment makes Cassie's eyes shine, but she sets her jaw and looks at me with an expression I've seen many times.

"You must be loving this, little sister."

I lower my eyes, hoping she'll leave the veiled dig between us.

"Dawn's always had a bit of an obsession with Shifters." Cassie grins as Tarek narrows his eyes. "It must be a fantasy come to life to have one like you at her beck and call."

"It's not like that, Cass-"

"Don't worry, sis, I'm not judging." She holds a hand up to

the side of her mouth, like she's telling him a big secret. "Our girl's never been into men."

"Cassie!"

"Come on, you know it's true." She pushes my shoulder like this is a playful exchange. "You chase anything with a tail. I bet you're having a blast now that they can do this." She gestures to Tarek, as if his body is a party trick.

Dammit. I should have known where this would lead. I should have turned him away at the door, or left with him if he refused. He deals with enough of this shit, he doesn't need to be subjected to it because of me.

"It's not like that."

Cassie wiggles her eyebrows and laughs like this is the funniest thing, as I melt into a puddle of hot shame. I can't even glance at Tarek, I'm too mortified.

Cassie's voice becomes distant. She's talking to my nephews. I turn and head back into the house, Tarek's heavy footsteps following behind me.

"What the fuck was that all about?" Tarek asks once we're alone inside.

"I'm sorry."

"Was it true?"

I'm sure my hesitation says plenty, because when I turn to look at him, his eyes are dark. "Not like that. Not the way she says it."

"Do you have a Shifter fetish? I've met more than a few of those types, but I didn't peg you for one."

"I'm not a fucking groupie." I scrub my hands through my hair, then lead him through the house and out onto the front doorstep. The last thing I want is Cass overhearing the argument she instigated.

I lean against the closed door, and Tarek folds his arms across his chest as he watches me. Holy hell, he's beautiful. I close my eyes. Checking him out in the middle of this argument doesn't exactly prove her wrong. But it's not because he's a Shifter, it's just *him*.

"You know I'm fascinated by Shifters. Your abilities, history, culture."

"I might not be human, but I'm still a man."

"I know. Fuck, Tarek, you know I know that."

"But you sleep with Shifters."

"No!" I don't know what we are right now, but I won't have him thinking he was some kind of trophy or name on a list of conquests. "I've never done anything like this. It's only you."

He's quiet, watching me with his arms folded while I still can't look him in the eyes.

"Why won't you let me get close to you?"

"I do, I-"

"No. You don't. You like to flirt, and you like to touch... but whenever I try to talk about how close I am to fall-"

"Tarek, don't."

"Exactly."

Oh, hell. I meet his emerald stare. "Why are you doing this? Why are you even here?"

His head jerks back, and I have to look away from the pinch of hurt in his expression. I have no reason to feel guilty. Cassie's bitter outburst aside, Tarek is the one who's not being honest here.

"How's your red-headed friend? Must be nice to have another dragon to *fly* with." Judging by their conversation, the flight was hardly the main event.

Now it's his turn to look away.

Tarek is amazing. And not just because he's a Shifter. But he's naïve if he thinks some declaration of temporary emotions will change who we are.

"Don't start talking about love, Tarek. It's fun until it isn't. Until life gets real."

He's silent for so long, I turn to head back inside.

"How long are you staying here?"

"I was planning to crash for the night, then head home in the morning."

"Let me fly you back tonight."

Holy hell. It wouldn't matter what was happening around us, that offer would knock me off my feet. But after Cassie's accusations, the last thing I want to do is take advantage of his Shifter abilities.

"I can take a cab."

MEMORIES

*W*hen my feet touch the earth, my legs are too numb to hold me. I fall to the ground, rolling onto my back and laughing up at the starry sky.

"Are you okay?"

Tarek stands over me, blocking half the sky and looking at me like he's concerned for my sanity.

"You're incredible."

A deep laugh shakes his shoulders, and he drops to the grass beside me. We're on the top of a low hill, surrounded by fields and forest. Somewhere along the stretch of farmland between Fentondale and Moridian.

After what happened with my sister, I couldn't stomach the idea of playing happy family for the whole night. I also didn't want Tarek leaving with so much tension between us. I care about him, and I know he cares for me. He doesn't need to pretend there's something deeper, and I want him to know I'm not upset that he has someone else. I'm happy for him.

It's impossible to dwell on any of those thoughts right now, after spending a half hour *riding a freaking dragon*. Fresh adrenaline surges through me at just the memory of his powerful body beneath me, his wings spread out on either side, harnessing the wind with ease and grace. Holy hell. I did that.

There are no words.

"I met Hunter a few weeks ago."

His statement jars me out of my high. He doesn't need to do this. We don't need to ruin this moment or make it into something bigger than it is.

I sit up and wave my hand in the space between us. "You don't need to explain. Whatever this is," I point between him and I, "It's fun. I like you a lot, and not just because you're a Shifter. We don't need to pretend it's something it isn't."

"We met in Dragon form and she wanted..."

Even with the starlit night casting his features in shadow, I can tell his skin is flushed. His eyes are unfocused. The way he's biting his lower lip would be insanely sexy if he didn't look so conflicted.

"You really don't need to explain anything."

"My dragon has a mind of its own. It has instincts and thoughts I can't interpret. Like when you remember emotions from a dream but can't name them."

I nod, even though he's not looking at me. He's staring off into the distance, and I can't help but appreciate the chance to drink in his features. I want to press a kiss to the tattoos on his neck, and to the spot where his pulse keeps pace with my own heartbeat.

"She wanted a mate, and my dragon responded. I barely controlled him, but we got the fuck out of there."

His statement tears me away from thoughts of tasting his skin. I've never heard anyone talk like this. Like the man and the dragon are two different creatures. A chill traces down my spine and I stay quiet, hoping he'll tell me more.

"I saw her at the Farm on the first day. She recognized me." He pauses again, breathing in and out like he's trying to keep calm. This conversation isn't easy for him. "She thinks if we let the dragons take control, they'll revive their species. I don't see that as a good thing, but she's determined. Finding me there gave her leverage. She threatened the Meadow, and to blow our cover if I didn't fly with her. If I didn't let my dragon free to do what it naturally wanted to do."

My stomach clenches as I remember her telling him about the secluded clearing that would give them privacy. It's not jealousy that's twisting my insides. Not anymore.

"She blackmailed you for sex."

He cringes, shaking his head in denial. "It wasn't about sex."

Now it's my turn to cringe. "Right. She blackmailed you for a baby."

He lets out a long breath as he scrubs a hand across the back of his neck. "I gave her what she wanted, but my dragon wasn't interested."

"You didn't..."

He shakes his head. For the first time since he sat, he meets my gaze. "Seems he's monogamous."

"Tarek..."

"I'm not going anywhere, Dawn. Not until you tell me to, and make it really fucking clear you're serious."

I don't know what to say. I've been nothing but clear that I'm not interested in anything long term. But his words don't make me want to run. I don't want to roll my eyes or laugh at the absurdity of his statement. I kind of want it to be true.

But it doesn't matter. His feelings may very well be real, and I know whatever I'm feeling isn't exactly a crush. It doesn't matter because I'm not putting my future on hold. I'm not giving up who I am to fit into any relationship.

"Sorry about my sister."

"I'm not your guardian, and I'm not your pet."

I shake my head. Even during the time I've spent with him in

Rocco's form, I've never thought of him that way. I could never see him as anything less than who he is.

"I know, Tarek. Shifters fascinate me. But I've gotten to know you, and the way I feel about you isn't about that."

He's picking at the grass, his big hands toying with the blades as his eyes reflect the moonlight with an ethereal glow.

"I want to enjoy this for what it is, but I'm not staying. I'll never be someone's wife. I'll never be a mother."

"Don't you want that someday? A home. A family?"

I snort at the idea. He's barking up the wrong tree, if that's what he thinks I can give him. "My sister's miserable. She hates her life, and she can't wait for those boys to grow up. Same as my parents. That's why she says the shit she does. She's jealous that I didn't fuck up my life by making commitments I don't really want."

"It's not always that way."

"It is often enough."

"I want that. Someday."

I turn away as I swipe a tear off my cheek. I can't help but be affected by what he's saying. Stupid female hormones.

"I can't give that to you." I turn back to him. "The trip I postponed isn't a vacation. It's a one-way ticket off-world. I won't be coming back."

His expression is unreadable. He just stares at me, and my body heats under the intensity of it. I'm such a hypocrite. I just told him there's no chance of a future for us, and yet all I want to do now is climb onto his lap and show him it doesn't change the way I feel right now.

His eyes drop to my mouth. As if he can read my mind, his hand moves to the back of my head, pulling me into a hungry kiss.

This can't last, we both know that.

He moves slowly, unfolding his body as he presses into me,

urging me to lay back on the soft grass. He hovers above, his arms braced at my sides as he kisses me rough and thorough. I'm breathless when his mouth leaves mine. He pushes my shirt up and the course stubble on his chin rakes across my belly. I gasp when he nips my hip bone, then bites my thigh through my pants.

"Tarek..."

"I want you. Now."

Holy hell. He's all I want. I don't care how much it hurts later.

He crawls back up my body, as I claw at his shirt like a crazy woman until he helps me pull it over his head. Tarek shirtless is a dream, but hovering over me like this, with his hair falling forward and the starry sky framing his silhouette, he takes my breath away.

He shudders as I run my hands up his powerful arms, the muscles bunched from holding himself up. His thick shoulders, his carved chest, his stomach.

He reaches for my shirt, slowly peeling it over my head. I lift my hips, so he can do the same to my pants. He stills, his eyes raking over my body as I lay in my mismatched bra and panties.

I reach between us, grasping the waist of his pants and fumbling with the zipper. His eyes meet mine, and for a fleeting moment, I swear he looks nervous.

He pushes up, rising to his feet with a playful smile on his lips. He makes quick work of his heavy pants, pushing them over his huge thighs. His boxers follow, and when he steps out of his clothes, I'm pretty confident I've breathed my last breath.

"You're beautiful, Tarek. Do you have any idea how incredibly perfect you are?"

His grin fades, and I scramble to my feet. I fumble with the clasp of my sports bra before tossing it to the ground, and waste no time getting my panties out of the way.

His lips part as he looks at me, and even in the dim light my skin prickles at the intensity of his stare. I don't move. I let him look his fill while I do the same, my eyes unable to drink in enough of him to satisfy.

As I take in every hard line of his body, memorizing every muscle and vein, I'm acutely aware of my body's reactions. The way the night air cools my skin and my chest rises and falls with each breath, lifting my breasts. The way my nipples have hardened in anticipation of his touch. The delicious ache and wetness between my legs.

I'm so ready for him, and he hasn't even touched me.

The grass tickles my feet as I step toward him, closing the distance between us and closing my hand around his thick shaft as he sucks in a breath. I had him in my mouth. I've barely been able to think about that night, because knowing it was the closest we'd ever get was just too painful. But I remember now. His taste. The sounds he made.

We don't need to be quiet here.

I tighten my grip, stroking along the length of him as he lets his breath out in a moan. I slide my thumb over the tip of him, over the first drop of his arousal.

He grasps my face and kisses me. Thoroughly but gently, he devours my mouth. His hands slide down my back as he kisses a trail down my chest to taste first one hardened peak, then the other. I moan my approval as he alternates, first kissing and sucking, then nipping the sensitive flesh.

He grips my hips as he nudges my feet apart, and I'm eager to guide him to the place I need him most.

He drops to his knees.

"Tarek, you don't-"

His tongue glides over my clit and my words die in a strangled *oh!* as I tangle my fingers through his hair.

I nearly come apart. If he does that one more time, I'm done for. I can feel the tremble in my knees, but his firm grip on my hips keeps me upright as he kisses my thighs, then my stomach, then so close to where I need him I nearly cry out.

I don't know what he's done to me. I've never cared for oral, let alone needed it so badly I'm willing to beg.

"*Please.*"

The word is barely a moan on my lips, but his tongue heeds my plea and I fly apart. I'm nothing but touch and feeling as my orgasm washes through me while his mouth coaxes me higher and higher. I can't feel anything but his hands, his arms, his mouth.

When the intensity subsides, I'm on my back and he's hovering over me again. He's braced on his elbows, his body against me, his forehead resting on mine as he looks into my eyes. I meet his gaze when I'm finally able to see straight, and then I feel the thick head of him pressed against my entrance.

There's a question in his eyes, but I've got no doubts. I'm so ready for this man. I wrap my legs around his hips and pull him closer. I watch his face as he sinks into me, stretching me further than I've ever felt before. The pleasure of his entrance far outweighs any temporary discomfort.

I can't take my eyes off his face. There are no words for his expression as he fills me, drawing the moment out like he doesn't want it to end. When he's fully inside me, his head drops. His breathing is ragged, his shoulders tense. I run my hands over his back, loving the sensuality of the moment but also dying to feel him lose control.

He moves his hips, cautiously at first and then more as I coax him with my legs. He takes my cues, pulling nearly out of me before burying himself deep once again.

The tempo he sets is slow, almost cautious. I want to tell him I can handle whatever he can give, but the feel of him moving inside me like this is too perfect. His kisses brush my neck and shoulder, his breath becoming a groan each time his hips meet mine.

I encourage him with whispered praise, meaning every word as I feel the pleasure building. He touches every part of me, filling me so completely as my fingers trail up and down his back.

When his mouth finds mine, his pace quickens. I moan against his lips at the heightened sensation, my fingernails digging into his shoulders. A growl rumbles in his chest as his hips move faster, and a gasp of pleasure rips from me. His eyes light up, and he shifts his weight to one arm, sliding his free hand behind my neck to anchor me as he thrusts harder and harder, all the while watching my face with wild eyes.

I struggle and moan and beg for more as he holds me in place, taking me to heights I never knew existed. I want it all. I want everything, but I can't take it anymore. My orgasm builds to the breaking point as he bares his teeth, burying himself inside me one last time as a roar rips from his chest and I come undone.

It's absolute bliss as we cling to each other, pleasure wracking our bodies in tandem as our breath mingles and gasps turn to kisses.

He's softened inside me, but he doesn't pull away. The hand behind my neck slides down my body, touching every part of me he can reach. His kiss deepens for a moment before he leans back, pulling out of my body as he settles by my side, tucking me tightly against the warmth of his body.

"That was... amazing."

"Yeah?" He props himself up so he can look down at my face.

I can't help but laugh at his expression, like he's amazed by my response.

"I'm sure you don't need me to tell you that."

"I didn't know for sure. I've never wanted that. I didn't want to hurt you."

He looks so vulnerable, I reach up and touch the worried crease on his forehead, trailing my fingers down the side of his face. "What do you mean? Was that... different? You didn't need to hold back for me."

He takes my hand in his, bringing it to his mouth to kiss my palm.

"What's that look for? Was that... was it good for you?" I move to cover myself, suddenly feeling a little too exposed. I was so swept away by him, I hadn't considered that I might disappoint him.

"I've never been with anyone else."

I swear my heart stops. "Are you serious?"

He shrugs. "I've never wanted to. Never cared one way or the other."

He looks at me, and my heart cracks wide open. No. We shouldn't have done that. I sit up, looking down at this beautiful man who's looking back at me like...

"Tarek, you shouldn't have given that to me. I don't deserve this."

"I'll never feel this way about anyone else. If you're not willing to be mine, I at least want this memory to keep."

Holy shit.

My chest hurts so much I think I might actually be having a heart attack. Tarek was a virgin. This moment is too much. It's too sweet. It's got to be a line. Maybe that's his thing, hooking women by convincing them he's been waiting for them... but he didn't do that. He didn't tell me until after.

I put my hand on my chest, as if I need to physically restrain the organ from jumping out and pledging its loyalty to this impossible man.

Don't do anything stupid. I need to chill out and enjoy it for what it is. Friends with benefits. Temporary.

"I've got a flash drive from Isaac. He wants me to upload it at HQ, to redirect the Centaurian fleet when they come. He said if I can do this, it'll buy us time and he won't need to destroy the Solar."

It takes a moment for Tarek's face to register my words, but when he does, his expression hardens. "Do you believe him?"

"I don't know. It seems convenient. If the solution's this simple, why go through the trouble of obtaining and arming a nuke?"

"Maybe there never was one."

"I don't know anymore."

"What are you going to do?"

"I can't do what he's asking. What if the bomb is a cyber-attack that takes out the anti-grav? I want to take it to Liam. He can tell me what it does, and I trust him to keep it quiet."

Tarek lays back, stretching his thick arms under his head. I can't resist the opportunity to drink in the sight of him naked and spread out on the grass.

Holy hell, the things I want to do to his body... travelling the cosmos suddenly seems dull in comparison.

Even soft, his cock is an impressive sight. I can't say I've ever considered that part of a man to be attractive, but just the sight of Tarek's makes my mouth water. He must notice where my attention's focused, because he hardens as I watch.

I keep still and quiet, loving the show his body's putting on for me. When he's fully hard and standing at attention, I climb over him.

If it's memories he wants, I'll give him a good one.

DRIVE

I could get used to this.

Dawn's warm little body fits perfectly against mine under the plush blankets. She murmurs in her sleep, and it's all I can do not to wake her and find out if sex from this angle would be just as amazing as missionary was.

Nothing could beat her on top, that I'm sure of. Riding my body as she touched herself. Watching her climax twice before I couldn't hold my own orgasm back a moment longer. Fuck, that is a sight I will never forget.

My cock's definitely on board with more experimenting.

Nestled between the soft swells of her ass, nothing but the thin fabric of our underwear between us... fuck. If she keeps squirming against me like that, I'm going to lose my mind.

Instead of ruining the sleep she clearly needs, I extract myself from her limbs and slide off the edge of the bed. We were both exhausted when we arrived at her flat in the early morning, but a few hours sleep is enough to keep me going.

She moans her disapproval at the loss of my heat, but doesn't wake.

I pull on my pants and shirt, then slip quietly from the room.

Rocco greets me when I enter the sitting area, and I crouch down to give him some attention. It's a little strange after spending so much time in his form.

"No one's ever gotten past that door."

I straighten at the sound of Liam's voice, tensed for an awkward conversation.

"It's cool." He puts his hands up, the grin on his face creasing the corners of his eyes. "Dawn's not stupid. If she picked you, I'm sure she knows what she's doing."

"But you'd rather she picked you." Might as well cut through the bullshit sooner rather than later.

His mouth presses into a thin line, but then he shakes his head. "No. Dawn's a good friend. I'd have to be dead not to try for more, but if she's with you, I respect that one hundred percent."

I nod. Alright then.

"She's been gone for a while. Everything okay?"

"I love her."

Why the fuck did I just say that to him? He looks at me like those are the last words he expected to come out of my mouth. Fuck.

I move to the couch, slumping back and scrubbing my hands over my face.

"Shit." I hear him settle into a chair. "Does she feel the same?"

"She likes me. I know she does. And we're... we're great together. But she..." Why the fuck am I talking to this guy like we're friends?

"But she won't let you past the door."

"Yeah. That's about it."

"For what it's worth, I doubt it's you. Dawn doesn't let anyone in. As far as she's concerned, family is conditional and love is a fairy tale. She doesn't think she needs either."

I lean back, sifting through his words. I barely remember

what it felt like when I was just Gideon's Shifter. Before the Meadow. The love I have for the family I chose, that's what makes life worth living. I don't know what I'd become if I didn't have that.

"You know she's not sticking around for long."

I just nod. What's the point? It won't matter how she feels about me, she won't trust her emotions enough to change her plans. Hell, I bet if she falls for me, she'll leave even faster.

Kelsey said I need to show her I can fit into her life, but how can I do that when she won't let me in? She's given me so much of herself already, but she's got these walls I just can't see past.

Rocco's ears perk up a moment before Dawn's door opens. He greets her with the same enthusiasm he offered me, and earns a thorough scratch behind the ears.

"Good morning." She looks at me with eyes that are all heat.

I see nothing but her as I cross the room in three strides and pull her into my arms, pressing a kiss to her mouth.

"Hungry?"

She glances toward Liam, but then smiles up at me. "I need to chat with Liam. Then I can order?"

"I'll put something together while you talk."

"Okay..." She sounds less than sure, and I wonder if she's doubting my cooking skills.

She heads over to show Liam the flash drive, and I start digging through the cupboards. Thirty minutes later, I'm dishing up four servings of omelettes and toast. Rocco looks a little uncertain of my offer for him to eat off a plate, but no way I'm eating in front of him while his only option is a bowl of kibble.

When the meal is done, Dawn joins me in the kitchen. She jumps up to sit on the counter, and I can't resist stepping between her legs and pulling her tight against me. Her little gasp melts into a hushed moan as I kiss her neck, kneading my fingers into her thighs.

"You can cook." She says it like it's the last thing she expected.

"I would hope so. I sure as fuck like to eat."

She laughs, and it's music to my ears. After everything we did and said last night, I didn't know if I'd get to hear that sound again. I didn't know if she'd let me get close, or if she'd decide arm's length was the safer option.

"Liam's going to look at the drive."

I nod, keeping my lips on her skin as I make a slow path down over her collar bone.

"I need to jump in the shower."

"That sounds like a great idea."

I start to peel her shirt up, but she swats my hands.

"Tarek!" She sounds annoyed, but her face is all smiles when I lean away. She points in the direction of the living room, as if I've forgotten we're not alone.

"I'm taking this into my room." Liam appears around the corner, his laptop open in his hands as he squints at the screen. "I need my setup."

Rocco's at his heels as he heads down the hall, and I turn my attention back to the woman in my arms. I hold her gaze until heat reflects in her eyes and a smile tugs at the corners of her mouth. She wraps her legs around my waist as I pull her off the edge of the counter.

When the bathroom door closes behind us, she slides to the floor and watches me with dancing eyes as I pull my shirt over my head.

Her eyes drink me in, sliding over every inch of my torso with open appreciation. I love every second of her attention. I watch her face as I unclasp my pants, pushing them down over my thighs.

Her attention snaps from my body up to my eyes, and then I'm the one lost in rapt appreciation as she pulls her own cloths off. She strips down unashamedly until she's naked in front of me. All I can do is stare as she turns on the shower, adjusting the temperature until she's satisfied.

She steps in, and as the water soaks her hair and cascades over her body, I have to brace against the counter to stay on my feet. Fuck, my woman's the most beautiful creature that's ever lived.

I watch her for as long as I can handle, as she washes her body without even glancing my way. When I finally step in and take her into my arms, her nails bite into my skin as our mouths collide.

We're both so worked up, it only takes a few strokes of my fingers to have her gasping against my lips, grinding into my hand as she comes. But I'm close, too. Her hands gliding over my wet skin, touching me like she can't get enough. It's more than I can handle.

The moment her eyes flutter open, I hook her leg over my arm and pin her against the wall. Our height difference makes it a little awkward to find the right angle, but in a moment I'm sinking into her and nothing matters but the feel of her body, the glide of wet skin, and the sound of our breathing.

The moment her body clenches around me, her nails biting into my shoulders as she whimpers through another climax, I let myself go.

Fuck, there's nothing better than this.

Neither one of us speaks as I dry us off, and she lets me carry her to bed. Skin to skin under the sheets, I explore every inch of her soft skin. It doesn't take long for me to be ready for her again, and when she discovers that fact, she pushes me onto my back and straddles my hips.

In this position, I can feel her strength and watch her as she finds her tempo, taking her pleasure from me until I can't stay still a moment longer. I grip her hips, urging her into a faster pace. The harder we collide, the more she seems to love it.

She told me not to hold back. She squeals as I flip her, putting her in the position I need. With one hand braced above her shoulder to anchor us both, and the other supporting her hips at just the right angle, I take her hard and fast.

She holds on with her thighs, clawing at my back as her moans and gasps mingle with words of praise. I think of nothing but the way she feels under me. Nothing but taking what I want from her body. My climax builds, and I grind my teeth to keep quiet as I empty inside her.

I press my forehead to her chest, feeling the wild beating of her heart for a moment before moving downward. She bucks against me as I seal that decadent nub in a kiss, tasting myself, tasting *us*. It's fucking paradise as I savor the aftershocks of my own climax while coaxing her into one of her own.

When I collapse beside her, she slumps over me, boneless and giggling. This is it, right here. This woman in my arms is all I need.

When her heartbeat calms and her breath evens out, I slide slowly off the bed. I could shift, removing the evidence of our lovemaking from my skin in an instant. Instead, I pull on my clothes and tread quietly out of the bedroom.

I knock once on Liam's door, but don't wait for him to invite me in. As long as he has that drive in his possession, I don't give a shit about his privacy.

The only sign that the room is a bedroom is the single bed in the corner, neatly made. A wide desk holding three curved monitors dominates the rest of the space. Liam's sitting back in a chair that looks like you could live in it, and he pulls off a headset to give me a nod.

"How's it going?"

"It's going." He gestures to the centre screen filled with type I can't make heads or tails out of. He pulls his glasses off and chucks them onto the desk, pinching the bridge of his nose as he leans back into the chair.

"What are you thinking so far?"

"I'm thinking I'd like to know what I'm looking at, because it's feeling like a whole lot of nothing."

"What did Dawn tell you?"

"Nothing. She said she couldn't tell me anything, she just needs to know what this does."

I nod, glad she didn't trust him with more than the basics. For her sake and his.

"Let me know as soon as you find something."

"It's gibberish. It's a lot of novice code and unnecessary strings and useless data."

"You're saying it doesn't do anything?" Maybe it's a test. A useless drive just to see if she'd do it.

"I don't know for sure. It's huge. I don't see anything yet, but if I had a rough idea what I was looking for-"

"I can't."

"Yeah." He retrieves his glasses and pulls them back on with an exaggerated sigh. "I'll let you know when something makes sense."

Dawn trusts him, and my instincts tell me he's a good guy. Doesn't mean I'm going to let him out of my sight for long while he has whatever that is.

I should go to the Elders with it.

Leaving him to his work, I return to Dawn's room. She's curled up on the bed just as I left her.

I strip out of my clothes and crawl in next to her, pulling her naked body tight against mine. She murmurs in her sleep, and it's not long before her steady breathing lulls me to join her.

I wake with a start at the sound of knocking on the door. Dawn jumps, but I get to my feet first and pull on my boxers. I open the door just enough to see Liam standing there, and he gives me a once-over with raised eyebrows.

"Got something?"

"Hell, yeah." He backs away and motions for me to follow. "You both need to see this."

"What did you find?"

I stifle a yawn as I enter Liam's room. I could have slept for days, but waking in Tarek's arms is hardly something to complain about. He's standing behind Liam's chair, arms crossed and watching me with a half-grin on his face.

Sex with Tarek is... wow. It's so much more than just sex. He makes me feel cherished. Like I'm the only woman in the universe he's ever wanted. And when he lets loose, holy hell I want more of that. I want all his fantasies.

It can't last. I know that. But I plan to soak up every ounce of this feeling for as long as we have.

I've never been the type to show affection outside the bedroom. Couples holding hands, kissing, it's not really my thing. But even with Liam right there, it feels so natural to slide my arms around Tarek's waist. To lean into his heat as he wraps an arm around me, squeezing me tight enough to let me know I'm welcome, but not so tight that I can't get space when I need it.

"I don't know where you got this, but it's nothing you should fuck around with."

"What is it?"

The code on the monitor means nothing to me. I can do some basic programming, but the jumble of words and symbols as Liam scrolls is far beyond my skill level.

"It wants to connect to the Solar's satellite relay. Someone's trying to make a call off planet."

I pull back from Tarek enough to look up at his face. He looks just as confused as I am. Why would Isaac-

"It's a message to Centauri B."

Tarek stiffens. I lean in closer, as if squinting at the screen will make it any clearer.

"Why would he... what's the message?"

I glance at Liam, still focused on the screen, then back at Tarek. His face is set in stone. I can't read him at all when he looks like that.

"I don't know yet. But whoever this is knows exactly how to piggyback the satellites without being detected. Whatever they have to say, they don't want anyone on Earth knowing what it is."

I press my middle fingers against my temples, trying to catch up.

What would he say to them? He's worried about an invasion, but what could he say to them that would stop that? And if he has something, why wouldn't he just take that to the Elders? Surely Tanikka isn't so bitter about their personal life that she wouldn't accept a diplomatic solution, even from him.

I look up at Tarek. This confuses the heck out of me, but he still looks stoic.

"Thanks, man." He slaps Liam on the shoulder. "Keep digging until you find that message. If this is what I think it is, you'll get compensated for your time."

"And if it isn't what you think it is?"

"I'll buy you lunch."

Liam laughs. I feel a little shiver of excitement at the evidence that they're getting along, but it fades when Tarek shoots me a *let's talk in private* glance.

We leave Liam to his work, and I lead the way back to my room. Once we're inside, he cups his hand around the back of my head and pulls me in for a deep kiss.

I pull back and he kisses my neck, nipping at the sensitive skin as a shiver ripples through me.

"Tarek..."

He laughs, a low rumble in his chest. "I swear this isn't why I wanted to get you alone. But fuck, I can't resist you."

He pulls me against him so I can feel his arousal against my belly. I grab handfuls of his shirt and grind my hips against him, making us both moan. "We have to talk about..."

His hand slides under the waist of my pants and I can't think about anything else. His fingers work my body like he can read my mind. Just the right pressure, just the right pace. When he slides two thick fingers inside me and hooks them just right, I come undone.

"I want to fuck you into oblivion every night."

His words rumble through me as I shudder with the after-shocks, his hand still cupping my sex.

"I want to make love to you every morning."

Holy hell.

"I want you by my side."

He pulls away, cupping my face in his hands. "I love you."

Holy shit. "Tarek..."

I can barely stand. In the afterglow of that orgasm, wrapped in his arms, all I want to say is *me too*. I want that. All of it. All of him.

Fuck. I can't fall for this. For these emotions that I know are temporary. It's biology. Hormones meant to ensure the continuation of our species. I don't want to be tied to anyone, or commit to something that will change when the hormones wear off.

I bite my tongue until the pain snaps me back to reality.

Leading him on would be cruel. It's only going to hurt us both.

"I can't." Goddamnit. I don't want to do this here. "I like you a lot more than I expected, but it's not love. You're incredible. Perfect. I'm just not wired that way."

I look up at him, bracing myself for his hurt, for his retaliation, but his face breaks into a grin and I'm not sure how to take it.

"You like me."

"What?"

"You like me a lot. Maybe you wish you didn't, but you do. It's okay if you can't say the words, because your body tells me plenty. Your eyes tell me more. I'm here, Dawn. You can use my body for all your Shifter fantasies..." He runs his fingers down my arm. I shiver with the chill even as my body heats. "I'll prove that you can still be free, even with me. That you can love me, without losing yourself."

His face goes blurry, but I don't try to hide my emotion. I wish I could make him understand. It's not that I don't want that with him, it's just not real. It can't be real.

"What if I don't? What if I can't stay?"

He shrugs his shoulders. "That's fine. I'll find another playmate when we're done."

My chest constricts so suddenly I can't take a breath. I try to push away from him, but he grips my arms and I'm helpless to move. I can't breathe as a wave of emotion overwhelms me. A fucking anxiety attack? What the hell.

"Is that what you want? Would you prefer I didn't care?"

I open my mouth to argue, but I can't lie. "No."

"Good. You're free, Dawn. I won't ask you for any promises. But I'm all yours. There's no female on this planet that could take my eyes off you. I don't care about sex, I care about you. I don't want a mate. I want you. When you decide we're done, I'll deal with it. There won't ever be anyone else."

"Tarek..." I swipe away the tears that I couldn't hold back if I tried. What can I say to that? He's giving me everything and asking for nothing. People don't do that.

He kisses me on the forehead and steps back. "There's nothing you need to say until you're ready to tell me to get lost."

He doesn't wait for me to speak, he just turns and walks out the door. I'm left feeling bombarded by emotions I don't under-stand. He's giving me a free pass to take what I want out of this and leave without remorse. That should make me feel free, but it doesn't. He thinks I want freedom, but that's not entirely true. I want to explore, see new places. I'm happy having no one who will really miss me.

At least I was.

I thought I could handle Tarek moving on with someone else. The idea of having this crazy romance, then taking off for the stars while he ends up with someone like Hunter. That's an ending I could be happy with. I think. Even the thought of that twists my insides now.

It's not Tarek moving on that bothers me the most, it's the thought of never seeing him again. Of not being able to hold him, kiss him, hear his voice rumble in his chest when he wraps his arms around me.

I'll miss him. I'll miss us.

But this is still new. We barely know each other, really. We're still caught up in the newness and firsts. This infatuation is consuming, but it's temporary. It's always temporary.

This is crazy. I've got bigger problems.

Another shower. That's what I need.

But even that simple task makes me think of what I have. What I'll be losing. Standing under the water, it's impossible not to think about Tarek in here with me. Holy hell, that man's beautiful. But naked and wet and wanting me... I take a deep breath. Infatuation. It'll pass. It has to pass.

He thinks he wants me. What he really wants is a family, a home, someone to share that with. I'll never be that for him. I've told him that, but he doesn't really get it. I *can't* be that for him.

"Dawn."

I jump at the sound of Tarek's voice outside the shower.

"Liam has something."

"Coming. I'll be right out."

I rinse off quickly, and Tarek's gone when I step out onto the towel that serves as a bath mat. My heart's racing, and not from all my love-life drama. Something in Tarek's tone tells me Liam didn't find anything good.

I find the men in the kitchen. Liam's nursing a steaming coffee, while Tarek stands with arms crossed and a knitted brow. He's tense, and when he looks at me, the expression doesn't soften.

"What did you find?"

"It's a message aimed at Centauri B. Just says *now*." Liam shrugs. "Only other thing I can get out of it is the coordinates. If you know someone with access to HQ's core systems, you can probably come up with a name."

Why would Isaac be sending a message to Centauri? Tarek's expression hasn't changed, but I'm clearly missing something.

"Your man's not trying to prevent an invasion. He's starting one."

REALIZATIONS

*H*ow could I have been so stupid?

I knew the Terran Defenders were the bad guys. I saw it firsthand when I stumbled across Tarek that night... but somewhere along the way I became just as brainwashed as the other idiots that follow Isaac.

He's got followers because of his fight against Shifters. He's got followers because of his fight to save us from invasion. And all the while, he's working with the Centaurians to help them take over our planet? It's crazy. It sounds like fiction... what kind of person would turn over their entire planet for, what? What could he possibly be getting out of it that would make it worthwhile?

"Why would he trust me with this? If it's proof that he's doing this, why would he take that chance?"

Liam clears his throat, holding up a finger to interject. "To be fair, whoever this is couldn't have predicted me. I'm kind of a genius. No one else would have found that message without triggering it to delete itself."

"You've got the clearance to access HQ's system. Maybe he doesn't have anyone else on the inside."

"He's got Daniel."

"Protectors don't have the access you do."

"I don't have that many privileges. I'm just a civilian."

"He's right. The Elder's security protocols are unique." Liam's eyes light up as he talks. "Protectors can download information, but they can't upload. You can upload because you have to input new employees and shuffle people around. You'd never get away with uploading something like a virus, but this is just a message. I doubt they'd even notice it during your shift, unless someone had reason to look closely at your logs."

That's what it all comes down to, then. Daniel targeted me because of my ability to upload their message. This was the plan all along. It seems so obvious now, but I can't bring myself to believe it. I don't know if Daniel's a good person, but he's not evil. He might be selfish and jaded, but he's got nothing to gain from sacrificing his entire planet.

"I want to talk to Daniel."

"Fuck no. We're going to Tanikka."

Tarek steps toward me. I take a step back, closing my fist around the tiny drive. The only evidence.

His eyes darken. "We played their games long enough. The only bomb is the one in your hand, and we're turning it in."

He steps forward again, and I back into the counter. Liam straightens, setting his coffee down slowly as his eyes flicker between Tarek and I.

This is it. This is where we end.

Good. It's a relief to get it over with. It would have been harder to say goodbye at the terminal, after three more weeks of nights and showers and confessions.

"Do what you have to do." I narrow my eyes, standing up straight and refusing to cower under his glare. "I don't expect you to understand, but Daniel-"

"You mean the asshole who enjoys beating Shifters and choking women?"

I shouldn't feel defensive. His statement is accurate, mostly. But it's complicated. "He's not-"

"I'm not taking you back to him."

"And I'm not giving this to you."

I slide the drive into my pocket and cross my arms. I'm fully aware that he can take it if he wants to. But he won't. He wouldn't lay a hand on me without my permission, and using that fact against him feels so wrong.

"Do what you think is right, Tarek. I'm doing the same."

I wish he'd get angry, but he just looks confused. I turn away from those emerald eyes.

One thing's for sure, he can get to Tanikka a lot faster than I can get to Daniel. I pull out my comm as I head for the door, sending Daniel a message as I load up the taxi app.

My heart stops when I reach for the door and Tarek's wide hand braces it closed. His thick arm is inches from my face, his body crowding mine and giving me no room to escape. I should be afraid, but I've never been able to fear him. Not in any form.

I look up, and he leans down to brush a kiss to my forehead. Then my lips. His hand brushes my cheek, melting me into a helpless puddle.

"I'll be above."

"What?" There's no humour in his expression. He looks raw. Resigned. "Aren't you going to Tanikka?"

He shakes his head. "That's what we should be doing. Going to Thomas first is wasting time. It's risking your safety, my job, and sacrificing any jump we might have on them."

Shit. Who am I to think I know better than an experienced Protector? But I know Daniel better than he does.

"I need to try. He doesn't know about this. When he learns what's really happening, he'll help us make sure Isaac doesn't get away. He'll give us more information."

"I hope you're right." Tarek doesn't sound convinced, but I'm not entirely sure I'm convinced, either.

He holds out his hand, palm up. "Give me the drive."

My hand covers my pocket as I press back against the door. "Tarek..."

"If this goes south, they'll find it on you. We'll lose the only evidence we have." He touches a finger to my chin, tipping my face up to look at him. "I'll keep it safe."

"If I give it to you, why wouldn't you just take it to Tanikka like you want to?"

Pain flashes in his eyes for just a moment, but I feel it echoed in my heart. "Because you mean more to me than any of this. Because I wouldn't lie to you."

I hold his stare, trying to feel angry, or suspicious, or even numb. All I want is to wrap my arms around him and forget this entire conversation.

"You only need to decide if you trust me as much as I trust you."

If I can't trust him, I can't trust anyone.

I slide the drive out of my pocket and place it in his waiting hand. All I feel is relief.

"You don't need to do this. Wash your hands of this, and of me. Sit in witness protection for the next few weeks until you cash your ticket and leave all this bullshit behind you. You've gone above and beyond to get this intel. You owe us nothing more."

His words should be liberating. I didn't ask to get tied up in all of this. I never wanted to get involved with anything or anyone that would tie me to this place. I never wanted a reason to stay.

Tears blur my vision, but I meet Tarek's gaze. "I don't want to see the universe if there's nothing to come back to. I don't... I'm not ready to leave you yet."

"Careful, you might be starting to care."

"It's not... I just..."

"Would that be so bad?" He cups the back of my head, pulling my forehead to his. "Maybe you haven't caught on yet, but I care a hell of a lot."

"Tarek..."

He pulls me into his arms, pressing my ear against his chest where I can feel his heart beating as fast as mine. "This is your home. Right here."

I feel myself stiffen.

"Home isn't the place you live. It doesn't tie you down. It isn't obligation, or servitude, or guilt. It's the place you go to unwind and find your centre again. It's love."

I don't trust myself to speak. I wrap my arms around his waist and let myself pretend, just for a moment, that I never have to let go.

ALLIES

"Thank you for meeting me."

"Of course." Daniel leaves his Jeep in park, turning in the seat so he can face me. "I was in the area. Believe it or not, I actually have to show up for work now and then."

"Are you going to HQ?"

"Not yet. I've got a minor mark I can stretch out for a couple days. Let him think he's got the jump on me."

"How do you still have your job?"

He shrugs, clearly past the point of self-reflecting on his work ethic. "I was good, back when I gave a shit."

The traffic moves by us at a steady pace on one side, while pedestrians flow on the other. The Solar moves like a well-oiled machine, carefully planned and built for efficiency.

It should be raining. Maybe a little thunder in the distance. I rarely think about the lack of precipitation up here, but now it feels out of place that the air should be so clear and still.

Tarek doesn't want me to do this. He doesn't think we should trust Daniel, and who am I to undermine him? He didn't stop me, but that wasn't because I convinced him of anything.

Maybe my instinct to trust Daniel is simply because, on some level, I see myself in him. He understands the futility of putting your happiness in the hands of another person. The temporary nature of the human heart.

He's a heap more jaded about people than I am, for sure. I'm not entirely certain of the logic in trusting someone who doesn't value loyalty. We might have formed a friendship of sorts, but that doesn't mean I wouldn't expect him to throw me under a bus if it served his own agenda.

"What did you call me for? Nervous about your task tomorrow? Need a little stress relief?"

His insinuation is too obvious, and the goofy way he waggles his eyebrows would be funny if I wasn't so nervous about this conversation. But that's why I trust him. Even as he's suggesting we hook up, his posture's relaxed. He's comfortable around me. He knows he can joke and I won't take him seriously.

Or maybe he's just that good at taking down walls.

Oh, hell. I clearly thought this was a good idea before I got here. Overthinking it now won't do any good.

"Do you know what it does?"

He looks confused for just a moment. "Isaac told you what it does."

"It's a code that will prevent the Centaurians from locking on and invading our planet."

He nods.

"Do you want the Centaurians to invade?"

His confusion returns, but now he looks wary. His posture stiffens. "What are you digging for, Blue?"

I cringe at his use of the nickname. A reminder that he's not all jokes and friendly banter. That his moral line is flexible when it suits him.

"Okay. I'll play along." He crosses his arms, flexing biceps that make the inside of his Jeep feel much too small.

"Why would someone want that? What would they have to

gain from it? A promotion? A fat payday? A private island to live out your life as a king?"

He cracks a smile, but then sobers when my expression doesn't change.

"You're serious?"

"Work through this for me."

"Okay. You're suggesting someone from Centauri offered me whatever I wanted in exchange for helping them invade?"

"Exactly."

"I'd agree, get all the info I could, and take it to the Elders."

I cross my arms, unable to resist scanning the sky for a moment. There's no sign of Tarek, but I know he's there. Watching, at least. Probably listening, too.

"Seriously. Think about it." Daniel tips his head, waiting for me to meet his eyes before he explains. "They're bigger, stronger, smarter, and they've already had us stock the planet with their shit. They don't need my help, or anyone's help. And if they do, they won't set me up on an island when they get here and keep me as a pet. Human's will fight for our freedom. We'll lose. Even if all I cared about was myself, I'd get far more by helping the Elder's prevent their arrival than I would from helping them get here and expecting gratitude."

"There must be something. Some reason they'd need you, and some reward."

"What is this, Dawn? Why are we doing this?"

This doesn't make sense. I'm missing something. Overlooking some obvious detail.

"That drive is a message from Isaac to Centauri. It says 'now', and there's thirty-six sets of numbers that look almost like coordinates."

I retrieve a slip of paper from my back pocket, holding it out for him to see the string of numbers I copied from Liam's computer screen.

"Like this one."

He takes the paper, and I swear his face pales. "Thirty-six of them?"

I nod, and he hands it back. His expression is unreadable, his eyes distant. I wait, quietly, hoping this is him deciding to do what's right and not him contemplating how to kill me and make it look like an accident.

"Daniel?"

"If anyone asks, we fucked in the back seat. You missed me, and I wouldn't turn down a booty call."

"Daniel."

"It's the only excuse he'll buy, if he knows we met. He never had access to your comm, but I'm confident mine isn't secure."

There's no hint of playfulness left in his expression. His posture's changed, the set of his jaw, even his voice has a commanding edge that's all business.

"What are you..."

"Go home. Act normal. When you go to work tomorrow, work for a few hours like normal, then take that drive to the Elder you trust most and tell them everything."

"Are you sure? Won't that get you in trouble?"

He meets my eyes, no hesitation or doubt in the icy stare he pins me with. "Everything. Do you understand? Skip nothing. Your involvement is minimal, and the intel you'll be able to give will buy your pardon and then some."

"What are you going to do?"

"I'm going to make up for some bad decisions."

"Are you going to confront him?"

His jaw tics. "Just do what I asked."

This is good, I think. But I don't like being in the dark. Something feels wrong. What if he pisses off Isaac? What if he confronts him and Isaac decides to silence him? I can't bring myself to get out of the truck. When he looks at me, the hard edges soften just a little.

"Why did you come to me with this? Why didn't you just turn it in?"

"I knew I could trust you."

His eyebrows raise. "You're not stupid, and I know you remember that night on the edge. What part of all this makes you think I'm someone you can trust?

I shrug. "Maybe I'm not as smart as you think I am. Or maybe good people do bad things. It's not one decision or one moment, it's a series of little ones until suddenly you look around and realize you're on the wrong side of the line."

"Do you think that's what happened to Isaac?"

"Maybe."

He nods, and I realize what it is I'm seeing. He's been betrayed. If all this is true, then Isaac's been lying to him.

"At some point, that doesn't really matter anymore. However he started down this road, at some point he realized exactly where it was leading."

"Thank you, Dawn. Go do your part. I'll do mine."

I put my hand on his arm, just briefly, then reach for the door handle. The screech of metal above us has Daniel drawing his weapon, and a moment later a hawk drops onto the hood of the truck.

He locks eyes with me for a moment before hopping to the ground and standing on human legs.

"What the fuck is this?"

I grip his forearm, refusing to look at the weapon held ready in his other hand. "Trust me."

I open my door, sliding out to stand beside Tarek. He doesn't take his eyes off Daniel.

"Shoot me, and I get to do what I've wanted since that night on the edge."

"Tarek!"

He shrugs like it's no big deal to antagonize a man with a gun pointed at you.

"Agent Thomas knows the score. He knows he couldn't take me in a fair fight."

Daniel's weapon clicks, and Tarek smiles. "Prove me right, so we can do this my way. She's the only one who thinks you're worth more than your weight in shit."

What have I done? These idiots are going to kill each other on the side of the road, and I'll have nothing to take to the Elders but my own word.

They continue some kind of male stare-down, then Daniel holsters his gun.

∼

"What now, Shifter?"

"Now I should haul your ass in and make you tell us every-thing you know before you run back to Durant and give him a head start."

Thomas nods. "Get on with it, then."

Dawn rests her hand on my arm, and I chuckle at the flash of confusion in his eyes as I wrap my arm around her waist.

"I trust her more than I trust my gut. If she says you're worth taking a chance on, I'm not going to argue with that."

He looks at me like I've lost my mind, and he might be right.

"Drop her off at home, then you can tell me what you need me to do."

Dawn's not pleased with being left behind, but there's no way in hell I'm taking her along for whatever this is going to turn into. Heat burns in my chest and my skin feels too small. I'm not the only one anticipating a violent end to this.

When we let her out in front of her flat, I jump down and pull her close for a kiss. I slip the drive into her hand.

"Tarek, why are you doing this?"

I hate the confusion and worry in her baby blues. Even though I'm still on the fence about trusting that asshat, the last thing I want is to leave her afraid.

"I heard everything, and maybe you were right to trust him. He'll need backup. If Isaac turns or runs, I'll make sure no one gets hurt."

She nods, drawing in a long breath and crossing her arms in front of her chest. "Be careful."

"Always."

I kiss her forehead and whisper an *I love you* before jumping back into the truck.

"What's the plan?"

"I'll do the talking. If I need you, you'll know. Otherwise, try not to blow this before I get what I need."

"One way or another, you'll be walking away from this. Your testimony's too valuable to waste."

"It won't go down like that. Not unless you fuck it up. Can you take the form of Dawn's dog?"

"I think I can figure it out."

The rest of the drive passes in silence. Long before we reach the ranch, I move to dog form and into the back seat.

When we park in the dusty farmyard shortly after noon, I follow on his heels into the house. He doesn't bother knocking or announcing his presence, just walks in and kicks off his boots before heading up carpeted stairs to the upper level.

"Well, look who's back!" Isaac sits on a wide chair in a small sitting room, a cup of tea in one hand and a tablet in the other. "Is Dawn here?"

"No. We need to talk."

"Okay. What's on your mind, son?"

Daniel doesn't answer, instead he turns and leaves with a whistle for me to follow. Once outside, he waits for Isaac to catch up.

"Where are the bombs?"

"You know I can't tell you that. It's for your own protection. The less you know, the safer you'll be."

Daniel walks, and Isaac keeps pace at his side.

"You never had a negative word to say about Centauri B. Not once. As early as I can remember, you told me stories about its perfection and superiority to Earth. Until shit fell apart with the TD. I could have taken over. I could have dealt with the Shifter issue, but you stormed in, talking about an invasion, getting us worked up and feeling like we had a bigger calling. Defending the earth from these invaders that would wipe us out or enslave us."

Wherever Daniel's going with this, Isaac isn't pleased. His face is hard, his hands curled into fists as he walks. "What's the point of this, boy?"

"I still remember my great grandfather. That one time you took me to see him, when I was, what, eight?"

Isaac nods, both of them falling silent as we pass a pair of farm hands.

"You were proud of Grandpa. He was an Elder. Of course you were proud. But the way you spoke of Great-Grandfather was something else. He was something else. The stories he told of his home world... they stuck with me."

"I grew up with those stories. Every day."

"And you shared them with me, the rare times we spoke. You didn't give a shit most days, but you wanted me to remember my heritage, even if I couldn't tell another soul."

Well, fuck. I did not see this coming. Isaac is Daniel's father? He catches my eye, but he's quick to look away.

"Great-Grandfather came here to make peace and open trade," Daniel continues. "His son, your father, became an Elder. You followed in those footsteps, mostly. Then there's me. Illegitimate. A disgrace to your otherwise perfect resume. Then you fuck up by getting involved in some stupid shit. Now you claim Centauri is going to invade.

All those years of talking about the beauty and perfection of Centauri B compared to the corruption and filth of Earth, then suddenly they're the enemy. Worth killing millions to save ourselves."

"You're pissed off. I get that. You might be a grown man, but you clearly still have daddy issues." Isaac puts his hands up in mock defeat. "My fault."

Daniel stops walking, waiting until Isaac turns to meet his eyes. "Then give me the respect to let me stand beside you. Centauri is in my blood, just as it is in yours. You're inviting them to make this planet their own, don't ask me to stand with the sheep. Respect me enough to give me my birthright. You owe me that much."

Isaac's quiet, but he reaches out to put a hand on Daniel's shoulder. "Forgive me, son. The circumstances of your birth were a disgrace to my father."

Daniel snorts.

"Centaurians conceive when they choose to conceive, it's not something that can happen by accident. A teenage boy knocking up his girlfriend was proof to my father that my human blood outweighed my Centaurian blood. I was more concerned with pleasing him than I was with doing right by you. He was right; I'm human. There's nothing in me that's anything more or less." Isaac puts a hand on both shoulders, staring into his eyes. "We are Centaurian, regardless of our human blood. We will have a place in this new world. They're coming soon. You'll greet them as my son, as it should be."

"What will happen when they arrive?"

"After they put down the initial resistance, it'll be a peaceful, gradual process as they terraform and mold Earth to greater reflect our own world."

"And humans? The ones that survive the initial resistance effort?"

Isaac shrugs. "Centaurians aren't cruel. There'll be no place for criminals or other useless members of society, but they'll be put down with compassion. Those who wish to adapt peacefully will do so, I'm sure."

"Who are you talking to? Who are you communicating with to know all this?"

"No one. Not anymore. Since your grandfather was removed from his office and I had to step down... our silence must concern them greatly by now. But Dawn solves that problem. She's got the access I needed. Now they'll know I'm still here. Still with them."

"Why would they need that? If Earth is ready, and they have the ability to attack, why does your message matter so much? What info can you give them they won't already have?"

"None. I sent them coordinates, but it's simply a show of good faith. Nothing they can't find on their own."

"Why do they need that message?"

"They don't. It's already in motion. Nothing can stop that now."

"And the bombs?"

Isaac shakes his head. "What point would there be to procuring a weapon like that? What's coming is far more effective."

That's it. That's all I needed to hear. I catch Thomas's eye, ready to bolt. He gives me a slight shake of his head, indicating he wants me to wait.

"How do you feel about this, son? It's a lot to take in, I'm sure. I've got some things to tend to, but don't leave until we chat some more."

"Sure."

Isaac walks off, whistling a tune as he goes.

Daniel doesn't linger, and I follow him behind the farmhouse to the furthest cabin. Once inside, he pulls out his comm to scan the interior and I sniff around for the subtle tang of electronics. He's clearly as suspicious as I am about the privacy here.

When he sets his device on the counter and pulls a jar of coffee grinds out of the cupboard, I shift.

"Son?"

Daniel grunts. "First time he's used that word."

"Can't say I saw that detail coming."

I pull open the fridge, finding what I need for a simple sandwich. While he waits impatiently for the coffee to brew, I make myself three and then take a seat at the small kitchen table to eat.

I can't help but picture Dawn here. She lived with him for nearly a week after I left. I can't focus on that, or I'll end up asking questions I don't want the answers to. Dawn says nothing happened between them, and I trust her completely. But I know damn well he wanted something to happen.

"He's always kept me at a distance. The Elders that knew about my great grandfather are gone. Keeping our bloodline secret was his priority, and it was never a question that if I told someone, we'd both be dead."

"Fuck. Nice family."

"Family's overrated."

"And your beef with Shifters?"

He tenses and takes a slow sip of his steaming coffee. Apparently that's a story for another day.

"What's our plan? We could kill him now. He clearly has no effect on whether or not this goes down. We could take him in. Our combined testimony will be enough to keep him locked up."

"What if there's more? You really think that bonding session made him vomit everything?"

"I need to take this back. The Elders need to know."

"How do I know you won't conveniently forget to mention I'm on your side?"

"How do I know you won't give him a heads up the moment I'm gone?"

"The last time I trusted a Shifter, he took off the first chance he had."

Fair enough. "The last time I trusted an Agent, I earned a brother."

HACKER

"You're certain about this?"

"We're telling you what we know. I wouldn't be here if I thought it was a hoax."

I sit quietly, feeling a bit like an afterthought in this conversation. But as Tarek fills Elder Tanikka in on everything we know, I can't miss the way she keeps looking at me. She's watching my expressions; my reactions to Tarek's claims.

"Do you have anything else to add?" She asks me, addressing me directly for the first time since we entered the room.

"No, Elder. Everything that Tarek said is accurate to the best of my knowledge."

"The delusions of a delusional man." She curses, a strange sound coming from her. "Excuse me for a moment. Wait here."

She leaves us alone in her office, and I look at Tarek. We haven't really spoken since he left with Daniel. When he knocked on my door, he had a taxi ready and waiting to bring us here. I learned what happened at the farm as he told it to Tanikka.

He looks stressed. Tired. Older than he did a few weeks ago.

I stand up and go to him, wrapping my arms around his waist

and sliding my hands under his shirt to touch the warm skin of his back.

He welcomes me without hesitation, wrapping his arms around me and resting his chin lightly on the top of my head.

"It'll all be fine. This will all work out."

"How can you be so sure? If they come..."

"I'm taking you to the Meadow. You're going to meet my family and see my home. I'm going to show you my bed, then I'm going to fuck you loud and hard until you need to catch your flight."

Holy hell. How does he do that? It's like no matter how serious the situation is, there's always a part of his brain thinking about sex.

"Oh. Well, I suppose the alien invasion will have to wait."

He tips my chin up and presses a kiss to my mouth. Maybe my mind's always half in the bedroom, too. When it comes to him, my body certainly is. Just one kiss and I'm lit up, ready for anything he wants from me.

The door opens and I push away, backing to a safe distance and smoothing my shirt. Tanikka's eyes flicker between us, and a soft smile plays at the corners of her mouth.

"Thank you for everything." She nods at us both, and it's clear we're being dismissed. "We'll be in touch to discuss fair compensation for your extraordinary efforts."

"That's it?"

"That's all you need to do at this point. You'll be contacted if we require anything further."

Tanikka's face is a mask, but Tarek isn't making any effort to hide the fact that he's growing more pissed off by the second.

"Tarek, you can report to Elder Tobias. You'll be an asset in the raid at the Farm. Then take some time off. You deserve it."

"Done. But that raid is the least of our worries. You need to prepare for what's coming."

"We can't overreact based on a hunch. We'll evaluate the evi-"

"It's not a hunch, it's fucking-"

She cuts him off with a steely stare, her honey eyes suddenly cold. "It's a hunch. This could all boil down to the crazy ramblings of a bitter man and the delusions of the people that choose to listen."

"You're biased. You're letting your personal history get in the way of your reason."

"You're crossing a line, Tarek."

"Did you know he was part Centaurian? Did you know your grandfather-in-law was Centaurian?"

"He kept those things from me. But that's irrelevant to this decision."

"Your ignorance is not irrelevant."

Holy hell. I want to shrink away from this, but I step closer to Tarek, putting my hand on his arm in what I hope is a calming gesture. Elder Tanikka looks ready to blow. I bet her face is burning red under that makeup.

"You know precisely what your pay grade allows you to know. Nothing more. Don't question my motives, my intelligence, or my ability to do my job." She takes a breath, then gestures to the door. "You're dismissed."

Tarek crosses his arms. How far can he push an Elder before they have no choice but to discipline him?

"Thank you for the intel. Dawn, thank you for everything. I will be in touch soon, and you'll be fairly compensated for your efforts, and your discretion."

"We're not leaving until-"

"You are leaving. Report to Elder Tobias."

"Let's go, Tarek." I squeeze his arm a little tighter, and when he tries to shrug me off, I move in front of him. Gripping his face, I finally get him to look at me. "There's nothing more we can do. Tanikka says she'll handle this, and I know you trust her. Let's go to the Meadow, take that little vacation you promised me."

A hint of warmth flares in his eyes as he touches my cheek, then takes my hand and leads me out of the office without another word. I look back at Elder Tanikka, meeting her eyes for a brief moment.

The concern I see in her expression haunts me as Tarek leads the way down the hall. His strides are so long I nearly have to jog to keep up. He's lost in his thoughts, still holding my hand but not making eye contact as we step into the elevator.

"Is there any doubt, Tarek? You were there, you spoke with Isaac and Daniel. Are we being deluded by a crazy man?"

"Maybe." He meets my eyes at last, and for the first time I glimpse a trace of fear. "The consequences of underestimating him are too big to ignore."

"Tanikka's hands are tied. The Elders can't react until there's more proof, and the only proof that's coming is a Centaurian fleet knocking on our door."

"If I could fly out there myself and stop them, I would."

"I have an idea. Can we go to an office?"

He nods, and I pull out my comm to text Liam.

Dawn: *Remember that time u got drunk and bragged about how u could hack the planet if u ever got in HQ's system???*

Liam: *I don't recall bragging. But yes. I could.*

Dawn: *Meet me at HQ if u want to prove it*

Liam: *Be there in 5*

~

I EXPECTED to find Liam looking a little nervous, but when I step out into the lobby, he's waiting with a grin on his face.

It takes ten minutes to get his visitor pass squared away, but then we're heading back to the time share offices where Dawn's waiting.

We find her pacing the floor, but she stops mid-stride and locks eyes with Liam.

"You sure you're up for this?"

"Hell, yes."

"It might get you arrested."

Liam shrugs, then pulls the handle of his bag over his head. "I'm way too valuable to lock up for long."

"What exactly are you doing?" I'm almost afraid to ask. I'd rather fly out to meet the Centaurians then have Dawn put herself in harm's way again.

"We're going to kill Terra-Link."

Dawn's eyes are wild. Tech is not my thing. I don't even carry a comm. I've got my implants and they work. That's all I need to know.

"You're shitting me?" Liam looks shocked, his upbeat attitude turning sober.

"Can you do it?"

"For sure. I'll know more when I get in, but I can probably get creative enough that it'll take them months just to find the problem. They'll have to hire me to figure out what I did."

I'm lost. "What's Terra-Link?"

"It's our end of the wormholes that allow deep space travel. If our end's gone, there's no more space travel. They'll know where we are, but pinpointing our solar system with any accuracy will be impossible."

"Can't they just follow a map?"

"No. They know where we are, but no one actually flies over those distances. That would take generations. The tech relies on the Link systems." She looks back to Liam. "You can walk away and pretend you didn't hear this."

"Fuck, no. I'm in. I saw that message. I can put two and two together."

Taking out our link to the universe... I don't need to understand tech to know a move like that would have consequences we can't take lightly.

"We need to run this by Tanikka."

Dawn looks at me like I've lost my mind.

"She won't go along with this. You heard her."

"She's doing what she thinks is best. We can't expect her to tell us what the Elders are thinking."

Dawn crosses her arms. "How do we know we can trust her? She was married to him. Maybe they're not so estranged as they appear."

"No. She wouldn't."

"How do you know?"

"I trust her."

"Do you even know her, or any of the Elders, personally?"

"I trust people who trust them."

Dawn rolls her eyes. "Trust is as good as faith, Tarek. It makes you feel safe, but you can't let it blind you."

She has a point. But as pissed off as I am that Tanikka shut me down, I'm not agreeing to a move like this without bringing her in on it.

"What about your ticket out of here? You'll be stuck with us."

She hesitates, her eyes dropping to the floor. The smallest grin pulls at the edges of her mouth, and when she looks back up at me, I swear my heart stops. "Maybe that doesn't sound so bad anymore."

I don't care that we're not alone. I step toward her and pull her against me, swallowing her surprised gasp with a kiss that leaves her breathless. When I let her go, those baby blues are huge.

Liam clears his throat. "Not to take sides, but I can't do this from here. I'll need to connect to the network through one of the Elder's offices."

"Come with me to speak with Tanikka. Both of you. If you're not happy with her feedback, I'll keep her quiet while you do what you need to do."

Dawn opens her mouth to argue, but I cut her off.

"Trust me."

She closes her mouth, her brow furrowing as she nods in agreement.

"Follow me."

"I APPRECIATE your trust in bringing this to me."

"To be honest, I wasn't so sure. But I trust him." I nod toward Tarek, who's standing by the door like a bouncer you don't want to mess with.

Liam's standing close, looking far less confidant and possibly even a little green around the edges.

Tanikka moves to the window. Arms crossed over her chest, she stares out at the city for long minutes.

"Terra-Link is our connection to the universe. Shutting it down will have devastating consequences on our economy. Depending on how long it's offline, the damage may be irreparable."

"We understand that."

"You understand the damage you'll cause by doing this? Even if it saves us from invasion, you'll never be able to prove it. You'll likely be regarded as terrorists."

She turns her gaze to Tarek, but he's expressionless. I'm not even sure he agrees with this plan, but he's not backing down.

"If I oppose you?"

"I wouldn't recommend that." Tarek's eyes are as cold as I've ever seen them. "I'll make sure it's clear you did everything you could to stop us."

Liam looks at me with the same flush of fear I feel.

The charged silence drags on, while Tarek holds the Elder's stare. She looks to me, but I drop my gaze, feeling a million times less sure.

I hear her suck in a breath, letting in out with a sigh that sounds a lot like defeat.

"My ex-husband was one of the first to suspect the true intentions of the Centaurians. If he'd cared more about the people than his own ambitions..." Tanikka's voice hitches and she pauses to take a deep breath.

"You knew about this?"

"I did."

A growl rumbles in Tarek's chest. The menace pouring off him makes me want to back away, but Tanikka seems unaffected.

"You may not like it, but there are aspects of our government, of our defence, that even the Elites aren't privy to. The three of you have no right to know what I'm about to tell you. Given that it's clear you'll do more damage if I don't, I'll accept the consequences of trusting you to keep what you're about to hear to yourselves. Do you understand?"

We all nod.

"Mr. Durant clearly doesn't understand the history beyond his own family's greed. When the first Centaurians came to Earth, it was with gifts of technology and offers of peace. We couldn't refuse. Our planet was suffocating and their aid gave us a second chance. For that, Earth is forever grateful.

But we were never naïve enough to let down our guard. We're ready. The only thing we didn't have was a timeline for their plans. We have Agents on Centauri B, of course, but communication is delayed. If I'd had any hint that Isaac was involved... We send the signal, and we wait."

"You're talking about war. How could you welcome that?"

"When they attack, it will be an act of war. But Earth won't see it. We're ready to greet them with targeted EMP's, then we'll send their soldiers home. A surprise attack was their only chance at defeating us. If they expected to invade a less advanced civilization, they should have come a decade ago."

EXECUTE

$\mathcal{B}$y the time we pull into the farmyard, a dozen armed Enforcers are already jogging toward the buildings. Even from my vantage point in the backseat of an armoured Jeep, I can feel the anticipation and energy of the raid.

Tarek squeezes my leg, and I look over at him. Damn, he's sexy. Sitting there in his full tactical gear, weapons loaded and hair tied back. He looks deadly.

And so, so sexy.

He spent last night at HQ, preparing for today. It feels like forever since I've had a moment alone with him.

It was a battle in its own right to get him to agree to me riding along. But in the end, he backed down. I'm starting to see a pattern. He'll fight to keep me safe, but he won't take away my freedom to choose.

"Stay here. Agent Rodgers will get you out if anything goes wrong."

I put my hand on top of his. "Be careful."

"Always am."

He slides out of the Jeep and closes the door, then walks

toward the main house with an almost casual stride. As two men start up the stairs, the front door swings open. Daniel steps out. My heart jumps to my throat when the Enforcer's weapons are levelled at his body, but he doesn't flinch.

It looks like they're talking. After a moment, the Enforcers lower their weapons and Tarek moves past him into the farmhouse.

I let out a shaky breath as movement in the upper window catches my eye. Isaac, maybe, but then a flash of pink hair gives him away. I'm not sure why Gareth would be there, but I'm relieved he'll be detained today along with the rest of them.

The only regrets I feel are for Ma. I can't imagine that woman has anything to do with all of this, and today's going to be devastating for her.

A piercing roar has me covering my ears.

"Sweet fuck." Agent Rogers curses, gripping the wheel with white knuckles.

I scramble to the other side of the seat, looking out and up to the roof of the biggest barn. A dragon perches at the top. Sleek and serpentine, distinctive striped markings glistening in the sunlight nearly as brilliantly as the metal roof. Her long tail snakes around and down the front of the building.

It's her. The woman Tarek met in the cornfield. The bitch who blackmailed him.

She roars again, this time accentuated by the screech of claws on tin. Her head swivels, her eyes taking in the Enforcers with mild indifference.

I give a whispered victory shout when Tarek emerges from the farmhouse, two Enforcers on his heels with Isaac in handcuffs. They stop in their tracks when they spot the dragon above, watching them with tendrils of smoke escaping past her bared teeth.

Tarek strides toward the centre of the yard with the same casual confidence in his gait. He crosses his arms. Waiting. The silence is excruciating, but he waits.

She just stares. The twitch of her tail the only sign of her agitation. Her excitement, maybe.

I hold my breath. He said he couldn't give her what she wanted, even though he tried. Maybe she's reasonable underneath all that bat-shit crazy, dragon-breeding shit.

She jumps. Like a cat pouncing toward a mouse, she pushes off and roars her intent. Gunfire erupts as Tarek's body expands in the space of a heartbeat.

Someone screams. Probably me. The massive bodies collide, teeth flashing and talons scrambling for purchase in the ground, and in each other.

Agent Rogers hits the gas, reversing us away.

"No! Stop!"

He ignores me, but even as we retreat down the long drive-way, I can still see the flashes of amber and emerald scales as they tear at each other. They take to the air, clawing and biting until they both hit the ground in a cloud of dust.

Why are they fighting like this? Tarek swore nothing could go wrong today. He promised me there were enough Protectors on the ground to handle any resistance.

My vision blurs and I swipe at the tears that appear on my cheeks.

For a moment, I can't see anything over the corn, but then Rogers hits the breaks as their massive bodies block the road behind us. A tail hits the side of the Jeep, making it rock, then they're in the air again. The female goes higher this time, with Tarek on her heels until they're nothing more than a speck in the sky.

Rogers doesn't attempt to drive again, he's too busy craning his neck to see just like I am. The speck grows. They're falling, and I can see the two of them locked together. She's trying to fly. Her wings are straining, but Tarek has his tucked tight. His weight is too much for her.

They hit the ground with an impact that rattles the jeep.

Now I know it's me that screams. I claw at the doors, but they won't give. "Let me out!"

"Not yet."

"Damn it! I need to-"

"No. My orders are to keep you safe."

I slump back in my seat and don't bother to wipe the fresh tears from my cheeks. My entire body is shaking.

He's fine. He's stronger than I can imagine. He knows his limits, and hers, and he wouldn't have done what he did if there was a chance...

I can't lose him. I just can't.

The Jeeps that arrived before us file by, the last stopping at our side. Agent Rogers rolls down the window as I lean over the back of the seat.

Holy hell. The other Jeep is mangled. Grooves that could only have been made by dragon talons mar the side. The back window is shattered and hanging. Its roof is completely gone.

"Sir. What happened?"

"It went apeshit, that's what happened. Tarek couldn't get a handle on it. After they fell, it turned on us. Tore through the Jeep to get at Thomas. Took him alive, as far as we can tell."

She took Daniel? Why would she do that?

"Where's Tarek?" I'm practically climbing over Roger's shoulder, but I don't care. I'll crawl over him and out his window if it's the only way I can get out of this fucking Jeep.

Rogers ignores me. The other man spares me barely more than a glance.

"All marks remaining on site have been detained, including Durant. Tarek's down. He hasn't shifted so we can't move him. Maverick's watching his back."

"Take me up there or let me out."

Rogers rolls up his window, his eyes meeting mine in the rearview. "I don't think that's a good idea."

"I don't give a shit what you think. Your orders were to keep me out of danger. You accomplished that, thank you. Now take me to Tarek!"

He sets his jaw, clearly contemplating the grey area of his orders. Keeping quiet while he works through his problem is nearly impossible, but it gives me time to think of some creative threats to get him to back down.

Finally, he puts it in drive and rolls forward. My stomach is in knots as the farmyard comes into view. Nothing looks out of place, other than the deep grooves in the packed dirt. Darker patches of mud make my stomach twist even more. Blood.

In the field beside the house, a glimmer of green filters through the tops of the corn. I jump out the moment the locks click, but Rogers grasps my arm to stop me from running ahead.

"Let me go!" I'm so fucking done with this shit. I twist out of his grip with a little move Daniel taught me, but he easily regains his hold.

"Stop fighting me and think! If he's not shifting, he's still breathing, but when he wakes up in that form, you don't want to be too close."

I twist out of his grip again and successfully dodge his next attempt to stop me. Thankfully, he doesn't bother chasing me as I push through the corn to emerge in a wide, flattened patch. Deep red stains the dry husks.

Tarek's enormous body is laying on its side, the sunlight glinting off his scales as his ribs rise and fall in a shallow, sporadic rhythm. He's bleeding from two ugly wounds on his side, and too many punctures on his neck to count. I put my shaking hands on his face, running my palms over his cold, silky cheek.

Why would she do this? Why would she fight so violently? He could have overpowered her easily, that I'm sure of. That he's lying here so broken means he did everything he could not to hurt her. It shouldn't surprise me. He doesn't have a violent bone in his body. I think the only reason he's so huge is to accommodate his giant heart.

I tuck in under his chin, resting my head against his neck so I can hear his heart.

She took Daniel. Why? Because they're working together? He betrayed Isaac by helping us, but maybe he had a bigger plan with her all along. Maybe he pissed her off. His playboy habits would certainly come back to bite him in the ass if he broke the heart of a dragon lover.

I run my hand over cool scales. Scales that should be warm and rumbling under my touch. I need him to wake up. I didn't want to get too attached, but it was naïve to think I'd have a choice in the matter. I don't believe in fate, but I think maybe he was always mine.

"I love you." I whisper the words. Testing them out. They don't feel wrong. What does that mean?

His leg moves, just a little. I feel a weak rumble in his neck. Carefully, I move around to the front of his face, keeping my hands on him but making sure he can see me when he opens his eyes. Getting accidentally crushed to death while he's waking up isn't exactly the happy ending I'm hoping for.

His lids flutter, opening to reveal the brilliant emerald of his eyes. I want to cry, and cheer, and hug his face with my whole body. But he doesn't look at me. He doesn't seem to focus on anything, as the pinpoints of his pupils dilate until the green is only a rim around the black.

He pulls his head away, and I take a few steps back. I'm not afraid of him. I could never be afraid of him.

He picks himself up and tests his legs, stretching his wings and growling until tendrils of dark smoke escape from his nose. When he turns his attention to me, my heart races.

Something's wrong.

"Tarek?"

He jolts at the sound of my voice, his claws crunching into the dry corn stalks.

I'm not afraid of him. I won't be afraid of him. I hold out my hand and step forward.

He moves so fast I can't process what's happening. An arm hooks around my waist as a blur of green passes in front of my face, a glint of sun on polished ebony claws.

"It's okay, I got you." The deep voice in my ear is vaguely familiar. He pulls me back as Tarek shakes his head and claws the ground. "It's Maverick. Tarek's friend. I won't hurt you."

I don't care who he is. I struggle to free myself from the arm around my waist, but he lifts me off the ground like a child. He pulls me back into the corn, hushing me to stay quiet.

His grip doesn't falter until we're out of the cornfield, standing at the edge of the deserted farmyard. I turn on him, but my anger fades the moment I see his expression. He's looking past me, and he looks just as worried as I feel.

He's dressed in full tactical gear. Basic implant tats as well as Stim, which explains why he could get to me before Tarek's claws hit their mark.

I shiver at the thought of what almost happened. Maverick's dark eyes snap to mine.

"Are you okay?"

I shake my head. "What's wrong with him?"

"That's not Tarek."

Not Tarek? "I don't understand..."

His jaw ticks. His lips press into a thin line.

"Tell me. Or I'm going back to ask him."

He smirks, his eyes drifting over me as if to point out how futile it would be for me to try evading him. Anger heats my skin. First Rogers, now him. He has no right to tell me what I can and can't do, just because he can physically overpower me.

I open my mouth to tell him exactly what's on my mind, but his cocky smirk warms as he shakes his head.

"A few months ago, some asshat hijacked a helo with a shipment of new BioSol weaponry, then crashed it on a fucking island. Serious shit that we needed to get back before it found its way to the black market. Tarek and I went after him. Figured we'd catch him by surprise. Tarek ended up in dragon form with injuries too severe to shift or fly.

Our mark was secure, and we had a ship on route to pick up the cargo and busted helo. But something snapped in him. The dragon took over, and it was pissed. Couldn't fly, could barely walk, nearly fried my ass when I tried to reason with him. All I could do was keep the fuck out of his way. Our mark was tied to a tree. I tried to get to him first, but..."

Holy hell. He told me he sometimes felt like the dragon was its own creature, but I never imagined something like this. "What happened? How did he get control?"

"I don't know what pulled him out of it. Exhaustion, maybe. He Hulked out for a good two hours until something clicked, and he shifted back into human form. Double fucked his leg in the process and passed out."

"The scar on his thigh." I feel my cheeks heat as I remember the night I discovered that scar.

Maverick nods. "He's lucky he has that leg. Medics have their limits."

"Did you tell anyone what happened?"

"No. I blamed it all on the fight our mark put up. Not like he was around to prove me wrong. It was two weeks before I got the chance to talk to Tarek, and I'm sure he had no memory of what happened. He remembered taking the hit to his leg, but nothing after."

"Did you tell him?"

"No. But I told the Elders I want on every high-level mission he takes. Told them being beside his dragon in a fight made me feel like I was on the edge of taking that form myself. They'd love to have another one of us with that ability."

"Why did you do that? Why cover for him, if you think he might be a danger?"

"Because I know what they do to anomalies. He doesn't deserve to be their fucking lab rat."

"But it's not like that anymore..."

"I hope you're right." He doesn't look very convinced. "We need to get back to HQ. I'll call us a ride."

He pulls a comm out of his back pocket, but there's no way I'm leaving now. Not until I know Tarek is safe.

"You can go. I'll wait for him."

He levels me with a stare that says I won't be given a choice in the matter, and I make sure my expression lets him know he'll regret trying to man-handle me again.

"There's no point in waiting here. He'll know where to find you when he calms down."

"I can't..."

"Tarek will kick my ass if I leave you here alone, and I'm needed at HQ. We're both needed, to give our statements and make sure none of those assholes walk free."

I nod, because I know he's right. But it still feels wrong to leave him. This wasn't how today was supposed to end.

Maverick types into his comm, keeping one eye on me like I might flee if he looks away.

"I'll wait inside." I gesture toward the farmhouse.

"I'll come with you."

"No." I hold up a hand, and he narrows his eyes. "I'm just going to the washroom. Please, stay here in case he needs help."

He nods in agreement, but I can feel him watching me as I walk away. It's an odd sensation. I don't feel threatened by him, but the way he watches me is unsettling. He's only just met me, but I think he wouldn't hesitate to put himself between me and Tarek if it came to that.

I shudder at the thought. But I saw that clawed hand pass in front of my face. If Maverick hadn't been there... Tarek would never hurt me, but he was right; that wasn't Tarek.

The house is eerily quiet without the ever-present sounds of Ma's kitchen. After I visit the bathroom, I can't help but peek my head in. I almost expect to see her kind face. Instead, I'm greeted by dishes and half-prepped food in disarray. A bag of flour sags on the counter, its contents spilled onto the floor and covering everything in a layer of fine dust.

Some of the men must have been in here when the raid happened, by the looks of the mess and carpet of footprints in the flour. My heart aches for what Ma must have gone through. It's not her fault her son's a psycho terrorist.

The creak of a floorboard jolts me out of my thoughts, and I spin to look down the empty hall. Faint flour footprints lead out of the kitchen, fading to nothing after a few steps. It's more than a little creepy. And now I'm tuned in to all the creaks and whispers an old house makes when there's no one awake to drown them out.

Hanging out with Maverick doesn't sound like such a bad idea anymore. I'll talk to Tanikka and pull what strings I have to make sure Ma has help getting this place cleaned up and running without the men she's lost today.

A cold hand closes around my neck and my body hits the wall. My vision swims with stars as pain erupts in my head. I claw at the hand, gasping for enough breath to scream for Maverick. A black mask fills my vision, but only for a moment before it's pulled off to reveal Gareth's laughing face.

"What's the matter, *Blue*? Isn't this what turns you on?"

I stop struggling, conserving my energy and praying he'll relax his hold if I'm not fighting back.

"That's a good girl." His eyes focus on my mouth, then drop to my chest. I want to spit in his face, but I close my eyes instead. "This is how Daniel got you to spread your legs, isn't it? Pushed you around a little, then you were begging to be his lapdog."

I try to remember the moves Daniel taught me. I'm not just relying on video game instincts anymore. I've got some actual self-defence skills I can use, if I can control the panic that's making it impossible to think straight.

"Where is he now? Where's your pet Agent, or your useless mutt?" He pauses, then laughs when I can barely swallow past his hand. "You did this, bitch. We were so close. But you were working for them all along, weren't you?"

He loosens his grip and I suck in air. I won't have this conversation with him. Maverick will come, I just need to stay calm and wait.

"Daniel lost his edge. He used to care about our cause, but now all he cares about is pleasing Isaac. We're sick and tired of playing nice. If we want to show the world what Shifters really are, we need the balls to spill some blood."

"How is it my fault Daniel's smarter than you?"

The back of his hand cracks against my cheek, making me cry out as my eyes water from the sting.

"The Terran Defenders didn't die today, but you're going to. As soon as I'm done with you."

He tightens his grip on my neck until I can't take a breath. His other hand grabs at the waist of my pants, pulling at the button.

Hell no.

I drive my knee into his crotch as I slam my forehead into his nose with a sickening *crack*. He yells out in pain as the walls explode with a deafening roar. I drop to the ground, covering my head.

The bomb.

It was here all along.

The noise stops as quickly as it started. I wait, curled in a ball, hearing nothing but my breath and racing heartbeat.

I move slowly, my neck aching and my body covered in splinters and Ma's trinkets. I look up to a row of razor-edged, blood-stained teeth. Tarek's massive head hovers through a gaping hole in the side of the house, as the air around him swirls with tendrils of smoke. He turns, and a black eye rimmed with emerald looks down at me.

"Hey!"

The dragon's head jerks out of the house with a sinister growl. He turns toward Maverick's voice, his wings flared as flames escape through those deadly teeth.

"Get the fuck out of here, Dawn," Maverick orders, backing away as the dragon begins to stalk him.

I retreat deeper into the house, tripping over debris and... holy hell. Gareth's body. Even covered in rubble, I can see it's mangled and broken.

Bile rises in my throat. Tarek roars.

I can't let him hurt his friend. He'll never forgive himself.

Seems he's monogamous.

He won't hurt me.

"Tarek!" I yell, stumbling my way out of the house and

refusing to give in to the fear that grips me when he pivots from his pursuit of Maverick.

Maverick shouts, but I keep my eyes on Tarek and he keeps his eyes on me. He jumps. In one cat-like leap he lands in front of me, and I hold my ground as his smoky breath surrounds me.

"You're beautiful," I say, then hold my breath as I stretch out my hand.

HOME

*W*here the fuck am I?

My eyelids feel like sandpaper and my body might as well be buried. Fuck. Maybe they did bury me.

My memory trickles back into focus. I knew that landing would take me to the brink, but she gave me no choice.

I didn't see it coming. Not by a long shot. Her loyalty to Isaac was stronger than her loyalty to her own kind. I didn't want to hurt her, but pulling her to the ground was my last chance to knock her the fuck out before I lost it.

Anger burns through my veins, heating my chest. Fuck no. This fucking reptile is not taking the reins now.

I can smell Dawn. Just a hint of that sweet, citrus scent. She's here. I need to make sure she's safe.

Hunter needs to pay for challenging me. I need to finish this.

Tarek

Dawn's voice. I swear I can hear her.

My hands are black. What the fuck? I push up from the ground, pain shooting across my ribs with the effort. I don't remember shifting. I sure as hell don't remember scorching the ground or... holy fuck.

"Tarek?"

I tear my eyes away from the devastated house and focus on Dawn's baby blues. The way she's looking at me makes my stomach turn.

What did I do? What did that fucking dragon do to make her look at me like that?

"You good, man?" Mav walks up beside her, and she gives him a small smile.

"I'm good." My voice sounds like gravel, but it's good enough for Dawn.

She lurches toward me, throwing her arms around my waist as I bury my face in her hair. She smells damn good.

"What happened?" I look up at Mav, catching the concern on his face before he schools his expression.

"The ranch is clear. Durant was detained. The other dragon's in the wind, and it took Agent Thomas. I'm sure we'll be getting orders to track them down once you're good to go."

What the fuck? She took Thomas? That doesn't make sense. But if they've got something going on behind the scenes, I'm in no hurry to figure it out.

"I'm not going anywhere. Not for the next few weeks."

Mav nods. "That's good. Take some downtime. You need to get your shit sorted out."

Fuck. So much for keeping my dragon problem under wraps. The charred ground around our feet is proof. I'm not just struggling to keep control, I've lost it.

"This isn't the first time I've done this, is it?"

Mav drops his eyes, crossing his arms in front of his chest. "No, man. It's not."

Fuck. "Who else knows?"

He meets my gaze. "No one beyond the three of us. Not that I'm aware of."

Dawn pulls out of my arms, her baby blues full of emotion. "You wouldn't have hurt us. He was just scared."

I run my thumb under a slight bruise on her cheek, and she flinches.

"What happened?"

She drops her gaze, and I take a step back. If I hurt her..

"It was some asshole from the TD," Mav jumps in. "You took care of him." He points at the wrecked front of the farmhouse.

"It was Gareth. He said the Terran Defenders didn't die today, but I... Your dragon saved me. He knew me."

Maverick chuckles, shaking his head. "I wouldn't bet on Hulk rolling over for a belly rub, but she might be crazy enough to try."

He pulls something out of his side pocket, then hands it to me. A medic shot. Fuck. I'm glad my dragon took care of that asshole, otherwise I'd kill him myself.

I hold the tiny syringe up and Dawn smiles. I soak it in as she pulls her sleeve up, giving me access. My dragon might have been the one who saved her, but it feels damn good to be the one who can take away her pain.

"He let me touch him, Tarek. Then you came back to me."

"It could have hurt you."

She shakes her head, the movement stiff. "No. He wouldn't. I'm sure of it. It wasn't you, but I could tell he cared. He let you come back when I asked him to."

I take her face in my hands, gently, and press a kiss to her lips. I've been pissed off and stressed out about my dragon, but if he's the reason she's standing here, I owe him everything.

"I'll head back and give my report." Mav smirks. "Most of it, anyway."

"Thanks, brother." I put a hand on his shoulder. "For everything."

"Yes, thank you, Agent Maverick."

"My pleasure, Miss Stevens." Maverick gives her a wink, then looks back to me. "I called you a ride." He points at the sky, then takes his phoenix form and jumps into the air.

"Are you okay?" Dawn asks once we're alone, her hands running over me to check for injury.

I didn't manage to bring back my tactical. That's a lot of gear lost. Sweatpants and a shirt are all I could conjure up, but I'd say my Medic did its thing in record time. Then again, it's not the first time I've noticed my dragon form ramping up my already accelerated healing.

"I'm good. I'll be fine."

"That was incredible. Seeing you in full battle-mode... you were beautiful. Terrifying, but beautiful."

I laugh, but my ribs remind me it's too soon. Worry flickers in her baby blues.

"Damn it, Angel. I love you."

She sucks in a breath, but I don't pause long enough to make her think I'm fishing for her to admit anything.

"You didn't need to stay. I would have recovered and found you. You should have gone home."

She steps close, putting her hands on my hips and resting her forehead against my chest. "I am home."

Her words stop my heart. I want to double check I heard her right, and it wasn't just wishful thinking. I carefully tip her head back to search her eyes. She looks so vulnerable, like maybe I'm finally getting a glimpse behind that wall she keeps around her.

I kiss her. Slow, soft. I kiss her until a tear escapes down her cheek and my own eyes sting from the rawness of the moment.

I know she's not promising forever. I've accepted that. But the fact that she cares this much here and now means so damn much.

"What's next?" I ask, pressing my forehead against hers. "We caught the bad guy. The Centaurians don't stand a chance. I think your mission is accomplished."

She smiles, but it doesn't reach her eyes. "I'm worried about Daniel..."

She looks guilty at her admission, but I'm not jealous anymore. I have her body, and even if she can't quite admit it yet, I have her heart. He's a lucky man if she's chosen to give him her friendship.

Assuming he's still alive.

"I'll find them. Once I'm back to full strength."

Worry flashes in her eyes. "You can't... if she attacks you again."

"She won't. This wasn't personal."

Her eyes widen, but she nods. She trusts my assessment of Hunter and my ability to retrieve Daniel. She trusts me.

"Then, I guess it's back to real life..."

I shake my head. "This is real life. The good and the bad. The joy and the fear. The fifteen-ton dragon at your disposal. Come home with me. Let me introduce you to my family."

Her eyes widen. "To the Meadow? Now?"

"I can't think of a better time. Tanikka knows how to reach me if she needs me. I'll be no good for much until morning, anyway."

"Are you sure you can fly?"

I shake my head. "I could, but I'll recover faster if I don't, and there's no way I'm giving him the chance to take over again, even if you did tame him."

She grins, a wide smile that's one part happy, and one part mischief. Maybe it's just my imagination, but I swear I can feel my dragon purr.

FAMILY

I'm trying my best not to geek out and embarrass myself, but my level of fan-girl bliss is through the roof right now. As Tarek helps me down from the double saddle, I can't avoid touching the silky black scales of the dragon that gave us a ride.

"Thank you," I say, once my feet are steady on the ground. It hardly seems adequate for allowing himself to be saddled and ridden.

He slips into human form and holy hell, I'd recognize that face anywhere.

Damon. Elite Whisper's partner. The first Shifter I ever saw take the form of a human. On that small stage, in front of everyone, he shifted from panther to man and confirmed everything I'd believed but couldn't prove.

"It's no trouble." He smiles, his dark eyes travelling over me for just a moment. I think he recognizes me, too. That makes me do a little happy dance inside. He turns his attention to Tarek. "You good?"

"Yeah. Long story."

"Hope's in the clinic."

Tarek waves him off. "Thanks for the lift."

Damon nods, then glances back at me before turning toward the village.

The Meadow. I can't believe I'm actually here.

We're standing in a cleared patch of ground at the edge, with Morwood forest at our back and gardens to either side. The village is a blend of modest cabins and tents; compact and unpretentious. The sounds of conversation and laughter reach our ears, without a trace of vehicle noises to drown them out.

"It's beautiful."

I can feel Tarek's pride as he watches me take it all in. His hand brushes against mine, and I lace my fingers with his. I take a deep breath, smelling herbs and earth and freshly cut lumber. It's perfection.

"Ready for a closer look?"

All I can do is nod my agreement. The weight of this making my breath shallow and my eyes blurry. He leads me toward the village, and we've barely reached its edge when we're swarmed by a pack of cubs, pups and kittens.

The cuteness is too much. I reach my hands down to them as Tarek drops to the ground. Some of them shift into young boys and girls to give him hugs he returns with gusto. He greets them each by name, acknowledging tales of accomplishments and reports of injury with praise and serious consideration.

Once each has had their moment, he lovingly shoos them away.

"You like kids." I saw it with my nephews, his natural way with them. The ease with which he met them at their level.

"I fucking love those little shits. We've got twenty-seven of them, from when the lab was shut down."

My heart drops. They're all orphans? I crouch down, eye level where he still sits on the ground. "That's awful."

"That place was. But those kids are good now. Most of them

have been adopted, but they all just run as a pack. We all look out for them."

"Don't they have to bond with someone?"

"No." Anger flashes briefly in his eyes. "That was a modification curtesy of BioSol. They'll get to live their lives."

My heart aches for them. I don't know a lot about the Lab. BioSol does great things with their medical tech, but that's far from their only speciality. The Shifter program created Shifters like Tarek, born in the lab to be paired with a human. Made to grow at an accelerated rate. Made to obey.

"I'm surprised they can shift so young."

"We all realized it when we took this form. This is our natural state, our natural mind. Our animal forms are part of us, but we were never meant to be confined to them."

I don't have any words. All those years. All those lives. Will humans never stop preying on those we deem less than us?

Tarek pushes up to his feet, his movements stiff. He's still hurting. I know his Medic implant will heal him fully soon, but I hate seeing him suffer through this part.

"Come on." He tugs at my hand. I don't even recall reaching for his again, but it's become such a natural thing to be near him. "I want you to meet someone before I introduce you to my bed."

A laugh bursts from me. He transitions so easily from serious to playful. I guess I do too, because a moment ago my heart was aching and now my body's heating at the reminder of our sexy plans.

He lifts my hand to his mouth, kissing me as his emerald eyes dance with promise. I wonder what exactly he has in mind?

He leads me through the village, over packed dirt paths that snake between the homes. Each is unique, some built for practicality and function, others intricately decorated with obvious love and care. Some are just tents, big enough for sleeping and not much else.

We pass cook fires surrounded by happy, hungry residents. We pass people making clothes or tools or trinkets. There doesn't appear to be any currency trading hands, and the more I watch the more I see people giving what they can and taking what they need. Compared to the overpriced, impersonal, hi-tech solar or dirty, overcrowded Moridian, this place is a utopia.

We come to a stop in front of a wooden structure, bigger than the others we've passed. Its plain wooden facade is contrasted by a sign that reads simply *Clinic*, colourfully decorated with a rainbow of little hand and paw prints.

Tarek knocks twice as he pushes the door open. "Hope? You in?"

"Tarek! Hey!" A pretty woman with pale blond hair emerges from a back room, beaming at Tarek until she sees me standing at his side. Her smile fades into a concerned frown. "Hi hon, are you okay? Do you need anything?"

"This is Dawn." Tarek snakes his arm around my waist, pulling me tight against his side. "My future mate."

The woman and I both gasp at the same moment, and I slap him on the stomach.

"I'm working on it," He confesses, and I cover my eyes with a hand.

Hope laughs. "Don't be embarrassed. Tarek's a good man, but he doesn't have much of a filter. You're a lucky woman if he's fallen for you."

"I know." It's the only response I can manage. Not because I'm embarrassed. Far from it. Because even though I know it can't last, I can't pretend I don't want it. I want it so damn much.

Hearing him say it like that. So open and unashamed. So confident. I need to be honest with him. I thought my ticket would be enough to discourage him from hoping for more. The clear boundary of a ticking clock to reinforce my words. But even though I've been clear from the start that this is temporary, he's still hinting at more. Still hoping for a future he can't have with me.

I need to lay it all out. I'll deal with that look of pity, the questions and useless suggestions, as if my very happiness as a woman is at stake. Once he realizes there's nothing that can be done, he won't be so eager to talk about forever.

I zoned out. I snap my eyes over to Hope's to find her watching me with a knowing look. Her eyes are too perceptive, too wise for her otherwise youthful appearance. She smiles and I get the feeling she'd be a friend if I stayed long enough.

The creak of the door pulls her attention away. "Speaking of lucky women..."

I follow Hope's gaze to the door as Elite Gideon steps through. He doesn't even acknowledge Tarek or I, he just crosses the room and scoops Hope up in a tight embrace. He presses his cheek to hers, and whispers something that makes her face redden.

When he turns, he smiles at Tarek. "Hey, brother." Then he looks at me and his smile widens. "Dawn? Strange, but awesome to see you here. With Tarek."

"Hey." I give a wave, and when he offers his hand I feel incredibly honored. When did I earn the right to be friendly with such titans? I take his offered shake, and he pulls me in for a quick hug that nearly makes me pass out. "If you're the reason for that look on Tarek's face, I'd say we're past handshakes."

I'm literally speechless. I feel my mouth open, but nothing comes out.

"Tarek, unless you need medical attention, take the poor girl someplace quiet so she can get her bearings." Hope's tone is confident, and I get the feeling her words hold weight around here. "Dawn, if you need anything at all you can usually find me here. And if not, just ask whoever you run into and they'll know where I am."

"Thank you." It's hardly sufficient for the welcome I just received, but it's all I can get out.

Along the walk to Tarek's home, we run into others. Tarek introduces me to each, and they all greet me with the same warmth. I'm blown away by how much this place is like one big, extended family.

Tarek's house is small, like all the others. A little cabin at the edge of the village, built with his own hands. It's turned at an odd angle compared to the rest. When I ask him why, he points at the setting sun. It's lighting the sky on fire in a brilliant display of oranges and pinks.

"I've always imagined I could chase it. In my dragon form, if I maintained just the right altitude and speed, I could watch the sun rise all around the world. I'm not even sure if it's possible, but..." He looks down at me, lifting his hand to my face. "I guess I've always been chasing dawn."

My breath catches in my throat. "Tarek, I don't know what to say when you talk like that."

"I'm sorry. Come here."

He pulls me under his arm and leads me into his home. It's cozy and warm, with a wide couch, a desk, and a single bookshelf overflowing onto the floor around it. There's one other room, and when I peek inside, it holds only a double bed.

"It's simple, but it's all I've needed."

"It's perfect." I mean it. Tarek's home is a space that's made for quiet down-time, but not for living in. He lives wherever he wants, goes wherever he's needed. This is just a home base.

"There's plenty of space around it. I can easily make it bigger."

"It's perfect, Tarek. But I'm not going to live here with you. When I thought destroying Terra-Link was the only option, I was prepared to stay on Earth. I meant what I said. But I can't just give up my dream because I care about you... I'd regret it. Someday."

"I don't want you to." He pulls me close, tipping my head back so he can look me in the eyes. "You don't owe me anything, and I don't expect anything. Don't compromise your dream. Don't give that up for anyone. I want you to be happy, even if that doesn't include me."

"But how can you say everything you do... you use words like mate and love. How can you say that, and then claim you'll let me go?"

"Do you trust me, Dawn?"

"Of course."

"Then be mine until you leave. I won't ask you to stay. I'll kiss you goodbye and be so fucking happy you're following your sunrise."

Holy hell. That's exactly what I want, isn't it? So why is my heart already aching with the loss?

"I'm afraid if you ask me to stay, I'll agree."

I didn't understand how I was feeling until this very moment. I want this life. I want Tarek, and the Meadow, and I... I want to be in love with this man and plan our forever. But I also want to cash in that ticket and step out into the unknown... explore new worlds and new cultures. I want both.

But what am I thinking? I can't have this. That option was taken from me a long time ago.

"I can't have children." I blurt it out, watching as the words sink in and understanding registers in his expression.

I didn't want to have this conversation. It's personal and completely irrelevant because I'm leaving. But if an expiry date isn't enough to convince him I'm not part of his future, my medical history will prove the future he wants was never on the table to begin with. Not with me.

"I was sexually active at a young age. I didn't use protection, and we didn't have access to good medical care. I got pregnant, but it was ectopic. The doctors, the facilities... the surgery didn't go well. My... I was damaged. I can't get pregnant."

I grit my teeth, waiting for the questions and pity and useless suggestions like my ability to reproduce encompasses my entire worth as a woman. Like I can't possibly be happy without the option of making miniature versions of myself.

His eyes drop, then turn to the window. He can't even look at me anymore.

"I've only ever considered taking a mate for the purpose of having kids. I never cared about sex. That was just something I'd have to do to make a family."

I snort. "Aren't we just polar opposites."

How did we even get to this point? Tarek's loyal to the core, settled down, ready for a family. I'm the definition of casual and temporary. We're the worst combination.

His eyes turn back to me, and I can't look away.

"Since you, I haven't thought of that once. I've only pictured having you in my arms and keeping you there."

I shake my head. He steps toward me, putting his hands on my hips and guiding me backward until he's pressing me against the wall. He leans down, brushing my mouth with the softest kiss.

He presses his hand to my chest, his eyes boring so deep into mine I'm sure he can see my soul. "Do you understand that I love you? Do you believe it, without any doubt?"

I don't try to stop the tears. All I can do is nod.

"Good. Because that love isn't conditional. It doesn't fade when galaxies separate us. And it doesn't depend on what you can give me."

"But you want..."

"There are other ways to make a family."

"Tarek..."

"Be mine until you leave. I promise I won't ask you to stay."

SMILE

When Dawn nods her head, I lose my mind. I crush my mouth to hers, gripping her ass and lifting her off the floor as she wraps her legs around my hips.

She's mine.

I don't care if it's a day or a week. I don't care that I have no clue how I'll survive watching her leave. She's mine for a handful of moments, and I don't plan to waste a single one.

I carry her into the bedroom and drop her onto the soft mattress, then reach up to pull the shirt over my head. She takes in the sight of my bare torso with wide eyes. I stand still for her inspection, loving the hunger and heat in those baby blues.

After that conversation, I should probably make love to her slowly. Ease into it to be sure she wants me. To show her I meant every word.

But I don't think that's what either of us needs right now. I want to be inside her. I want to make her scream.

I finally understand the difference. Making love to Dawn is beautiful. It's far more than I ever imagined it could be. But right now, I just want to fuck her.

"I want you naked."

Her eyes snap to mine, and I cross my arms over my chest. My heart's racing a mile a minute, but I'm not wasting time being nervous. For the first time in my life, I know exactly what I want.

"Now."

For a moment, I think she might not obey. Maybe that was too much. Maybe she won't like-

She pulls her shirt off in a slow, deliberate movement, then lies on her back to wriggle out of her jeans. My mouth waters and my cock pulses at the sight of her on my bed like that, eyes uncertain, hands shaking as she pulls off her socks and then reaches behind her back to unclasp her bra.

When her perfect, round breasts are exposed, my restraint cracks. I grab her by the ankle and pull so she falls onto her back with a squeal. I flip her onto her stomach, pull her up to her hands and knees, and free my aching cock.

She's watching me over her shoulder, heat in her eyes as her breath comes in ragged gasps. I grip her shoulder with one hand, her hip with the other, and push the tip of me into her.

She moans as she rocks against me, asking for more. But I like this too much. Holding her pleasure in my hands, knowing the bliss that's just around the corner. I pull out of her body and she whimpers in protest, I push back in and she moans a needy *yes*.

Knowing she wants me inside her as badly as I want to be there makes me want her even more. I drive myself deep into her perfect heat with one smooth motion.

She screams as she grips the heavy quilt that covers my bed, and I keep her held in place with my hips flush against her gorgeous little backside.

"You good?"

She nods, her head tipped downward. Eyes closed as she breathes in heavy gulps. Arms shaking.

"I don't want to hurt you. Tell me to stop, and I will."

She nods again. I grind my hips against her and she gasps. I don't want to hurt her, but I definitely want to make her scream like that again.

"Talk to me, Angel."

"Fuck me, Tarek. Please."

That's music to my ears. I pull back and slam into her. Her carnal scream becomes an affirmation, and I don't hold back. Words of encouragement punctuate her moans, letting me know I can take this from her; use her body as violently as I want.

"You're mine." I growl my possession as I take my pleasure from her body. Owning her in this moment and knowing I'll do anything to possess her heart just as surely.

Again and again I pull away and drive deep, as she claws at the sheets and encourages me with a stream of *yesses* and *oh gods*. When I slow to check on her, she presses against me and begs me not to stop.

She screams my name as she comes, her inner walls tightening around me as her voice takes on the lilt of blissful orgasm. I keep my pace until I feel her body slacken, then bury myself in her and hold on as I'm hit with the most intense orgasm I've ever felt.

When I slide out of her body, I scoop her into my arms and collapse on the bed with her held tight to my chest. I'm utterly spent. I've worked a fifteen-hour day hauling logs and never felt this bone-deep spent.

And I sure as hell never felt this happy.

"Are you okay? Did I hurt you?"

She laughs, a manic chuckle that sounds as drunk as I feel.

But she doesn't answer. I tip her face toward me, searching her smile and her blue eyes for evidence that I went too far. Took too much.

"If I hurt you..."

She turns her body toward me, wrapping her arms around my

neck and throwing a leg over my hip. She kisses my mouth, my neck, my chest.

"You can't hurt me. But you can't fuck me like that and expect rational thoughts or conversation after."

Pride swells in my chest. I make her feel that way. I put that dopey, happy, satiated look on her face.

"Where did that come from?"

I laugh at the awe in her tone. "I'm not sure what you mean."

She props herself up on my chest so she can look me in the eyes. "Seriously. You're all cuddly teddy-bear, never-been-kissed. Then you get me into your bed, and you turn all sex-god, alpha male. Either I've been hustled, or you've had a seriously rich fantasy life."

"Sex god, huh?"

She rolls her eyes. Damn, I love teasing her. But she needs to know she's not some prop. I roll her onto her back, hovering over her, and lock her gaze with mine.

"You're the only female I've ever wanted. The only woman I've ever imagined doing this with. I want to hold you down and use you until you can't take anymore. And I'll gladly submit to whatever you want to do with my body."

She shudders beneath me, the playfulness gone from her eyes.

"Are you okay?"

She nods.

"Did I hurt you?"

She shakes her head.

"Good. Because I'm nowhere near done with you yet."

Her eyes widen as I pull her legs up and around my hips, letting her feel that I'm ready for more. A perk of my Medic implant.

"I want to make love to you. If we have a day or a lifetime, I want you to feel how much I love you."

She sucks in a breath as I press inside her body, not once

breaking eye contact as we move together at an unhurried pace. I don't know how much time passes, but when her body stiffens and her eyes close, I let myself go. We come together, and when the aftershocks fade, I nearly weep at the thought of losing her.

But I push that emotion away as quickly as it comes. There's nothing to be gained from thinking about a future I can't change. I meant what I said to her. I don't know how I'll survive it, but when she's ready, I'll let her go with a smile on my face.

TICKET

"*D*amn it! I'm dead."

I pull my headset off and toss it aside. It's been so long since I've gamed, I'm getting rusty. But that's not entirely true. I thought I missed the escape of a good game night, but I really don't. It's empty compared to a night with Tarek.

My body heats at just the thought. Holy hell, that man is insatiable. And creative. Last night he took me-

Oh fuck, here I go again. After a week of spending every moment together when I'm not at work, I told him I needed a night to myself. A night of normal. A night of...

I don't even remember why I thought this was a good idea. I miss him. That scares the shit out of me. Shouldn't we be tired of each other after this long?

I reach into my pocket to feel the familiar pattern on my ticket, but it's not there. Guess I forgot it in my room. The truth is, every time I try to imagine getting on a transport or stepping off onto another world, I find myself thinking about the Meadow instead.

My comm vibrates on the coffee table, and I reach for it with

a groan. The unknown caller makes me hesitate, but I'm actually in the perfect mood to spar with a scammer.

"Hello?"

"Dawn. This is Elder Tanikka Durant. Can you meet me at HQ?"

"Sure, yeah..."

"Excellent. Come directly to my office. Security will let you through."

I stare at the screen for a moment after she disconnects. My gut is twisting and my heart's racing. My hands are sweaty. Something's wrong. Very wrong. I should have known it would be too good to be true. The Centaurians had something up their sleeve. Isaac found a way to warn them about our defences.

I wipe the potato chip crumbs off my shirt and finger-comb my hair until it looks fashionably messy, not haven't-showered messy.

Holy hell. Since that last day in the Elder's office, and the raid at the Farm, I've been completely focused on Tarek. But I catch myself now and then, looking up at the sky and wondering if they came, if they're above us getting sent home with their tails between their legs and a reminder that humans aren't so vulnerable, after all. Or maybe they came, and it was us who underestimated the enemy.

At HQ, security greets me immediately. With my nervous system in full panic-mode, I walk into Tanikka's office.

"Dawn!" She doesn't look nearly as stressed as I feel. Her makeup is perfect, her eyes bright and alert.

"Elder, I..."

"It's done. They came, and our greeting went off without a hitch."

I feel my entire body relax. "Really? Are you sure?"

She laughs, walking around the table to grip my shoulders and look me in the eyes. "I'm sure. Thanks to you."

Her hands drop, and I'm not sure what to say. "How's Ma, ah, Mrs. Durant?"

There's a warmth in Tanikka's eyes at my mention of Isaac's mother, and she smiles before answering. "She'll be fine, and so will the farm. I ensured the house was repaired, and there's family on the way to help; children from her second marriage."

Good. It's a relief to know she won't have to pay more than she already has for her son's mistakes. I didn't know her for long, but she's a good person. A strong woman, literally and figuratively.

"This event has opened our eyes to some security issues we've overlooked. We'd like to offer you a position as manager of a new cyber security team, which at the moment consists solely of Liam."

"Manager?"

"Until now, it's been contracted out. We'd like to move it in-house. I want someone who cares, someone who wouldn't be afraid to suit up and head into the shadows if that was what it took. Initially, your primary focus would be in building the team; ensuring a balance of skills and personalities."

"Elder, I appreciate..."

I can't say the words. *I appreciate the offer, but I'm leaving*? What the hell am I thinking? I've wanted to leave for as long as I can remember, but since meeting Tarek... The thought of going doesn't make me happy anymore. He makes me happy. He loves me, just the way I am.

I love him. All of him.

GRIPPING THE COLD METAL RAILING, with the Solar at my back, I look out over sprawling Moridian and the endless expanse of Morwood in the distance. In the past, I'd drink in this view to feel a little less claustrophobic. It rarely made much of a difference, because no matter how big the world looked from up here, I was still stuck to the ground.

Now, I have wings.

A blast of air hits me as a wall of green scales erupts from below. Tarek flares his wings before dipping down to land gracefully. My heart soars as my body hums with anticipation. I waited until this morning to send him a message. I wanted to sleep on it all... to be sure I wasn't making a terrible mistake. But there was never a moment of doubt.

Black eyes meet mine, and a thrill races up my spine.

Since that day at the farm, Tarek's let me get to know his dragon. Far from the Meadow and always with Damon ready to intervene, but there was never any danger. He just wanted to be free. He wanted to be acknowledged. Now that Tarek lets him take over to stretch his wings, and get some attention from me, he has no problem taking a backseat when asked nicely.

"Hello, beautiful."

He rumbles deep in his chest as he pushes his nose against me, nearly knocking me off my feet. I slide my hands over his face, loving the feel of him as much as he loves my touch.

He nudges me backward, then shifts.

I drink in the sight of him. Heavy boots and cargo pants, a white t-shirt that stretches across his chest and biceps. His hair tied back, with loose strands falling around his face. And those eyes. Emerald green and blazing with emotion as they rake over me.

His expression is appreciative, warm, and when I take the first step toward him, he closes the distance in two strides and pulls me into his arms. His mouth crushes into mine, kissing me senseless.

When I pull away, gasping for breath, I step out of his arms. I pull the ticket out of my pocket. It's just a piece of paper now. I refunded it first thing this morning.

I hold it up, and his expression falls.

"Today's the day, Tarek. It's time for me to take the life I want."

His gaze drops as he offers a smile that doesn't reach his eyes. I tear the ticket in half.

His eyes widen, a look of panic replacing the sadness. "What are you doing?"

I rip it again and again before I let the wind take it. He stares at me, eyes wide.

"I love you, Tarek. You're my home."

He's still for a moment, then I'm swept up in his arms as he showers me with kisses and nips and growls that leave me laughing and wishing we were somewhere a lot more private.

When he finally calms, he grips my face in his hands, looking into my eyes with intensity.

"I love you. I don't want you to choose between me and your dream."

A tear escapes down my cheek, and he brushes it away with a thumb. My heart cracks a little more. "I don't dream about that anymore. I dream about you."

His jaw clenches as his eyes turn glassy. If he cries, I'll lose it.

"You've waited your whole life for the chance to cash that ticket, don't you dare give it up for me."

My heart stops as understanding hits me like a kick in the gut. He wanted me to want him, but he never meant for me to choose to stay. My leaving made this a safe bet for him. He never had to worry about commitment.

I feel like such a fool.

I swat his hands away and step back, wiping the stupid tears off my cheeks. "God, I'm so stupid. I thought this was... I thought you were... Fuck, Tarek. Just forget everything I said. It's been a crazy night. I got carried away..."

His expression goes from confused to pissed off. I stop talking and he steps toward me. He doesn't touch me, just leans in close and locks his eyes on mine.

"Don't fuck with me, Dawn. Don't tell me you love me, then take it back like it was a slip of the tongue. Which is it?"

Holy hell, my emotions are all over the place right now. But I can't lie about that. "I love you."

He closes his eyes, his face relaxing. I don't know what he's thinking. I don't know if I fucked up or made the best decision of my life. All I can do now is be honest.

"I refunded my ticket and took a new job at HQ. I want to stay with you, if you want me."

He presses his forehead against mine. "Then we have a problem. I quit my job and bought a ticket off-world."

I jerk back, but his face is dead serious. We stare at each other like that for a while, and then he bursts into laughter. It takes me a moment longer to clue into what just happened, but then I'm laughing along with him. He scoops me up into his arms, kissing my neck, my face, my mouth.

This is really real. *We're* real.

OUR STORY

uck handshakes. We're so much more than handshakes.

I pull G in for a tight hug and keep him there. He's a part of me. My first memory is of his face and his voice as he named me. His consciousness shaped me. His memories and knowledge made me who I am. Through everything, even after the artificial bond was severed, our true bond never wavered.

I love you, brother.

I fucking love you, brother.

I knew it would be hard to say goodbye, but seeing the emotion mirrored in his eyes as I take a step back is harder than I thought.

Oh fuck, we got the women going now.

G tips his chin, and sure enough, Hope and Dawn are wiping tears from their cheeks as they watch us. Seeing them together is almost too much. How did I end up with a mate that's so fucking perfect? She fits in with my family like she's always belonged here. I'm so damn lucky.

I lock eyes with Dawn, and we share a private smile.

I love that woman. She loves me.

She also loves my dragon, and the feeling is most definitely mutual. It's a little odd. I catch myself feeling jealous when they're having a moment. But I was losing control, and she brought me back. She connects my human side and my dragon side, and both are stronger because of it.

"You know you're coming back in six months, right?" Whisper's hands are on her hips, her big belly giving her almost comical proportions.

I tear my eyes off Dawn and press a hand against Whisper's stomach, instantly greeted by a hard kick. My heart might just explode today.

"I'm sorry I won't be here when she comes."

Whisp puts her hand over mine. She doesn't need to say anything for me to feel the love. But damn, this is the hardest part. I'm gonna love the hell out of this little kitten. I'll spend the next six years making up for missing her first six months. Gideon won't stand a chance at keeping the favorite uncle title once I get back.

I grab Damon and pull him in for a quick one, slapping him on the back.

"I'll miss you, too, brother."

He nods. I know he feels it. We're family. All of us.

I couldn't ask for better.

Next, I pull Hope into my arms. I love her for so many reasons. For the light she brought to Gideon. For the remnants of the connection she shares with all of us. Just for being her.

We'll be back in time for this baby's birth, if all goes well. Interstellar travel isn't without its risks, which is why I'm saying a proper goodbye to all of them, just in case.

"Remember something for me, okay?"

I tip her chin up, and her eyes turn misty again. She nods as her chin quivers.

"Tarek is a really strong name."

She slaps my arm, swiping at her cheeks as she shakes her head. "You can't do that to me!"

"Her name's Luna." Gideon's tone is firm, but Hope rolls her eyes.

"It's a boy," I remind him.

"Fuck no. She's a girl."

"You're both overgrown children." Hope shakes her head, pressing fingers into her temples like our ongoing debate is giving her a headache. It probably is. "I'm not telling either of you what the sex is, because it doesn't matter!"

I look back at Dawn, and everything else fades away.

This is it.

Our story began the day she kissed my dragon. Or maybe it was that night on the edge. Either way, this is where our forever starts.

We don't need a wedding or a baby to tie us together. We're going to wake up every morning in each other's arms and *choose* forever all over again. Then we're going to fall asleep each night knowing we're exactly where we want to be.

"Are you ready?"

She nods, holding her hand out for mine.

FOREVER

*D*espite the thickness of the glass, the view outside is clear and unobstructed in all directions. It's breathtaking. A sapphire sky washed in shades of purple as the blue sun sinks low over a watery horizon. A flock of wyverns hunt for their meals, tempting fate with each dive into the inky waves.

On this planet, it's the underwater view that attracts tourists. Vibrant, thriving coral reefs. Countless species of marine life. Behemoths that dwarf anything Earth's fossil records have to offer. Everything here exists in a spectacular balance of life and death, free of civilization beyond the handful of terminals and resorts that dot its equator.

One of the many worlds I'll never forget.

Arms slide around my waist, and I lean back into Tarek's warmth. We watch the view in silence until the wyverns have had their fill. They climb toward the clouds, heading to rocky nesting grounds far from here.

"Are you ready to go home?"

I can't stop my smile. I can't believe six months have passed already. This trip has been the most incredible experience.

Sharing it made it so much sweeter. But going back to Earth; back to the Meadow... no words could capture how right that feels.

I tip my head to look back at him. "I am home."

He covers my mouth with a kiss, and I forget about the view outside. I turn in his arms, sliding my hands around his neck, pulling him down into a deeper embrace. I pour every ounce of my love into it. We kiss like this every day. We make love like it's the first time. We remind each other how happy we are together. Nothing has faded. Our love hasn't diminished with time, and in many ways I think it's even grown stronger.

I barely remember what it felt like to doubt him. I don't know how I ever thought life could be complete without this.

A melodic chime precedes our boarding announcement, and Tarek's face lights up. Seeing that look makes my heart swell. I never imagined I'd be experiencing this with someone. I didn't think I even wanted it, but here we are and just like everything else with Tarek, it feels so right.

"Are you ready to be a father?"

His smile consumes him, and he grips my face, looking deep into my eyes with such intensity it burns. "I am so ready. You're amazing. We're going to be great parents."

Parents. I'm going to be a mother. It's still so surreal.

The message from Gideon came in about two weeks ago. They discovered a BioSol facility that was still creating Shifters and selling the babies on the black market. Fucking disgusting. Gideon said they shut it down after rescuing nine young from its labs.

Nine babies needing homes, and I happen to know for a fact that Tarek's arms make a great home. We talked it over, slept on it, tried to convince ourselves it was too much, too soon. But it didn't work. Every cell in my body wants this new adventure with him.

When we get home, we'll be the parents of two beautiful babies. My heart has never felt so full.

The boarding call chimes again, and we join the crowd of fellow galactic tourists heading to their next destination.

The transports between systems are always compact, but comfortable. On my own, I would have been in a seat with a window. Tarek wasn't having that. He upgraded us to a sleeper bunk on each leg, and the moment we secure our backpacks for the trip, he reminds me exactly why it's worth every extra penny.

He steps behind me, snaking his arms around my waist and moving his hips just enough to let me know he's ready and wanting me. I press back against him, reaching up to pull his head down until his lips are against my neck. His teeth find that sensitive place behind my ear, making me weak in the knees as his trim beard tickles my skin.

He holds me tight against him with one arm, while the other works on my jeans until he can push them out of his way. Skilled fingers know exactly what I like, and the combination of his mouth on my neck and his hand working my body has me nearing the edge in mere moments.

He pulls away.

I curse him as he leaves me standing there with my pants around my ankles, gasping for breath. I spin around to glare at him, finding him already naked and so damn hard.

Two can play that game. I kick off my pants, then toss my shirt and bra. I can work his body just as well as he can mine, and I know exactly how to make him beg. I take a step toward him, debating whether to start with my hands, or just drop to my knees. Oh, I definitely want to taste him.

He moves too fast for me to react. Spinning me around, he presses me to the wall and kicks my legs apart, then buries himself inside me in one swift motion. The pain is exquisite as my body resists the sudden invasion. He holds me firmly in place as he takes me relentlessly, the discomfort lasting only a moment until the pleasure consumes me.

The intensity of his total domination over my body. My utter helplessness beneath the power and strength of this man. My climax crashes into me, sending me to a place where nothing exists beyond the pleasure only he can give me.

When I'm again aware of my own breathing, of the heat from his body and the chill of the air, I'm curled up on his chest. My legs straddle his hips and I can feel him like steel between us. He didn't finish. I smile against his skin, lifting my head to kiss his mouth. When he takes me like that, without warning or consent, he won't let himself come with me. Even though he knows how much I love it, he needs to make sure I'm okay before he can take his own pleasure.

I lift my hips, not wanting to make him wait a moment longer. I'm a little sore as I slide down onto his thick and impossibly hard length, but it's quickly forgotten when he growls and grips my hips, letting me set the pace as I ride him to the edge and beyond. His climax rips out of him with a roar, his face a beautiful mask of pure pleasure.

"I love you, Tarek. I love you so damn much."

His eyes open, their emerald depths blazing. He pulls me down, holding me tight against the heavy beating of his heart. We stay like that, as he softens inside me and I drift off to sleep.

I wake to the feel of him growing hard again, and the odd sensation of zero gravity. I grind my hips against him, letting him know I'm awake and earning a delicious moan that I can feel rumble against my ear.

My stomach growls, and his sound of pleasure becomes a laugh.

"Should I feed you before I fuck you again?"

I slap his shoulder, but another rumble from my midsection answers for me. "That might not be a bad idea."

He pushes me off him, an effortless task without gravity. "Good. I'm starving."

We use the many well-placed handles on the walls to move around as we dress, then strap on the magnetic boots that will allow us to walk throughout the transport without floating away. On the trip away from Earth, we could hardly move in them, walking around with stiff, measured movements. Now, we're old pros, strolling through the hallways as easily as if we're home.

The food on these trips is always good. It's not gourmet by any means, but we're not picky eaters to begin with. All-you-can-eat fast food fare and salad bar, sweets, and smoothies. And that's just in the Terran dining area.

We keep to ourselves mostly, never taking part in any of the social events offered or attempting to get to know some fellow travellers. We're more interested in staying naked in our room than we are in making friends. And now that we're returning home to work and responsibilities and babies of our own, well, we're working overtime to soak up every sexy moment we can.

"Thank you, Angel."

I look up from my burger, meeting his eyes that are suddenly soft with emotion.

"For what?"

"For letting me experience this with you. For letting me in. For letting me love you, and for loving me back."

I couldn't stop my tears if I tried, and seeing his own eyes turn glassy doesn't help.

This man. From the moment I first saw him outside HQ, he's captivated me. The moment he let me touch him, I was done for. I can't believe I ever doubted this love. He's my forever. And I'm going to spend the rest of my life showing him exactly how I feel.

THIS LIFE

*H*oly hell, those little troublemakers!

"Dustin! Casey!" The guilty parties freeze. They know to mind when Grandma raises her voice. "If I catch you stalking that poor chicken one more time, you'll be cleaning the coop for the next month."

They giggle as they run off, likely planning to find another hapless animal to practice their hunting skills on. They're good boys. Wouldn't hurt a fly, just give it a good scare. They're not half the trouble their father was, that's for certain. That little bear gave me a few too many grey hairs when he was on the edge of adolescence.

I tug at the heavy quilt around my shoulders, pulling it a little tighter around my neck. Autumn is invading our warm evenings, bringing its chill with the fading sun. We'll have to ensure the community centre's stocked sooner rather than later. Last winter was a long one, and even though the boys didn't complain, I don't want to see them hauling firewood in a blizzard again.

Across the lawn, a certain grizzly stalks my way. That man can still warm my soul after all these years. I can't help but grin at the stiffness in his gait and the tense set of his jaw. I do my best to keep it hidden. Wouldn't want him to think I find his troubles amusing.

He climbs the steps to our front porch, circling behind me to put his hands on my shoulders, kneading gently but firmly. He still warms my body, too. I reach up to place a hand over his, and he threads his fingers through mine.

We're both quiet for a few moments. He's taking in the view of the setting sun and the children playing, the neighbor's houses and the people walking about their business on the road. Soaking it all in as I feel his tension ease.

"Did you finish?"

"Yes, it's done. Finally. Why they think they need one room for each cub is beyond me. Ours did just fine sharing a bedroom. It's wasteful."

I can't help but laugh. Used to be he'd come home from a day of construction with a smile on his face and a spark in his eyes. My old bear's getting tired.

"Oh, I recall a certain little one that despised sharing his space with three siblings. Zeke begged you every year for his own room."

"It was wasteful then, it's wasteful now."

"He just wants to give everything he can to his own. He's a good father. Takes after you."

"You're ruining my sour mood, woman."

"Good. Life's too short to be sour."

He huffs, coming around to sit beside me at last. I wrap my blanket around him as he pulls me close.

"Are you happy here?"

I look up at him, a bit taken aback by the question. He hasn't asked me that in many years. His gaze searches mine, like my answer is the very thing that gives him breath.

Time has changed him. It's changed both of us. Each line on his handsome face tells a story; a chapter in a life fuller and more vibrant and bursting with love than I could ever have wished for.

"I love you, Tarek. You've given me an exquisite life. I wouldn't change a single moment."

He leans in, his soft lips brushing mine and sending a shiver clear through me.

A tumble of limbs and giggles barrels up the stairs, the little dust bunny hardly able to contain her excitement.

"What is it, child?" Tarek scowls at the interruption, but the love in his eyes is unmistakable as he watches the little one bounce.

"Nana!"

I hold my arms out, and our youngest grandchild crawls onto my lap. Her little body fits so perfectly in my arms as I hug her tight, knowing well how fast it all passes into memories.

This little one holds a special place in my heart. Her papa was the last baby we took in, a few years after we said we were done adopting. He came to us quite unexpectedly, his cries waking us late one night after someone left him by our door. We never learned how he came to be there, but we knew he was ours the moment we held him.

"Can we have a sleepover with you tonight?"

"Did we not just spend the last month building you the biggest house in the Meadow?" Tarek's exasperation only makes her giggle.

"Did Mama and Papa say it was okay?"

She nods, her dark eyes wide.

"Papa says we can sleep over with you, so they make sure the house sounds right." She shrugs her little shoulders, innocent confusion furrowing her brow.

Tarek throws his head back in laughter, and I stifle my own. Those kids. It warms my heart to know our boy found that kind of love. It sure is rare.

"Go pack your things, kitten. I'll make cookies."

Her excitement is contagious as she scrambles off my lap to spread the good news.

"And tell your Papa we've got enough grandkids!" Tarek calls after her, and I slap his stomach to hush him.

"You were just the same in our younger years, Grandpa."

The reminder makes his eyes dance, as he returns for the kiss that was interrupted.

"I still would be if we hadn't traded a houseful of kids for a houseful of grandkids."

To prove his point, he kisses me breathless on our front porch. Holy hell, if I didn't have cookies to bake...

"Maybe it's time we went on another vacation." His voice is rough as he nuzzles into my neck.

"Do you think? I hate to leave them."

"We're not getting any younger."

He's got a point. We've seen so much in our lifetime. Exploring the planet on family vacations was incredible. I thought I'd seen it all, but with Tarek at my side and the kids taking it all in for the first time, we made some great memories.

Once the kids were grown, we ventured much farther. Three trips off-world within those five years, each time visiting new sights and old favourites. Making friends and making love. After that, the grandkids started arriving. Our trips got a lot less frequent, until we eventually just stopping daydreaming about going anywhere at all.

It's been about fifteen years since we left the Meadow for any length of time, and not once have I felt that wanderlust that used to flow through my veins. Nothing has ever come close to the view from our own front porch.

"Maybe next year," I say.

A smile softens his features. "Maybe next year."

We sit for a long while in comfortable silence, but the sun's getting low and if I linger here much longer, I'll be late. I stand and fold my blanket, gathering up my knitting supplies.

"I've got some cookie dough ready in the freezer."

"You spoil them." Tarek presses a kiss to my forehead, and I can feel the smile on his lips. "I'll check the stew."

He heads to the big pot of deer stew I left warming on the stove. The recipe never changes, but the pot's gotten far bigger over the years.

The Meadow's grown, but these Friday night potlucks at the Community Center keep us all in touch. It's important to Hope, and to all of us, that the Meadow remains a close-knit family, no matter how big it gets.

The Center is warm and inviting, humming with the promise of life and laughter to come. I join Hope and Whisper, and we jump into our usual routine to ready the eclectic feast. Tarek joins Gideon and Damon, setting up the tables and ensuring everything is clean and welcoming.

The door swings open, the chilly air causing the lamps to flicker. It's a good thing we're getting a head start on the wood. Maybe an extra cord or two wouldn't be a terrible idea.

"Hunter!" I hurry to greet my dear friend with a hug, offering my cheek for a kiss from Daniel. "What a surprise! I didn't think you'd make it this week!"

They come as often as they can, but the trip down from the mountains isn't as easy as it used to be, and they have their own prolific brood to tend to in their lovely little valley.

Daniel joins the men, handshakes and half-hugs all around. Hunter joins us in the kitchen, prepping and serving as our families and neighbours pour in.

Soon, the air is filled with the drone of conversation, punctuated by the sounds of children playing between and under the tables. It fills my soul to watch and listen, soaking up the love I have for the community that welcomed me so eagerly, so many years ago. There was a time I thought I didn't need any of this, and imagining where I'd be now if I'd walked away...

"Dawn?" A concerned voice jolts me out of my drifting thoughts.

"Liam." I grasp his hand, giving him a smile before scanning the room. "I didn't see you come in. Is River here tonight?"

I spot her two tables over, and wave as I catch her eye.

"You were lost in thought. Everything okay?"

I pat his shoulder, gesturing for him to grab a plate and help himself. "Just daydreaming, you know me."

All too soon, bellies are full and the conversation has come to an end. Dishes are washed, tables are cleared, and we've said heartfelt goodbyes to everyone, even though we'll see most of them many times before we meet here again.

It's after midnight by the time the grandkids are finally asleep. Four little treasures, tucked in tight and dreaming of whatever their hearts desire.

"Thank you, Angel."

Tarek's voice is smooth and warm against my ear, as his arms wrap around me. I smile, lacing my fingers in his.

"For what?" I know his answer by heart, but I never tire of hearing him say it.

"For giving me this life. For sharing it with me. For letting me love you, and for loving me back."

My vision goes blurry, and I blink away the tears. It's silly, after all these years, but I sometimes still can't believe he's mine. I turn in his arms, letting him see the emotion on my face. He smiles, pressing his forehead to mine.

"I love you."

A NOTE FROM THE AUTHOR

Thank you for reading Dawn and Tarek's story!

Would you like to hear about my future releases and be the first to get freebies and sneak peeks? Subscribe to my newsletter at www.CharlenePerry.ca

If you enjoyed this book, please consider leaving a review wherever you can. As an indie author, reviews are critical for helping my books find the readers who will love them. I adore hearing what you think of my work. It gives me confidence, motivates me to push through the hard parts, and inspires me to keep adding to the series you love!

For more information about me or my stories, be sure to check out my website! (www.charleneperry.ca)

Find me on Facebook! @CharlenePerryAuthor. I love to chat and am always delighted to receive feedback :)

Thank you so much for spending this time with me,

Sweet Dreams!
   -Charlene

Printed in Great Britain
by Amazon